A CLOCKWORK CAROL

BILLY O'SHEA

a

CLOCKWORK
CAROL

BLACK SWAN

ISBN 978-87-996426-2-5

Songs and melodies mentioned in the book:
'The Teddy-Bears' Picnic', written by John Walter Braaton and Jimmy Kennedy, pub.
Sony/ATV Music Publishing LLC, Warner/Chappell Music, Inc.
'Nellie The Elephant', written by Ralph Butler, pub. Hal Leonard - Digital Sheet Music
'If You Knew Susie (Like I Know Susie)', written by Eddie Cantor, Joseph Meyer and
B.G. De Sylva, pub. Shapiro Bernstein Organization
'Maple Leaf Rag', written by Scott Joplin, pub. Sedalia: John Stark & Son
'Breakin' In A Pair Of Shoes', written by Dave Franklin, Ned Washington and Sam H.
Stept, pub. Sony/ATV Music Publishing LLC
'Round Midnight', written by Theolonius Monk, pub. Thelonious Music-BMI
'Alley Cat', written by Bent Fabricius-Bjerre, pub. Multitone ApS

Front cover illustration:
Andrey Dorozhko (www.andreydrz.com)

Originally published in Denmark by
Black Swan, Copenhagen (www.blackswan.dk)

For Dad, who always said so

By the same author:
Kingdom of Clockwork
It's Only A Clockwork Moon

A Clockwork Carol is the third book in the series.

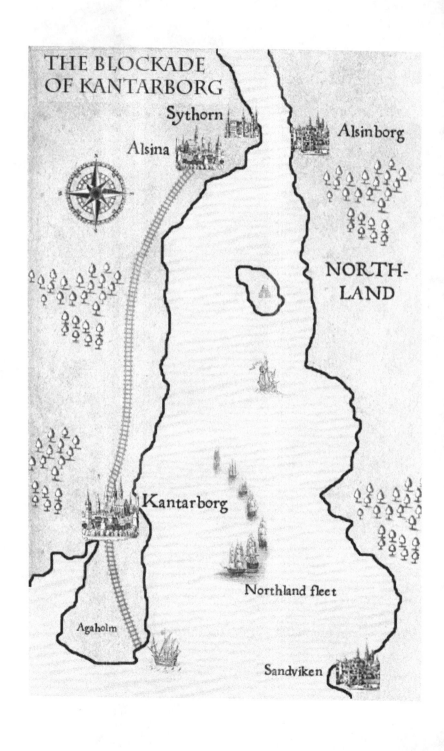

The King sent to his lady on the thirteenth day of Yule...

CHAPTER ONE

'Karl, he has got to go!'

Marieke stomped about the kitchen, packing her basket with the last produce of the garden. It was Saturday, and she was on her way to help out at Berendina Jansen's market stall. In the next room, the strains of *The Teddy-Bear's Picnic* started up on the wind-up music box. I sat at the table with my morning cup of tea.

'Marieke, be reasonable. He has nowhere to go.'

'And how is that our problem? Has he no family?'

'He does. But ... it's complicated.'

'Ah, so *they* threw him out! Well, I'm not one bit surprised. And then he comes to you, of course.'

If you go down to the woods today, you'd better go in disguise...

'He sits in there all day, playing those discs,' she growled. 'And those are valuable originals, Karl! If he wears them out, you won't be able to make any more impressions from them. And he *smells*. He doesn't even wash!'

'He does wash, I've seen him.'

'But he never changes his clothes! I gave him a fresh set yesterday, and he hasn't even put them on. He just keeps going about in that ridiculous costume. He's a stinking, disgusting old tramp. And high and mighty with it.'

He had got off on the wrong foot with Marieke from the start. On his first evening here, she had opened a bottle of our best wine at dinner in honour of this old friend of mine from Kantarborg who had fallen on hard times. He knocked back the first glass almost in one gulp, put it down, and looked at her expectantly. I quickly reached for the bottle and refilled his glass, but it was too late. She had caught the look. After that she said very little and went to bed early. From there on, things had gone downhill fast.

'I can't just throw him out on the street,' I said. 'Especially not at this time of year.'

'At this time of year or at any time of year, Karl, he has to go! I mean it.'

The music in the next room changed.

Nellie the Elephant packed her trunk and said goodbye to the circus ...

I could barely repress a smile.

'You think this is funny, Karl? I'm serious.' She pulled on her cloak, picked up her basket and plucked a few of the larger ripe tomatoes from the plants inside the kitchen window. They were acceptable vegetables even for orthodox Northlanders, and by now would practically be worth their weight in gold.

'...for thereby some have entertained angels unawares,' I murmured to myself, in Kantish.

'I heard that, and I know my Bible too, Karl Nielsen. He's no angel. Get him OUT before I come back, or I will not be responsible for my actions! You know me!'

Another change of music from the adjacent room.

If you knew Susie like I know Susie, oh, oh, oh what a girl...

Marieke slammed the apartment door and clattered down the stairs in her clogs. I sighed and opened the door to the living-room. He was lying on the bench bed listening to the music, dressed in his red and white tunic with a wide black belt. He had not even taken his boots off. I wondered if he slept in them. The beard was long and white, but was starting to show dark roots, which spoiled the look a bit. I walked over to the music box and lifted the needle off the disc.

'That was mean of you,' I said. 'And not at all funny.'

'What on earth do you mean, Karl? I was just trying out your lovely machine. Quite remarkable reproduction. Much better than my little music box, much as I love it.'

I ran a finger over the brass plates and rosewood case. It needed dusting.

'One of our latest models. Expensive, though. We haven't sold many of them.'

'It's beautiful. I must commission one of them from you.'

'One day, perhaps.'

'One day very soon, I can assure you of that, Karl.'

I sat down on a chair by the dining-table.

'Well, you heard her. She wants you out. Today.'

'Yes, I'm sorry. I have worn out my welcome. Forgive me, Karl.'

He was silent a moment.

'I don't suppose, if you intimated to her that, you know, in a way, I am the person who was responsible for you getting this lovely apartment..?'

'That most certainly would not help. If she suspected who you really were, she'd kill you. And I mean that quite literally.'

'Hah! A fine situation for us to end up in, isn't it? Your wife wants to kill me, and my wife tried to kill you. But really, why would she take against me so? Is she a radical or something?'

I shook my head.

'Not at all. She blames you for me getting into debt. And for all the trouble that caused. Including my imprisonment and near-execution, if you remember.'

'Oh, that,' he said, as though it were a mere bagatelle. 'I rather thought I was responsible for getting you *out* of debt, was I not?'

'She thinks you sent Hapgaard.'

'I most certainly did not!'

'I haven't told you who Hapgaard was, yet.'

'Oh, very clever! Well, think what you like. I can see I shall have to go. A man must keep his wife happy, I suppose.'

Keeping my wife happy had been a little difficult of late. I suppose it would be fair to say that Marieke and I were going through a rough patch. I had very little idea of what was the matter, though I suspected that our inability to produce children after five years of marriage might well have something to do with it. Whatever the reason, Marieke seemed to have a lot less patience with her husband and his schemes than she used to do. Lowlanders value thrift, hard work and practicality, but my business ventures had shown very little return and were putting something of a strain on our finances. More than she knew, actually. And then, having this unwanted guest lying about the house had been close to the last straw.

'I can give you some money,' I said. 'And couldn't you put some other clothes on? If you looked normal, the Watch wouldn't notice you.'

'A man must have a profession, Karl. This is my professional outfit.'

'Begging is hardly a profession. And the Yule Father is supposed to give things to people at Yule, not take things off them.'

'Begging is illegal, Karl, may I remind you. I'm collecting for the poor, and who is poorer than I? And by the way, you're not supposed to call it Yule any more, did you hear that? It's Nicholastide now, says the Church. Hah!'

'Yes, I heard. I thought the Church disapproved of the solstice celebrations?'

'Well, they're politicians in cassocks, aren't they, Karl? If you can't beat them, they think, better join them. So now they have a new saint of the solstice. Nicholas the gift-bringer. Which is a bit ironic, because old Pope Nicholas never gave anything to anyone, I can tell you. Least of all to me. And he was anything but fat and jolly. Miserable old bugger.'

'Anyway, I'm not paying your fine if you get arrested again. And I'll be obliged if you do not mention my name next time.'

'Yes, I'm sorry Karl. I had no choice. They thought I was a thief, can you believe it? They would have put me on the next boat across the Sound. And that would have been my sentence of death, you know.'

'Well, if you don't want to be thought a thief, don't steal anything!'

'I merely borrowed those discs from your shop, you know that.'

Marieke had made her first acquaintance with him a week earlier. She had watched in astonishment as a man dressed as the Yule Father ran into our shop, stuffed several music discs into his sack, and ran out again, shouting 'Merry Yule!' She was able to give an unusually precise description to the Watch. They found him in the market square, where he was augmenting his mendicant business by playing jazz records on a music box and accompanying them in improvised scat, much to the bewilderment of passers-by.

'Count Basie and the Earl of Hines. Wonderful stuff. That little music box you sent me is my most treasured possession. Well, my only possession, actually. It has practically kept me alive. But I only had three discs, and the public does grow a little tired of them. I would have brought them back, honestly. The Watch would not believe I was your friend.'

'Sometimes I can hardly believe it myself.'

He sat up, swung his legs off the bench, and fastened his puppy-dog brown eyes upon me.

'Look, Karl, I can see I must leave your house. But I want to ask you something. As a friend, not as your king.'

Here it comes, I thought.

'Could you accompany me to Kantarborg? I know it's a lot to...'

'No! I am *not* taking any more chances for you. I have my wife to think of. You can make your own way there. I will give you the fare.'

'Karl, you know very well I cannot cross into Kantarborg alone. If I am picked up at the border I am a dead man. But you, on the other hand, are a respectable merchant. If I am your travelling companion, I will go unnoticed.'

I raised my eyebrows.

'I mean, at this time of year!' he protested. 'You could say you were bringing me along for some special Yule promotion for your business. Surely you owe me that much? After all, if it were not for me, you would not be living this comfortable life now.'

I decided to let that lie.

'Why do you want to go back there, anyway?' I asked. 'There's nothing there for you now.'

'I still have some loyal allies in the kingdom. And I have a plan.'

'And what is your plan for me, if I am caught trying to smuggle the ex-king back into the country?'

'I am still the King, Karl! But yes, I suppose you would be taking a certain risk. Is there nothing I can offer you by way of recompense?'

'Absolutely nothing. Even if you had anything to give me. Which you don't.'

'I have a few things hidden away over there. And there is one thing in particular that I think would interest you greatly.'

'I'm sorry, there is nothing you could possibly offer me. I have everything I need here.'

He stood up, walked over to the shelves, and looked at my collection of recordings.

'These are the discs I gave you in Kantarborg, are they not? Lovely. And you make copies of them? Are they popular?'

'The wax impressions sell very well, along with the wind-up players, although the copied discs are of very poor quality compared to the originals. I've been trying to work out the technique for making recordings myself. Without much success so far, I'm afraid.'

'And these are the only original discs you have? Then the range must be rather limited.'

'I have a grand total of forty-seven in all. But yes, the public is crying out for more. It's becoming something of a craze around here. I am told they are even starting to hold jazz dances in the Three Bells.'

He looked out of the window at the distant spires of the city of Kantarborg, on the horizon, across the Sound.

'What if I told you that I know of a collection of several hundred of these? All ancient jazz discs and popular songs of the very finest quality?'

That brought me up sharp. But only for a moment.

'It's been years since you've been back in the Kingdom. They've probably long since been plundered or confiscated.'

'Not these discs. They're hidden somewhere no-one would think of looking. I could show them to you today, if you come with me. You could take a few as samples, and be back here again tonight.'

It was tempting, certainly. That many recordings could keep my business going for a long time.

'And while we're there, you could also deliver that remarkable toy of yours. And collect your payment.'

The 'remarkable toy' was a commission I had been working on for the past two months. One morning in early autumn, when the rain was dancing off the cobbles outside and there were no other customers in the shop, a red-haired, bearded man from Kantarborg had come in with an unusual request. A certain Lady Amalia of the Kantarborgan nobility wished me to construct a miniature replica of the clockwork locomotives of the city, which I had devised and which were now famous throughout the known world. (Were they? That was news to me.) The model was to be a Yule gift for someone, so it would have to be ready in December, and it was to be made in 1/43 scale.

'1/43? Why not 1/50?' I asked. But he went on talking as though I had not spoken.

It was to have a durable clockwork motor and to run on a suitable length of oval track, the latter to be made in flexible rods of extruded steel strengthened by suitable slats. The whole to be produced in a degree of quality suitable for representative purposes at the highest level.

'And the outer casing of the model locomotive is to be made in gold.'

'Gold!'

'Yes. Is that a problem?'

'Well, no, but ... gold is a quite unsuitable material for such work. It is soft and malleable ... and also extremely expensive.'

The red-haired man placed a large, heavy leather bag on the counter.

'Half now, half on completion.'

I undid the drawstrings and looked inside. It contained a quite extraordinary number of coins of the realm. I picked one up. It looked genuine. It was dated the previous year, and stamped with the new arms of Kantarborg: three towers and the sign of the moon and star. No royal profile on the other side, just the denomination.

'All legal tender and pure gold,' said the man. 'Best quality coinage of the new regime.'

I thought I saw a glint of contempt in his eye, but I didn't know if it was for me or for his new rulers.

I naturally accepted the commission. No-one knew the locomotive better than I, and to construct such a model lay well within my area of expertise. And it was extremely well paid. At that price I could even subcontract some of the turning and casting work to Eriksson the toolmaker, which left me free to concentrate on the assembly and the finer details. I spent all my evenings working on the model, somewhat to Marieke's irritation, and devoted a great deal of care to it – mostly, I admit, for the sheer pleasure of making something beautiful.

The driving mechanism was essentially simple, being much less complicated than a clock, but I equipped the open footplate with levers to stop and start the device and change its direction of travel. Making the bodywork in gold allowed for great detailing, but it had to be strengthened by a brass underlay. It could be wound up from the side, using a key that fitted directly onto the ratcheted hub of a coil spring, and once wound up it would run for about three minutes on the small piece of track I had made up for it. As a final touch I gave it a small bell that tinkled gently as it ran. When it was completed I was so pleased with it that I placed it in the shop window as a temporary decoration.

Our guest, when he saw the finished model, was fulsome

in his praise.

'Why, it is absolutely marvellous, Karl! A truly wonderful device.'

'It's just a simple thing. Like the toy locomotive you once showed me. But I have taken some trouble with it.'

'You are too modest, you always were. You are a true genius of your profession.' (I had learned to be on my guard when he called me a genius.) 'And it's for Lady Amalia?'

'So I'm told. It was supposed to be a Yule gift for someone, presumably some very privileged child, but now it's nearly Yule and I have heard no more.'

'Really? Well look, she's a personal friend of mine, and I was going to try to get back to Kantarborg anyway. I could deliver it for you, and make sure you get paid.'

'That is kind of you, but I think I would prefer to wait. I have already been paid half the amount, and if the rest doesn't come, I still have the piece as security.'

The truth, of course, was that it would be a little hard for me to explain to Marieke why I had entrusted a work worth hundreds of sovereigns to a man we had found begging on the streets.

And there the matter had rested – until Marieke's ultimatum had brought things to a head. And what Marieke did not know was that, in truth, we were rather relying on that final payment to come through. The bills were due for my experimental investments in music box technology. But I could not just give the piece to him and hope for the best.

'This Lady Amalia,' I asked. 'Do you know where she lives?'

'She normally lives near Alsina, but she is having her portrait painted at the moment, so she is residing in her town house.'

He seemed remarkably well-informed, considering he had not been back to the kingdom for quite some time. But no doubt he had his contacts.

'And I could be back here by tonight? You're sure?'

'The last ferry sails at ten. You'll have plenty of time.'

I pursed my lips for a moment, then made my decision. I went into the hallway to get some writing-paper and leave a note for Marieke. On the hall stand, I saw something I had not noticed before: a letter addressed to *Mr Horologist Karl Nielsen, Sandviken*. Postmarked Kantarborg. Perhaps a message from my customer at last. I brought it back into the living-room to open it. The envelope contained a greeting card, with a picture of the Yule Father on the front, standing by his sleigh in the snows of the far north. It was not signed. Inside were just a few enigmatic words in Anglian, written in a neat hand. I read them out:

'*I am looking forward to my gift. Hurry down the chimney tonight.* What the devil is that supposed to mean? Is this from Lady Amalia?'

He came and looked over my shoulder.

'Well, it looks like her hand. I suppose it means we'd better hurry,' he said.

CHAPTER TWO

'I will scale the blue air and plough the high hills,' said the monk, pointing at the grey massing clouds above the mountain.

'You will all that and more,' said Karval the blacksmith, sending the sparks flying from the anvil with his hammer blows. His apprentice brought water in a bucket.

'There's wine from the royal pope upon the ocean green,' the monk declaimed.

'There would be, I'd say,' said Karval. 'Sure no doubt Pope Rurall will be sending you a bottle or two for your next birthday.'

He quenched the hot metal in the water and held it up in the tongs for the monk to inspect.

'Now. Will that do you, do you think?'

The monk narrowed his eyes to peer at the steaming metal. It was a small, crooked fitting of indecipherable purpose.

'It's not the worst, but it's not been bettered,' he said. 'I'll take it.' He turned around so that Karval could drop the still-warm piece into the hood of his habit.

'Don't forget your drawing,' said Karval.

'Keep it. I might want another.'

The monk jumped up on his bicycle and cycled off up the lane. The blacksmith watched him go, stuffing the drawing absently into a pocket of his overalls. His apprentice came over and stood beside him, wiping his hands on a cloth.

'Is he cracked, that fella, or what?'

'As dry mud,' said Karval. 'But he's a good customer.'

'But what's he making at all? With all them little pieces?'

'Did you not hear? The brothers of the Rock are looking for gold. They're going to make a big balloon to fly all the way to America. Like St Christopher Columbus did in the Hindenburg.'

'America? Sure there's no such place!'

'They seem to think there is.'

'He seemed in good spirits, anyway.'

'And why wouldn't he be? Sure isn't he getting married?'

CHAPTER THREE

Extract from the diary of astronomer Johannes Brorsen

The wind is from the east now; wet and muddy autumn is gradually subsiding into wet and muddy winter. There is no frost yet, but we are keeping the roads swept, for nothing is so treacherous to the island carthorses as frozen leaves in the ruts.

I was at my desk today, working at my calculations, when I heard something of a commotion outside. I stood up and opened the window a fraction, and saw Peter Rasmussen, my captain of the guard, coming up the pathway from the jetty, and shooing away curious villagers in that island dialect that I pretend not to understand. Yes, it was from Kantarborg, no, he did not know what was inside. I watched as he impatiently opened the gateway into what I like to call the castle courtyard – though in truth it is more of a farmyard – and, shutting out the onlookers on the other side, he entered the tower through the pantry door.

I closed the window again and sat down at my desk, waiting for the knock. When he came in I took the letter, looked at it in what I hoped was a bored manner, and put it aside. I knew what it was, of course: confirmation of my coming position.

'Thank you, Peter. I will read it later.'

Peter remained standing where he was.

'Was there ... anything else?' I asked.

Of course there was, there was the matter that he and the whole island had been talking about for weeks. But Peter is a shy man, and so he spoke of something else first.

'Pastor Skrivenius wishes to see you, sir. He says the schoolhouse roof is leaking again.'

That priest and his damn schoolhouse. He has a little hut close to the presbytery where he terrifies the village children. The presbytery is Church property, but the schoolhouse is mine, having been built by one of my predecessors, and so I am responsible for its maintenance. It seems to have a leakier roof than any other property in the parish.

'I will call on him this afternoon, if that is suitable.'

Finally, Peter managed to broach the matter that was on his mind.

'Sir, I was wondering if we might discuss ... the matter of the future arrangements.'

'You mean, who will take over while I'm away?'

He said nothing. I sighed and put aside my work.

'Peter,' I said, 'you shall be my rock.'

He looked at me uncomprehendingly.

'Pastor Skrivenius represents the spiritual powers. You represent the earthly ones. I am relying on the two of you to keep order here in my absence. You will administer justice and lay down the law. He will threaten any transgressors with hell and damnation. I think it will work admirably.'

'Will you be gone long, sir?'

'Just a few months. Until after Yule. Then we'll see. But I will remain lord of this island, whatever happens.'

There is a persistent rumour that I am planning to sell the entire estate to some Kantish noble. I deny it, of course – but privately, after all that has happened recently, I know I might well consider it if the price was right. Indeed, I might have no choice.

Peter left and I returned to my horoscopes. Pluto was beginning its transit of Capricorn. Wars and rumours of wars, the fall of dynasties and the rise of others. All very well, but which ones would triumph? On that salient question, the heavens were silent.

I believe I am a shrewd man, and, if I may say so without false modesty, somewhat skilled in hypocrisy. My greatest achievement during my period of tenure as lord of this isle has been keeping us out of the upheavals that have burned and raged up and down the coasts of both our neighbouring kingdoms.

By long tradition, this territory has been semi-autonomous; and so I have praised the wisdom of Northland and the justice of Kantarborg – or was it vice versa? – paid tribute to them both, and on more than one occasion paid taxes to both of them at once. Through my diplomatic contacts, I have given both kingdoms the impression that I was secretly on their side. As a result, we have remained pristine and at peace. It is thanks to me that the mothers of this island can expect to see their children grow to adulthood. And it is a skill for which I am, of course, entirely unappreciated.

But now, it seems the time for vacillation is drawing to a close. Northland has refused to recognise Queen Ulrika as its overlord, and conflict is threatening. Their first move will probably be against Kantarborg, which is formally in alliance with the northern Queen. And this island in the Sound is not without strategic value. To try to remain neutral in such a situation would be to invite occupation, plunder, and conscription. So a decision will have to be made – to lay ourselves under the protection of one power or the other. Northland is of course closer to us in geography and culture, but Kantarborg has more to recommend it politically, and it is a nation I know well. It is true that I left the court under something of a cloud when I fell out with the Young King, but now he is gone, whereabouts unknown, and is thought to pose little danger. That idiot Kramer has since become prime minister, but Commander Johansson is said to be the real power. And it was he who had written to me.

I had not seen Johansson for some years and was surprised to receive the invitation. He gave a good impression of himself when last we met – a man of some intellect and dynamism, though I greatly doubted the wisdom and seaworthiness of his political project. He also showed a degree of respect for my position and office that, sadly, has been somewhat lacking elsewhere in recent years. I had of course also heard about him from other sources, but as always the question was how much to believe and how much to discount as common gossip. He was said to have instigated the overthrow of the Young King, which shows a certain level of cunning, at least. He was in any case a rising star in Kantarborg, and like any rising star he would probably eventually fall. Unless, of course, he had the right advisors. And given the chance, I believe I can prove my worth to any person of power.

'It seems we are to be colleagues,' I said to Skrivenius as I sat down to tea in the presbytery. I enjoyed the moment of fear and confusion that passed across his face. He knew me to be a protégé of the Pope, at least in theory.

'I mean, I am to become a teacher. Or a tutor, to be precise.'

Skrivenius covered his relief by pouring the tea.

'For some noble child, I take it, my lord?'

'For the highest noble. For the crown prince of Kantarborg.'

Skrivenius is enough of a snob to be impressed, as I knew he would be. He did not congratulate me.

'And an advisor to the Minister of Defence', I added. True, that part of the job was more implied than actually stated in my contract, but I for my part am enough of a snob to wish to be considered more than a mere schoolmaster. And I would in any case be a courtier again.

'So I'm leaving you and Rasmussen in charge. Don't go starting any revolutions while I'm gone, will you?'

Skrivenius laughed uneasily.

'I'm sure I don't know what you mean, my lord.'

'I'm sure you do.' I held his gaze. 'Go easy on the people, Skrivenius. They've been through a lot.'

'I will go as *easy* on them as the Lord our God would expect,' he replied. 'The Lord is a loving God. He is also firm and severe in his love.'

'Just make sure they are fed,' I said, with some weariness. 'I want to come back to an island with a fit and healthy population.'

'Of course. But their spiritual welfare comes first, my lord, as always. That is where my duty of care lies, as their pastor.'

I was in ill humour as I strode along the muddy track back

to the castle. The blasted man always puts me out of sorts.

I should explain.

The people of this island, although they do not know it, are mainly Northlandish in their culture and habits. Like their mainland neighbours to the east, they have by long tradition relied on a diet of meat, milk products and rye bread, with comparatively few vegetables. Recently, the clergy have tried to make a virtue of this custom by declaring bread to be the proper food of good Christian folk. (The clergy in the northern lands have ever been opportunistic in this manner with respect to popular tradition. I should not be surprised if one day, the Church declares shaking hands in greeting to be an expression of doctrinal rectitude, and the doffing of one's hat, by contrast, to be of the devil. But I digress.)

When old Pastor Sørensen died we were sent this young man – slight, prematurely balding, and with pince-nez – who had studied at the university in Kantarborg and was rumoured to be of the Lunarian persuasion like that fool Kramer.

At our first interview Skrivenius was deferential and assured me that he was, no, of course not, in no wise a supporter of the tendency of Prime Minister Kramer. So all was well – until a month later, when he got rid of all the paintings and statues in the church. The stink of burning oil paint still remains in my nostrils. The organ was next to go – a beautiful instrument that was centuries old. All music besides sung psalms was sinful, apparently. The interior of the church was to be bare and painted severe white. Some of the islanders came to me in distress, but I could not interfere in Church matters – something they had difficulty understanding.

There is no tavern on the island, but in summer the locals are in the habit of meeting up at crossroads here and there for a dance and a few drops of *akvavit*. This is technically against the law, though I used to turn a blind eye to it. But these gatherings, according to Skrivenius, were an occasion of wickedness, since not only was such music an abomination to the Lord, but *akvavit*, being distilled from potatoes, a plant cultivated under-ground, was of the Evil One. (The Lunarians perceive some obscure theological and etymological connection with the 'apple' of Adam, since in some languages the potato is known as an 'earth-apple'.) The gatherings were banned, and the young people were forced to post look-outs and to flee whenever the priestly cape was seen approaching.

But all this was as nothing compared to what was to come. For as I said, it had been a wet year, with a poor harvest. By long-established custom and tradition, the rye grown on the island is milled in the estate windmill and the flour given back to the tenants as part of their wages. 1 Timothy 5:18 and all that. I paid for a doctor to come over from the mainland when Rasmussen's youngest child was poorly, and in that connection I showed him the granary, expecting praise for my progressive ways. Instead, he picked up a handful of the stuff and pronounced it rotten and unfit for consumption. The damp had ruined it.

'You will have to destroy it all.'

'All of it? But what will people eat?'

'I'm afraid that's your problem. But they can't eat this. It's full of mildew.'

And so I acquired a great many sacks of potatoes and carrots from Lowlander merchants on the mainland, as a replacement. But then, to my astonishment, Skrivenius began to preach against the consumption of root vegetables. They are grown by heretics in the Irrational Layer, he said, in the realm of the devil – they draw their nourishment from evil in the darkness. You cannot eat at the Lord's table and at the table of demons, too, says St Paul.

I complained to the bishop, but he was rumoured to be of the Lunarian tendency himself, and did nothing. So I deliberately left the storehouse unlocked – and sure enough, many sacks of vegetables disappeared. Then Skrivenius began directing his sermons against those who would lead others into sin, how it was better that a millstone be tied about their necks and that they be cast into the sea, etc. The people grew hungry, and hungry people are restive and unruly.

Eventually, at great expense, I brought in sacks of wheaten flour, and peace was restored. But the episode had near ruined me. People always assume that the lord of the isle has reserves of gold hidden away somewhere. They would be amazed to see me sighing over my accounts by candlelight, trying in vain to balance the books. (And a tallow candle at that – no beeswax!)

The irony, of course, is that Skrivenius and I actually have a great deal in common. We are both book-educated, both unmarried – my wife, from whom I inherited this estate, died many years ago – both of us exiles from the intellectual life where we feel we belong. I suspect I know what is at the root of much of his restlessness. Lonely men are a danger to the world.

And so I look forward to taking up my new position at the court of Kantarborg. It will be a delight once again to converse with others about matters other than the weather and where to spread the horse dung. Most of all, it will be good to be *useful*, to be able to apply my not inconsiderable skills in matters of moment. I intend to make myself quite indispensable.

There is another way to enter the kingdom now – one of the new railway lines has been built all the way up the coast, linking the capital with the garrison at Alsina, where the Sound is narrowest and there are plentiful ferries. Margretha the shopkeeper assures me that it is a safe and convenient route, as well as inexpensive. She has a Kantarborgan robe that is the envy of the village. But I am an old man and set in my ways. And to be honest, the thought of an astronomer of the court sitting in a mechanical contraption with a second-class ticket seems to me a little undignified. Let Skrivenius strive to enter by the narrow gate if he wishes. I will take the wide gate: the sea. Besides, I hunger to see the towers of the city appearing gradually over the horizon, as in the days of my youth. They always seem to promise so much – even with what I know now about the ways of the court.

Mikkelsen the fisherman, who will be my ferryman, tells me the trip will take most of the day. It will be cold, he says, I should wrap up well. His concern for an elderly man is well intended, but I find it irritating. I have had a long life of survival. I am not as fragile as I look. Far from it.

CHAPTER FOUR

Brother Christopher was coasting his bicycle gently down the long hill, the new rudder bearing stashed in his hood, when he caught sight of a long black rowing-boat gradually materialising through the fog in the harbour. The sight had an instantly galvanising effect on him. With an ecclesiastical exclamation – of sorts – he stamped on the pedals and sped down towards the boathouse, outside of which a rather peculiar-looking craft was hanging suspended in chains from a wooden gantry. It looked something like a foreshortened boat, but was equipped with stubby wings and propellers, with a large section of glass panels in the bow. He threw the bicycle down on its side in the grass and began to run.

'Joe! Joe! Where are ya?'

'I'm over here, doing the tarring. What's the panic?'

'Scarper, get out of sight, quick! The abbot's coming.'

'Arrah feck it. Where am I going to hide around here?'

'Get inside! I'll hoist her up.'

Joe crawled up through a hatchway into the craft. Brother Christopher began hauling on a clanking chain attached to a pulley on the gantry, which gradually raised the contraption a few feet off the ground. Then he picked up the brush and can.

'Hard at work, I see, Brother!' said the small, grey-haired man cheerfully as he approached, leaning on the arm of his acolyte.

'Ah, Father Abbot! Good to see you. I was just tarring the hull.'

'We rather miss you on the Rock, Brother. How long has it been now, nearly four months?'

'Around that, I suppose. But we've been very busy over here, as you can see, Father. What do you think?'

'Quite a fine piece of work! Though I must say, it looks more like a boat than an airship.'

'This is a boatyard, Father. Whatever you ask them to build, it always seems to end up looking like a boat.'

'Well, it will undoubtedly float, Brother, but will it fly? That is the question.'

'It's lighter than it looks. It's made of canvas on a wooden frame, stiffened with tar. A bit like the underwater boat, but lighter.'

'It looks a little ... odd. It's not upside-down, by any chance, is it?'

'Ah no, Father Abbot, sure that wouldn't make any sense. If the glass bit was on top, you see, you wouldn't be able to look down at the ground. It's based on a design Joe found in one of the manuscripts.'

The abbot placed a hand on one of the wooden propellers.

'And what are these windmills for?'

'The ancients might have had motors in them, Father, like the Jarl's clockwork engines, but we use them to stir the ballast, so that the water won't freeze. I hear it gets mighty cold in the upper atmosphere.'

The craft shifted slightly in its chains. The abbot watched the movement expressionlessly.

'Have you considered a name for the vessel?'

'I was actually thinking of *Stella Maris*, Father.'

'Ah, most appropriate. After the Virgin.'

'Er ... that's right, Father.'

'And not, of course, after the house of ill repute where you were born. I believe that was endowed with a similar moniker. But I take it that is pure coincidence?'

'Ah, that's it, Father Abbot. Pure coincidence.'

'I'm glad to hear it. Would it be possible to take a look inside?'

'Not at the moment, Father. Not when it's covered in wet tar, like. But I can show you what it's like. Wait till you see what Joe has rigged up in here ...'

Christopher led the abbot into the boatshed and showed him a strange contraption that looked a bit like an inverted dining table with pulleys and wires attached – largely because that is what it was. Above it, suspended all the way from the roof of the boathouse, was what looked like a giant spring. In the middle of the device was a seat and various control levers.

'Joe calls it a simulator. Apparently the ancients used to have them. It means you can train a crew in the controls without having to actually fly.'

'Ingenious!' said the abbot. 'How does it work?'

'Well, it kind of imitates the way the craft will react. This yoke here, for example, controls the altitude ...'

Christopher leaned over and pulled back on a lever in the cockpit, then leaped swiftly out of the way. With a loud shriek of metal, the device shot up towards the boathouse roof on its spring, and dangled there, leaping and dancing about like a fish on a line. The abbot, startled, stared up at it.

'Ah, it needs a bit of adjustment, Father,' said Christopher. 'I forgot the water ballast.'

'Indeed,' said the abbot. 'We would prefer the brethren not to be martyred before they actually leave our shores.'

'Joe says it will be safe, Father. Safer than actually flying. The idea is to be able train crews for the missions without risking either them or the airship.'

They walked back out into the daylight, where the abbot's acolyte was waiting.

'Yes, the talented Brother Joe. Where is he, by the way?' asked the abbot.

'She ... he went down to the village after nails, Father.'

Joe, hearing the name mentioned, peeked curiously out of a porthole. Christopher waved frantically at his companion to get back, then converted the gesture into a flapping motion.

'It'll fly like a bird,' he said hurriedly. 'It'll still need a pretty big balloon to lift it, though. How's that coming along over on the Rock?'

'The brothers have been hard at work in the sewing workshop. We expect the balloon to be ready the day after tomorrow.'

'Ah, that's grand Father Abbot. But there's no great rush, you know. Joe and I will be busy for the next while, what with our wedding and all.'

'Yes. Well. About that. I'm afraid I must ask you to delay your plans.'

Christopher turned and stared at the abbot in astonishment.

'But ... I got the letter ... from the Pope in Birmingham! I'm to be released from my vows. And Joe can become a woman again.'

'Yes, when I perform the necessary rites for you both. But I'm afraid an urgent situation has arisen, and the Church needs your help. The Pope has asked for you and Joe personally. He wants you to travel to Kantarborg straight away, with an important message for the king of that country. You will need to go there in this craft. We can regard it as a test flight. And I'm afraid I must ask you to do this before I can give you leave to marry.'

Christopher looked dumbfounded.

'But we've been waiting a whole year! Couldn't you at least turn Joe back into a woman again first?' he asked, a note of desperation entering his voice.

'Not on a Church mission, Brother! You know the rules. Monks must be men, celibate and chaste. No women allowed. But if you perform this one last task for us, I promise you there will be no further impediments. Joe will be returned to his former feminine state, and you will be free to marry with the full blessings of the Church. I will even perform the ceremony myself, if you wish.'

Christopher opened his mouth, then closed it again.

'It's just a quick trip, Brother!' the abbot continued sternly. 'Over to Kantarborg, deliver the message, then back. In an airship, it should not take you more than a month. Two at most.'

'But what about the mission to America? You had a team picked out and everything.'

'Yes, but it needs funding, Brother. The king of Kantarborg

has been in negotiation with the Pope for some time, and has offered a very large donation of gold for our charitable and scientific purposes, in return for certain concessions. You are aware of the precarious financial situation of the Church. And it seems our silver is no longer as respected as it once was.'

'Jaze, you're telling me. I've had the devil's own time paying the boatwrights. Ah, saving your presence, Father Abbot. They won't take our silver anymore.'

'How have you been paying for the work, then?'

'With beer, Father. A few barrels. From the brewery.'

'Beer!'

'Well, the thing is, Father, it's a solid currency. Whatever way the silver market goes, beer keeps its value. The boat builders sell it down in the village and they hold a grand hooley. Ah, so I hear.'

'Do they, indeed? And all this is the work of the Lord, do you consider?'

'Whatever it takes to get the job done, Father.'

'Hmph. Well actually, that is precisely the reason why your trip is of such importance. If we are to continue our missionary and scientific work, we must have funds. This could be the answer to our prayers.'

He smiled at Christopher's downcast expression and laid a hand on his shoulder. 'Cheer up, Brother! You know the old saying: Abstinence makes the heart grow fonder! I will come back and see you again shortly.'

Chuckling to himself, the abbot turned and offered his arm to his acolyte, and they began to walk down the harbour steps towards the waiting boat. Christopher watched them go with an air of disbelief.

'Joe!' he called out, as the long rowing-boat pulled away from the dock. 'Joe! You can come out now, he's gone. But I'm afraid I've got some bad news. You're going to have to stay a man a while longer.'

Joe emerged from a hatchway onto one wing of the craft, the

monkish habit failing to conceal the round protuberance of her belly.

'I heard. Well, it's a bit fecking late for that now, isn't it?' she said.

CHAPTER FIVE

How does he do it? How does he always do it? I asked myself as I stood leaning on the railing of the ferry', staring out over the stern at the receding Northland shore. The day was overcast and blustery, and some lackadaisical snowflakes were drifting around the boat. I was glad I had brought my warm cloak. Marieke would not be well pleased at my sudden departure, although she would find my note. But she would at least be glad to see the back of our visitor, I reasoned to myself. She would probably start fumigating the place at once.

The ferry was one of the modern clockwork models, powered by Hansen pods, and so produced little noise and no smoke. I was pleased; it was about time they got rid of those dirty old steamers. I wondered who the engineer had been for the project. Tillonsen, perhaps. I had heard rumours that he was the new clockmaker royal.

My companion was standing at the other end of the vessel, his sack at his feet with my precious model locomotive inside. *In the Yule Father's sack, of course, Karl! What could be more natural? You don't want to have to pay duty on this item, I can tell you!* He was gazing at the approach of what had once been his kingdom. I wondered what melancholy feelings that might inspire. I need not have worried; his mood was buoyant, as usual.

'Come over here, Karl, look! Look at all those windmills! Enough to charge thousands of pods! That is one part of my legacy they cannot deny.'

'They do look magnificent, your Maj ...' Force of habit. My voice trailed off awkwardly.

'Just call me Rex. They won't get the joke.'

I nodded, though neither did I. We watched as the windmills drifted by. There seemed to be an immense host of them, like an army of four-armed warriors at the ready. I liked to think that they were partly my legacy, too. But I kept that thought to myself.

The boat reversed its engines as we approached the quay, throwing up foam as the men threw the ropes to shore. One stevedore on the dock popped a lighted pipe into the pocket of his dark blue jacket as he grabbed and tied the hawser with his heavy-gloved hands. I looked about for the clockwork locomotive, and was gratified to see it standing ready to receive us at the quayside, looking resplendent in its red livery.

We stepped down the somewhat unstable gangplank and joined the queue at the station ticket office. Behind us, a collection of small spruce trees was being unloaded from the boat and stacked up along the platform.

'I've never understood the point of all that,' said Rex, looking at them.

'Yule trees? People put them inside their houses to celebrate the solstice.'

'Yes, yes, I know that of course, but whatever for?'

'For good cheer. They hang decorations on them. And candles.'

'And that's it? They pay money for that? How extraordinary.'

'The Northlanders do good business with them. Some of my neighbours grow them for the Kantarborg market. It's an ancient custom.'

'An ancient custom invented by some canny Northlander merchant, more like.'

I had given Rex some coins before we set off, with which he now insisted on treating us to a first-class compartment. We had it to ourselves – at one stage a gentleman in a top hat opened the door and poked his head in, wrinkled his nose, and hurriedly withdrew.

The Yule trees were loaded onto the last wagon of the train, and then the locomotive was wound up – which is to say, the Hansen pods were loaded into it – and we set off. The train seemed to squeak a lot more than I remembered.

'Lubricating oil,' I said. 'It was always hard to come by.'

'Remind me of that when I get my throne back. We shall have to do something about it.'

I looked away, out of the window. When he said things like that, the potential enormity of what we were doing kept trying to sneak its way out of the corner of my mind where I had buried it. I had almost succeeded in convincing myself that I was merely taking a short trip to a neighbouring city with an old if slightly peculiar friend. But it was unlikely that the Kantarborg Watch would see things quite that way, if we were discovered.

Rex seemed lost in his own thoughts as the train clattered across the snow-covered fields of Agaholm, but he became abruptly galvanised when we halted outside the city ramparts and he caught sight of the banner flying above Island Gate: three yellow circles on a red background. He jerked to his feet, pushed down the window, and stared out in disbelief.

'What the devil's that?'

'It's the new flag.'

'But they can't just change the flag of the Kingdom! How dare they! It was a thousand years old!'

'They say it's the original flag of the city. I don't know what they base that on.'

'Traitors! Bloody traitors! That's not the flag of Kantarborg!'

Outside, on the platform, I could see a Watchman walking along the train, checking on the passengers in their compartments. He looked up at the commotion. I dragged Rex back from the window.

'Please, your Maj ... Rex! Please, I beg of you, be quiet!'

'I'll see them all hanged! Hanged!'

'SHUT UP!'

The Watchman put his head in the window and stared in some confusion at the sight of someone apparently trying to strangle the Yule Father.

'Merry Yule!' bellowed Rex sourly. 'Ho bloody ho!'

The Watchman moved swiftly on.

'You almost got us arrested!' I gasped, as the train started up again and rattled through the echoing archway beneath the ramparts.

He flashed me a surprisingly cheerful smile.

'Relax, Karl. No-one ever comes near a lunatic. Trust me, I've learned that.'

In Sandviken, Marieke stood at the hall table, holding the unsigned Yule card from Kantarborg. *I am looking forward to my gift. Hurry down the chimney tonight.* It looked like a woman's hand.

CHAPTER SIX

Sitting in the cockpit of *Stella Maris*, Christopher was trying to eat a bowl of porridge, but was having some difficulty guiding the spoon to his mouth. He put out a hand to steady himself as the craft lurched to starboard again. This didn't feel much like the simulator.

'Joe, far be it from me to criticise, but aren't we getting a bit fecking low?'

'Maybe a touch.'

'You can see the wave tops!'

'Well, they're big waves, CC.'

'Somehow that doesn't make me feel a whole lot better.'

On the advice of Brother Thomas the meteorologist – who had also studied the planetary alignments and pronounced them favourable – they were attempting to ride a cyclone to the north. This meant following the winds south-east in the first instance, with the hope of being swept north-east and eventually north-west by the vortex. 'Like riding a panther,' Brother Thomas had said, with his gap-toothed smile. 'You'll be there in no time.' But the trouble with riding a panther, reflected Christopher, is that it's a heck of a rough ride and the beast may decide to eat you along the way.

The craft swung violently from side to side again as the wind buffeted it. Raindrops, mingled with snowflakes, spattered against the glass panes of the cockpit, almost obscuring the view of the sea beneath them.

'Could we not try to get a bit above the weather, at least?'

'The thing is ... I think we might have a bit of a leak in the balloon,' said Joe, pointing at the pressure gauge.

Christopher made another attempt to get the spoon into his mouth, missed again and gave up. He put the bowl aside.

'Well, isn't that just flipping typical? See, that's what happens when you try to get monks to sew a balloon. Sure those days are gone. I told the Abbot, I said to him, we should have got one from the Jarl. A modern one, in rubber. They're all one piece, no seams. But he wouldn't hear of it.'

'We'll put that on your gravestone, boy. *He was right.*'

'Well, how's this contraption supposed to get to get halfway around the globe if it can't even get across the Anglian Sea? If we go down here, we've had it. We'll have to swim home.'

Christopher narrowed his eyes to peer at where the horizon ought to be, but it was hard to distinguish the sky from the water.

'Isn't there anywhere we can stop for repairs? Any monastery nearby?'

'Take a look at the chart, it's in the drawer.'

Christopher opened the drawer and unrolled the parchment map. It was decorated with mythical beasts in red and blue inks.

'Well, this is a great help.' He turned it around and examined it from another angle. 'There's the brothers at Mont-Saint-Michel. Same order as us. They ought to be within an hour's flying time of us.'

'Can you give me a course?'

'According to this fine piece of creative art from the brothers at Kilkiernan, we turn right at the next sea monster.'

Christopher stabbed his thumb at a drawing of a well-endowed mermaid sitting on a rock.

'We can ask your one here for directions.'

'But seriously. Do you think we can we find it?' asked Joe.

'There ought to be two islands around here, fairly large. They used to be part of the Unintended Kingdom.'

'The what?'

'Did you not learn any history in Kilkiernan? The Unintended Kingdom. Founded by William the Confused.[1] Anyway, if

1 According to *A History of the Ancient Kings of Anglia* by Anton of Bow, William the Confused (also known as Will the Unwilling, a phrase that later became the family motto), Lord of the Isles of Gerns and Jers, was returning from a journey to the Frankish emperor when he was blown off course and landed on the coast of Anglia. Believing himself to have arrived home, he was horrified to find his duchy full of strangers, and set about slaughtering the native population. After many massacres, he was eventually declared King of Anglia and the Isles, later known as the Unintended Kingdom. Historians

we can find the islands and keep them on our port side, we should go straight there.'

He looked up from the map, and his eyes widened.

'Jaze, Joe!'

They were now no more than a mast-height above the waves.

'I know. I'm doing my best. Flaps are on full. We don't have enough lift.'

'Could we not let go some water ballast?'

'We only have half a tank left. I'm saving it for emergencies.'

Christopher lifted the spyglass and studied what could be seen of the horizon.

'No sign of land. Visibility's bad. But there's a boat up ahead. We could ask the way.'

'Very funny.'

'I'm serious. We're on the same breeze, we can match their speed. Go on, give it a try.'

A mile ahead, a small, single-masted fishing boat was heading south, its sails billowing in the fractious winds. As they approached, they could make out the figure of a man in oil-skins, standing at the wheel. Christopher unbolted the side hatch and opened it.

'What if he doesn't speak Anglian?' asked Joe.

'Looks like a Frankish crab boat. Don't worry, just leave it to the old sailor here.'

Stella Maris drew gradually closer to the boat, which was making difficult headway in the heavy seas. The man at the wheel was fully preoccupied with steering his craft and had not noticed that he had company approaching from the stern.

'I'll try and get his attention,' said Christopher. He picked up his box-like monkish hand bell, held it out of the side hatch and rang it vigorously. The man on the boat gave a glance over his shoulder, then turned around and stared in open-mouthed disbelief. Christopher took the loud hailer – a conical brass instrument embossed with the figures of angels – and stuck his

---

differ as to the true extent of William's confusion.

body halfway out of the hatch.

'*Allô! Allô monsieur! Où est l'abbaye de Mont-Saint-Michel? Dans quelle direction?*' he called down.

'*Allez vous faire foutre, bande d'imbéciles!*' the man shouted back.

'*Merci monsieur!*' Christopher climbed back in and closed the hatch. In front of them, the mast of the boat suddenly swung into view, much too close.

'Jaze, mind out we don't hit her, Joe!'

'I'd better let go the ballast.'

Joe wrenched at a lever and the airship's remaining water ballast cascaded onto the deck of the boat below, drenching the man, who roared up at them, shaking his fist. *Stella Maris* jerked upwards and began to ascend.

'What did he say, anyway?' asked Joe.

'He said it's straight on,' said Christopher.

'Bit of a change from the Rock, eh, Joe?'

Christopher glowed with the kind of approval that only a full stomach can give. Colourful covers lay on the two beds in the cell, and there were religious pictures and hangings on the wall. He sat down on one of the beds.

'Clean sheets and a feather mattress. Fecking brilliant. Fair play to the abbot here, he knows how to treat a guest. He reckons our airship will be repaired by tomorrow, and they're pumping up fresh water for the ballast tanks. All in one night. That's continental efficiency for you.'

Joe looked doubtfully at the other bed, then began to haul the covers off and dump them on the stone tiles of the floor.

'What are you doing?'

'I'm going to sleep on the floor.'

'What? Are you joking me? What in the heck would you

want to do that for?'

'I didn't join the brethren to sleep in a feather bed, boy.'

'Ah for feck's sake, Joe, it's only the one night. And you're a... you're with ... I mean, in your ... , '

He waved his hands incoherently in the air. Joe looked at him with sceptical amusement.

'I'm a lay brother of the brethren of St Michael until the Pope declares otherwise, Brother Chris,' said Joe. 'I took vows of poverty, chastity and obedience. And *this* is not what I call poverty.'

She began to spread the blankets on the stone tiles.

'Well, we're hardly in a position to point the finger, are we? That belly of yours isn't exactly a sign of chastity,' said Christopher, and instantly regretted it. Joe's eyes flashed.

'That was a misunderstanding.'

'I've never heard it called that before.'

'Call it deception, then, if you prefer. You told me, you *assured* me, that I was a woman. But it turns out I was a man all along. And a monk!'

Christopher held up his hands.

'All right, all right, *mea culpa*. We jumped the gun a bit. But these lads are monks of St Michael too, you know, same as us. And they don't seem to mind sleeping in a bed.'

'They're on the slide, boy. Luxury and decadence.'

Christopher sighed.

'Could be, I suppose. Did you hear their abbot? He could hardly speak Anglian. The abbot! I had to speak Frankish to tell him who we were and where we came from.'

'It's not so much their language I'd be worried about. They eat lunch, boy – bread and cheese! And they drink wine! They even have warm water to wash in. I couldn't believe it.'

'Well, being comfortable is one thing. But it's the language that worries me. If they lose that, Joe, they lose everything: science, technology, history ...'

'And the Good Book.'

'That, too. Although they have a translation in Frankish.

They read from it while we were eating.'

'Is that what that was? Isn't that heretical?'

'Apparently they use the Anglian version at mass.'

'I should flipping well hope so. Sure these fellas aren't real monks at all. They're just living off the fat of the land.'

'Well, maybe so. Anyway, we should be off by tomorrow afternoon. They have plenty of hydrogen to fill her up again, and they've refilled the water tanks. But the abbot says there may be more bad weather on the way. The glass is falling.'

'Doesn't matter boy, the sooner we're out of here, the better. This place is a nest of corruption.'

Joe lay down upon the floor and drew the blankets around her. Christopher patted his bed and sighed. Then he, too, began pulling the blankets off and throwing them on the floor.

'Nest of corruption,' he muttered to himself.

'Is that it?' asked Joe, pointing at the spires up ahead. She had to shout to make herself heard above the wind. Snowflakes danced around *Stella Maris* as the craft swung back and forth in the storm. 'We'll have to get her down soon, or we'll be wrecked.'

Christopher was looking out to port. He seemed distracted.

'Well is that the place or isn't it?' said Joe.

'Yeah, that's it. Look at that, Joe.' Christopher pointed out of the window at a long row of warships at anchor in the sea, not far from the city.

'Never mind that, we need to bring her in. Look out for a mooring tower.'

'They're flying the Northlander flag. I think we might be arriving in the middle of a war or something.'

'Great. If the wind doesn't get us, the cannonballs will.'

'There's supposed to be a round tower in the middle of the city where we can moor. Can you see it?'

'I can't see a thing with this flipping snow.'

'There it is – see it? It's over there to starboard. Give me the helm a second.'

Joe relinquished the helmsman's place to Christopher.

'We're going too fast,' she said. 'We'll need to slow down for docking.'

'I know, I know. I'll just take her around the tower to lose speed.'

They crossed the perimeter walls of the city; snow-covered roofs began to race past beneath them. The tower suddenly loomed very large ahead.

'Chris! Watch out, for feck's sake!'

'It's higher than I thought!' said Christopher, as he banked the craft urgently to port. There was a scraping sound, then a loud bang.

'Did we lose anything?'

'The controls are gone. I can't steer her.'

Stella Maris began to rotate slowly in the wind.

'Take her up again, fast,' said Joe. 'We'll have to land outside the walls.'

Christopher released the water ballast, which splashed down onto the streets below, and the craft lifted, still gyrating helplessly, and cleared the city walls.

'There!' said Joe, pointing. 'Put her down quick.'

'That's woodland, Joe. We'll crash.'

'No choice! Let out the gas! Easy, now.'

Christopher jerked a lever to release the hydrogen, and the ground came up much too fast to meet them.

CHAPTER SEVEN

At the train stop in the city centre Rex eagerly hoisted his sack on his back, opened the carriage door and jumped down. I followed him across the canal bridge and into the winding High Street. Although the day was cold and grey, the shops and stalls seemed to be doing good business. Some light snow had fallen and the city looked delightful in its seasonal garb, with garlands hung across the streets, emblazoned with hearts and stars. Braziers had been lit and the sweet aroma of roast almonds seasoned the air. Street musicians, acrobats and magicians were competing for the attention of the crowds between the market stalls, where all kinds of trinkets, some home-made, some purportedly from the Orient, were on sale as Yule gifts. I made a mental note to look for something nice I could bring back to Marieke. It might appease her for my sudden disappearance.

I saw several other people dressed up as the Yule Father, like my companion. A few were ringing hand-bells and beckoning to passers-by, cajoling them to enter shops or taverns, while others were telling fortunes or simply begging.

'You would fit right in here,' I said.

'Too much competition,' he muttered. 'Oh, and just look at that blasted nonsense!'

A large banner bearing the words 'MERRY NICHOLAS-TIDE' flapped in the breeze above the street. Alongside the words was a crudely-painted image of St Nicholas the Gift-bearer, looking fat and resplendent in his red and white robes, seated on a giant sleigh drawn by a team of reindeer.

'I'm pretty sure it didn't look anything like *that* when they handed him over. I've never seen a sleigh like that up north, for a start. You'd never get it through the forest. And that "Nicholastide" rubbish.'

'Most of the other signs still say "Merry Yule", sire.'

'Humph. Give the Church an inch and they'll take a confounded liberty. They need to be kept on a tight leash.

Remind me of that.'

I drank in the atmosphere gratefully. Kantarborgans celebrate Yule for the whole month of December; candles burn brightly in the windows, and there is feasting and merriment every day. I have always loved this season.

'I've always hated this season!' said Rex loudly. (A woman passing by glanced at the Yule Father in some surprise.) 'It's nothing but a drinking orgy. No-one does any work! The cost to the kingdom in lost work time is incalculable.'

'Well, people need to relax and enjoy themselves once in a while.'

'Once in a while? It's the whole damned month! Do you know, when I was ... at court, every day of Yule, as soon as it began to get dark – and that's the middle of the afternoon, you know, at this time of year! – everyone would disappear. Off they would all go, to the taverns. Tradition, they said! Servants, courtiers, guards, the lot. I'd be practically alone there in the palace. If an enemy had decided to attack us at that moment, we would have been utterly helpless. Luckily most of our neighbouring kingdoms are just as foolish about the solstice as Kantarborgans are. Blasted superstition.'

'But surely it's only natural to celebrate the darkest point of the year? Just before the days begin to brighten again.'

'Yes, yes, all right, but couldn't one day be enough? We could call it Big Yule Day, or something. Or two days at most: First Yule Day and Second Yule Day. That ought to be enough for any...'

He stopped abruptly and placed his hand on my arm.

'Karl, listen!'

The faint strains of some lively piano music could be heard drifting on the wind.

'My God ... that's ... that's *Maple Leaf Rag!*'

He set off marching towards the sound, his boots scuffing in the snow.

We traced the joyous jangling to a basement tavern on a

corner, where we stood outside, listening. A peeling blue poster announced that ˌMiss I. Andersen would be playing the new *jazz music* today. The sound that emerged from within undeniably resembled jazz – and by the sound of it, it was getting an enthusiastic reception.

I followed Rex as he descended the steps and cautiously pushed open the door. Inside, by candlelight, a large group of Kantarborgans of all ages sat listening to a very respectable-looking lady hammering out some chirpy tunes on a battered upright piano. She appeared to be playing from handwritten sheet music. I had heard rumours that some of the melodies on my discs had been scored and were circulating as pirate copies, but I had never imagined that the craze might have spread to Kantarborg.

'Come on Karl, let's have a drink, now that we're here,' said Rex, fishing some more of my coins out of his pocket. 'My treat.'

After a glass of *gløgg*, the traditional hot spiced wine, my companion's Yule spirit improved considerably. He sat entranced by the music, tapping his fingers to the beat and occasionally humming along.

'Isn't it wonderful, Karl? *Breakin' In A Pair Of Shoes!*'

Almost all of the tunes I had heard so far seemed to have originated in my meagre collection of discs – but not quite all of them, which puzzled me a little. Was there some other source of jazz melodies around here? Or perhaps they were even writing their own?

Rex sent me up to the bar to get more drinks. These would have to be our last – I was worried about the time.

As I picked up the glasses and walked back to our corner, someone called out a toast to the pianist. She stood up and bowed shyly to the assembly. Rex, meanwhile, had struck up a conversation with the man beside him.

'You think *you* have problems with women? I have TWO wives! And either one of them might attack me at any moment from an airship! Oh, you can laugh, but it's perfectly true! Ah, there you are, Nielsen.'

'Rex, we'll really have to ...'

He snatched the glass from my hand, and to my horror, leapt up onto his chair.

'I will give you a toast!' he shouted out to the assembly. 'To the Young King, a true lover of jazz!'

An awkward silence fell across the room as its occupants stared at the crazed man in the Yule Father costume. Rex, seeing that no-one was about to share his toast, shrugged and knocked back his drink. The pianist hurriedly sat down and began to knock out another merry tune.

A man pushed his way through the crowd towards me.

'I don't know who you and your friend are,' he murmured urgently in my ear, 'but I think you should leave now. We don't want any trouble here. This is not some royalist saloon.'

I nodded, picked up my companion's sack, grabbed Rex by the elbow, and manoeuvred him out of the door and up the steps into the snowy street.

'What did you do that for?' he complained, shaking off my guiding hand as we walked up Woolmerchant Street. 'I was just starting to enjoy myself!'

'Perhaps you could try to enjoy yourself a little less, Majesty? Before you get us both killed?'

'Oh nonsense, Nielsen. You were always such a stick in the mud. You should relax more.'

'Could I give *you* some advice, sire, for a change?'

'Well, why not, Karl? You are my one remaining counsellor, after all.'

'Give up this crusade. It's hopeless. Kantarborg has moved on.'

'But I am the rightful monarch of this kingdom! What would you have me do? Go back to begging on the streets?'

'Well, *I* don't know. Learn a trade? Become a musician?'

'Indeed, why not?' he laughed. 'I was taught the piano in my youth, you know? Old Petersen the music tutor with his metronome and compendium of Anglian and Kantish folk melodies. *Alley Cat* and all the rest of them. Every Saturday afternoon at the palace, dear God. But unfortunately we can only be who we are, Nielsen. And follow that path wherever it leads. Don't you agree? Hm? Are you listening?'

'Er, sorry, Majesty ... yes, I suppose you're right.'

I had been a little distracted by an odd sight. The King followed my glance, and stared.

'Tell me, Karl, have my wits deserted me entirely, or was that a pregnant monk?'

CHAPTER EIGHT

'You can't go walking around in sandals like that in this weather,' said Christopher, as he and Joe trudged down Wool-merchant Street in the snow. 'There's plenty of shoe stalls here. Let me get you some proper boots, at least.'

'Mortification of the flesh,' replied Joe. 'Prescribed for the brethren and good for the soul. You should try it, you oul' sinner.'

'Joe, for crying out loud, you're a pregnant woman.'

'Ah, don't be going on. I'm a lay brother of the Order of St Michael, and proud of it. And I'm also a pregnant woman.'

'I'm not sure that's possible.'

'*With Man this is impossible, but with God, all things are possible.*'

Christopher gave it up. Theology was not his strong point. Snow was snow, however, and Joe's feet must have been freezing. He himself had breeches and boots on underneath his monk's habit, and a cloak around his shoulders, and he still felt the cold. Hopefully it would not be too much further.

Their dramatic arrival had not gone unnoticed, and the battered remains of *Stella Maris* had swiftly been surrounded by a party of armed men, who conveyed them to the nearest town gate. The papal seal had caused a bit of a commotion when they presented their papers, and a guard had been dispatched on horseback, with the documents in his satchel. After an hour, he returned and told them to walk down this street to the palace and present themselves. It seemed to be going on forever. This was the biggest city Christopher had ever seen. It must hold fifty thousand people, at least. Maybe more. Something flapped above his head and caught his attention.

'Ah jaze, wouldya look at that!' he said in annoyance, pointing at the banner.

Joe peered up.

'Is that supposed to be him?'

'It is, Joe. Pope Nicholas himself. Riding on his sleigh, bringing gifts to the world.'

'Sure that doesn't look notton like him. And there's no sign of us anywhere.'

'Ah well, we're only minor characters in the story, aren't we? Like the wise men at the Nativity.'[2]

'The ass and the cow, more like.'

The winding street eventually led them to a canal, where a vast, grandiose building rose up on the other side, larger even than the Palace of the Holy See in Birmingham, which it was said could hold nearly two hundred people.

'That's some kip,' said Joe. 'Is that it?'

'That's what the fellow said. Down Woolmerchant Street and across the canal.'

'Holy God! Look at that!'

Along the street beside the canal, a large machine was making its way slowly towards them, its front end pushing aside the snow like the prow of a boat. It squeaked to a halt beside the palace, and the passengers disembarked.

'That's one of them clockwork trains,' said Joe in wonder.

'Yep, like we saw up north. Great little yokes. Long as you have the windmills to wind them up.'

'Well, we've got plenty wind back home. And they're of the angels, you know – they use only the fruits of the air.'

'Yeah, so you keep saying. But you still need a load of metal for them, Joe. Iron and steel, for the engine.'

'It's the power source that matters, boy. Long as that's alright, the Church says it's allowed. Even for monks.'

'Maybe one day. If the Order ever gets enough money.'

They crossed the canal by a stately bridge and stood staring up at the grey stone façade and its galaxy of windows.

'And this is where we meet the King?' asked Joe.

'Not sure how the protocol works. I think in the first place, we just turn up and tell them who we are. Ambassadors of the

---

2 Anglians celebrate the Nativity on 30 September.

Church to the Kingdom of Kantarborg, diplomatic courtesies, if you please. But remember, we don't pass on our message to anyone except the King himself. Those were the abbot's explicit instructions.'

'Why's that?'

'The abbot said it's a sensitive matter. Something to do with their internal politics here. So until we meet the King in person, we're just envoys from Birmingham, on a friendly visit.'

'They'll never believe that. Sure we're just a couple of monks. Not, like, cardinals or anything.'

'They will, they will. Our papers are in order. Papal stamp an' all. They have great respect for that sort of thing, the Kantarborgans.'

They passed beneath an archway into a courtyard, and found themselves at an imposing entrance, clearly of ancient construction. Christopher, with Joe following behind him, skipped up the broad granite steps and pushed open a tall wooden door.

'Chris, you can't just ...' began Joe, and stopped.

Inside was a vast hall with a chequered black and white tiled floor and wide marble stairways, filled with a motley collection of figures in silken jackets and scarves. All of whom, it seemed, had ceased doing whatever they were doing to turn and stare at the newcomers. There was a silence.

'Which one of you gentlemen is the King?' Christopher called out in the echoing space.

A large uniformed guard began striding towards them, his weapons belt rattling.

'Are you the King?' asked Christopher.

By way of reply, the guard drew his sword.

'Woah, woah, go easy there now Your Majesty,' said Christopher, backing away with his arms raised. 'We're envoys of the Pope!'

A tall, blond-haired man wearing a rather fine-looking scarlet tunic hurried over and said something to the guard, who sheathed his weapon reluctantly, while continuing to eye Christopher and Joe with suspicion.

'You're our two visitors from Birmingham, I take it?' said the tall man. 'Come with me. We can talk in my office.'

They followed him up a broad staircase and down a long hall adorned with portraits of aristocrats and generals.

'Sorry about your reception down there. The guards get a little nervous sometimes.'

'Are you the King?' asked Christopher.

'Ah ... no, not exactly. We don't actually have a king at the moment, you see. Not as such. I'm surprised that Birmingham wasn't aware of that.' He opened a door. 'After you.'

The room was lined with chairs and bookshelves. A military officer was seated at a desk. The tall man waved a greeting at the officer and led Christopher and Joe through to an inner office which was large but sparsely furnished. There was just a simple desk by the window, with a single chair behind it. He called out for extra chairs, which the officer brought in.

'Now, my name is Commander Johansson,' he said when they were all seated, 'and I'm the minister in charge of the armed forces of the Kingdom of Kantarborg. And I am also Head of Security.'

He spoke Anglian well, though with an odd accent.

'I'll come straight to the point. Frankly, I want to know what you're doing here.'

'Well, we're ambassadors of Pope Rurall,' said Christopher. 'You've seen our papers?'

'Yes, I have. Very nice, and with the papal seal, too. But what puzzles me is, we weren't expecting you. We had no word of your coming, and your documents don't mention why you're here.'

'The Holy Father is aware that there have been some recent upheavals in your kingdom,' said Christopher confidentially. 'It would have been unwise to be too specific. This is not an official mission to Kantarborg. More of an exploratory trip. A reaching out of the hand of the Church. In friendship.'

'I see. And you are both in holy orders?'

'I was a monk of the Order of St Michael. I've been released from my vows.'

'No you haven't, ya fibber!' said Joe.

The minister raised his eyebrows.

'Well, I will be soon,' said Christopher. 'It's a bit complicated. And Joe here is a lay brother of the Order.'

'Forgive me,' said Johansson, looking at Joe. 'I do not wish to be rude, but I was not aware that a lay brother in the Church could be with child.'

'It can happen to anyone,' said Joe indignantly, shooting a reproachful glance at Christopher. 'If you're not careful, that is.'

Johansson considered this reply in silence for a moment.

'Indeed. And you will be staying with us here for how long?'

'Until we meet the King. Those were our instructions from the Holy Father.'

'Well, I'm afraid the Pope appears to have misunderstood something. The King is in the far north and is not expected to return to the kingdom for some time. In his absence, I and the Prime Minister represent the crown. Anything you can say to the King, you can say to me.'

Johansson looked from one of them to the other. Neither said anything.

'Of course, it is entirely up to yourselves whether you wish to co-operate with us or not. I understand your craft is damaged?'

'Bleedin' banjaxed,' said Joe.

Johansson looked confused.

'Wrecked,' Christopher translated. 'We had a bit of a hard landing.'

'Yes, so I heard. And you nearly demolished one of our public buildings. So you will no doubt be requiring our help to repair the airship?'

'That would be most kind,' said Christopher.

'Well, we will most certainly try to assist the envoys of the

Pope in whatever way we can. But I'm afraid it might be quite expensive. Is the Holy Father prepared to recompense us for that?'

'Well, to be honest, at the moment the Church is a bit ...'

'Yes, I rather thought as much. As is our kingdom, and with a hungry winter on the way, too. So the question is, how do we finance this? Hmm?'

'I suppose you might have some suggestions,' said Christopher resignedly.

'Well, first of all, let me tell you what I've been able to learn about the two of you from our archives. It seems that you were present during the handover of the previous pope in the north, and are well known to our friends the Albans. They say that you, Brother Christopher, are an accomplished sailor and something of an explosives expert.'

Christopher tried not look startled. They had been pretty quick finding that out.

'In another life, your Ministership. But yes.'

The minister turned to Joe.

'And you, Brother Joe, are an artificer, I believe, and the inventor of a very special type of weapon. A boat that can travel beneath the water.'

Joe winced.

'It was not designed as a weapon of war, Minister.'

'Well, in any case, these are technical skills that I believe might well prove useful to us in our current situation.'

'Er, situation, Minister?'

'I'm afraid you have arrived at a rather tense time. We are being threatened by our Northlander neighbours, who are unhappy at having to pay tolls to pass through our waters.'

'We saw the warships out in the Sound,' said Christopher. 'It looked like you were under blockade.'

'Regrettably, that is correct. Since this morning.' The minister sat back. 'So, what I had in mind was this. I can assign a team to work on your craft. We are experienced in airship construction, so it should be no problem. We will have it up and running in no time, and then you can return to Birmingham with our best greetings to the Pope, and our apologies for the absence of the King. But it would be a shame to waste your talents and your time while you are here, as I am sure you will agree. So in return, we would like you to do a little work for us.'

'Let me guess. Weapons.' said Christopher.

'Given your field of experience, and our current peril, that would certainly be one possibility.'

'My colleague here might have a problem with that, Minister. Brother Joe objects to weapons. On principle.'

'I object on principle to you messing about with fecking explosives, you mean,' muttered Joe.

'As I say, it's entirely up to you,' said Johansson. 'But you must understand that under the present circumstances I cannot justify devoting a large part of the resources of the kingdom to the repair of your airship without obtaining at least something in return.'

'And without our craft, we'll be stranded here.'

Johansson spread his hands apologetically.

'Well, perhaps. Unless the Pope can arrange for your return journey by sea, of course. Although that might prove somewhat difficult in the present situation. But let us meet up again soon and talk about it. In the meantime, the Prime Minister has expressed an interest in meeting you. He is most anxious to repair relations with Birmingham after the regrettable rift of recent years. As you have no doubt heard, he is a devotee of a certain strand of belief within our broad Anglian church.'

'Yeah, we heard he's a Moonie,' said Joe.

The minister's face twitched.

'That is the popular name for the Community of Celestial Concord and Peace, but I would ask you not to use that term in his presence. Do you have time today?'

'We don't exactly have a very full calendar at the moment, your Ministership.'

'Excellent. Then perhaps you could see him now?' He rang a handbell to call a servant.

'What was all that guff about co-operation?' whispered Joe as the boy led them down one long corridor after another.

'Nation of merchants and pirates, the Kantarborgans,' replied Christopher. 'Everything's a deal or a barter to them. *Nugget for nugget*, they say here.'

'And what does that mean?'

'It means, "You give me a nugget, I'll give you a nugget". Of information, like. Or gold. Their highest compliment is to call you a good *collaborator*.'

'Sounds a bit weird to me.'

'It's all give and take, Joe. Negotiation. Bartering. The trick is to let them think they're getting the better end of it.'

They paused at a corner, where the boy indicated that they should wait while he entered a room. He returned after a moment.

'The Prime Minister will see you now.' It sounded as though he had been rehearsing the Anglian phrase.

Christopher and Joe walked through the outer office and into a large room with tall windows and a parquet floor. A chandelier made up of small electric bottles strapped together hung from the ceiling, the light coming and going intermittently. Despite the fire burning in the grate, it was draughty and cold in the high-ceilinged room – like, it seemed, everywhere else in the palace. The Prime Minister, a small, dark-haired man, sat behind his desk, busy with his papers. He looked up as they entered.

'Greetings, Prime Minister!' said Christopher cheerily.

The reaction these words produced was somewhat unexpected.

Prime Minister Kramer stared at them, his eyes widening. Then he stood up, turned as pale as the papers he was clutching, and backed away towards the wall.

'You!'

Christopher and Joe exchanged glances.

'Er, yes, Prime Minister. It's us.'

'Have you ... come for me?'

'Wha'? Ah no, we haven't come for anyone. We're just envoys from the Pope, that's all. Not kidnappers or anything. Take it easy.'

The Prime Minister made an effort to compose himself. He gulped visibly, and put down his papers.

'But you are ... who I think you are?'

Christopher gazed at the man more carefully. He had grown a scraggly black beard, but the scar on his forehead was familiar.

'My God! Joe, it's Ambassador Ekramer!' he laughed. 'What a pleasure to see you again, Your Excellency. We always wondered what had happened to you. It's good to see you're alive. And now you're the prime minister. Well, well!'

Kramer gave a rather strained smile in return.

'I am, by the grace of God. But what are you doing in Kantarborg? Did you come here in your ... craft?'

'Ah, not the same one you saw us in last time,' Christopher replied. 'We came by air this time. But we had a bit of a crash landing, you see.'

Kramer looked uncomprehendingly at them.

With her hand, Joe mimicked the action of a crashing airship.

'Whoosh ... bang! Like what happened to you in the sea, that time.'

Kramer nodded nervously.

'So ... you are stranded here? In our world?'

'Well, temporarily, at any rate.'

Kramer came out from behind his desk and looked from one to the other. He pointed at Joe's midriff in astonishment.

'But ... I did not think such things were possible for ... such as you.'

'Jaze, not another one!' said Joe. 'Doesn't anyone do it around here?'

The Prime Minister looked confused again. Joe raised her hands to demonstrate with a gesture.

'And how have you been since we last saw you?' asked Christopher hurriedly.

Kramer turned to him with sudden urgency.

'Do you have ... a message for me? From *over there*?'

'Ah well, no, not really. Like I said, we weren't really expecting to see you here. We didn't know if you were alive or dead. I must say, you seem to be doing very well. Prime Minister, eh?'

'I have introduced great reforms in this kingdom,' said Kramer proudly. 'I have preached the true gospel. I have taught the people that they must turn away from sin and the underground, and that their true home is on the moon.'

'Ah ... right. Gotcha. And have you had much success with that?'

'The Kantarborgans are a stiff-necked people. They say they believe, but true faith is hard to find.'

'Right. Same as everywhere else on Earth, then, eh?'

'Indeed. This entire planet is a realm of sin.'

Behind the Prime Minister's back, Joe was now making gestures of a quite different kind.

'I suppose it must seem like that, all right,' said Christopher, improvising to hold the man's attention. 'For someone like yourself, who has seen ... other places.'

Kramer smiled warmly and nodded.

'It's so good that you understand! But we must celebrate your arrival here. How long are you planning to stay with us?'

'Well, just until we can get our craft repaired, then we'll be off again. And I hope you don't mind me mentioning this, Prime Minister, but it's freezing cold out there in the woods and we don't have anywhere to stay at the moment, except our craft, which has a few holes in it.'

'There's feckin' snow coming in through the roof,' said Joe. 'And me in my condition.'

'We have an apartment reserved for honoured guests of the

Kingdom,' said Kramer. 'It's in the Round Tower, where the airships moor. You will be most welcome to stay there. Talk to Mr Tillonsen, the royal clockmaker. He has the key.'

'Well, that's very kind of you, your Prime Ministerness. We will accept that offer with gratitude. It will be good to get out of the weather.'

'We will talk soon again. Concord and peace!' said Kramer.

'Er ... right you are.'

CHAPTER NINE

The moonpenny

The King and I were walking up Woolmerchant Street in the direction of the Round Tower. The day was already growing dark, and I was starting to wonder whether the promised music discs would ever materialise.

'So what now, Rex?'

'Well, first of all, we must find a numismatist.'

'A what?'

'Someone who deals in old coins and sells them to collectors.'

'People collect such things?'

'People collect all kinds of strange things, Clockmaker. You'd be surprised. As I recall, there used to be just such an establishment down here ...'

He pointed down a grimy-looking side street, lit by a couple of oil lamps. It was hard to believe that he had ever walked down there as a reigning monarch, even in disguise. But who could tell, with the King? It was more of an alley than a street, barely wide enough for us to walk side by side. But to my surprise, it did indeed contain a small, crooked shop with old postage stamps and coins in the window. *Frederiksen Stamps and Coins*, said the sign. *Gold and jewellery bought.* We stood outside while he scrutinised the display.

'One of the privileges of being a monarch, my dear Nielsen, is being able to design your own coinage. But I do not see any coins from my reign here. Perhaps there are some inside.'

A bell rang as we opened the door– it sounded rather rusty, as though it did not ring many times in the course of a day. As we stamped the snow off our boots on the mat, a grumpy-looking, middle-aged man in a dark blue tailcoat came out of the back room and stood behind the tiny counter. He had side whiskers and a bald head. If he was unaccustomed to receiving visits from the Yule Father, he did not show it.

'Yes?'

'My friend here is interested in stamps and coins,' said Rex.

The man simply raised a hand, as though to say: *Look around you, idiots.*

'We were wondering ... would you perhaps have some coins from the, er, former regime?'

'Which of them?' asked the man in a bored voice.

'Well, do you have anything from the reign of the Young King?'

The shopkeeper looked suspiciously from one of us to the other. Then he bent down and brought out a small book-like folder, which he opened on the counter. Inside, inserted into a number of pockets, were some coins of the realm, bearing the likeness of the King.

'This is what I've got.'

'Anything from after the restoration?'

'After the restoration? What would you want them for? They're much poorer quality.'

'How so?' I asked.

'That's when the mint started debasing the coinage.'

From beneath the counter, he produced a small cardboard box with a few loose coins inside.

'See these, they're not pure gold, silver or bronze, they're full of junk. The gold and silver is impure and there's too much tin in the bronze. Lead, even, sometimes. The Kingdom had run out of money. The King spent it all sending the Prime Minister to the moon, heh heh.'

'He wasn't the Prime Minister then,' said Rex testily. He lifted a bronze coin from the box. 'So how much would a coin like this one cost?'

I took the coin from him and examined it. It was quite large and heavy. On its reverse side it showed an image of the moon, along with the mooncraft that I had designed. I felt vaguely gratified – I had not seen the coin before, nor even known of its existence.

'The moonpenny, we call that one,' said the shopkeeper. 'Commemorative issue. It's a bit bigger than the others. It'll cost you half a sovereign.'

The King looked at me. I had only taken a sovereign with me – enough for the day. Reluctantly, I drew it out of my pocket and placed it on the counter. The shopkeeper sucked in his breath between his teeth when he saw Queen Gudrun's profile.

'That's Northlander coinage, friend. I can't take that here. Not anymore.'

'It's all I have.'

'Well, I can give you the value of the gold, that's all.'

He took the sovereign and weighed it on a set of scales beside the counter.

'Four seventy-five. All right, I'll give you the moonpenny for that. That's doing you a favour, mind.'

'We'll take it,' said Rex, before I could protest.

'Now for the next part of the plan,' he said, once we were outside again. 'But let's get something to eat first. I have a little money left.'

A little of my money, I thought. Now I was broke. But perhaps I was being petty. After all, the man had paid me well enough in the past. (But then again, had that debt not been repaid? And not just once, but many times.)

In a nearby tavern we ate herring sandwiches, which Rex insisted should be accompanied by a glass of *akvavit*. Then he took out a pencil and began to sketch something on a napkin.

'Have you ever been in a gaming hall, Nielsen?'

'Once, sire.'

It was back when I was a student. A large, wood-panelled room, full of well-dressed young people. It was very quiet, save for the rattle of dice and the *thock* of wooden balls being knocked across green baize. It had all looked very tranquil, though it was said that the sons and daughters of the aristocracy could lose an entire estate in an afternoon in such places.

'I will need you to visit one today.'

'I hardly think we have time for that, er, Rex.'

'Trust me, it will not be a waste of time. There are many machines there that I am sure you will find fascinating.'

'Machines, sire? I thought people played billiards and cards in such places?'

'Yes, well, this is a slightly different kind of gaming hall. A bit more proletarian, if you know what I mean. Now, what I want you to look for is this.'

He drew a kind of angled cabinet.

'This is a gaming machine, of a type made by the ancients. I used to have one in the palace. Do you remember it?'

'I once saw such a machine in the workshop, sire. Was it not electrical?'

'Yes, partly battery-powered and partly mechanical. Coin operated. Perhaps you played a game on it?'

'Unfortunately not. That was back in Handrasen's day, and he wouldn't let me near it.'

'That's a shame, it would have made things easier. I donated it to a gaming hall towards the end of my reign, in case I found myself deposed again. Which was prudent, as things turned out. Anyway. The machine you are looking for is called Demon Fire. To play, you put a coin in *here*, in this slot. Now the thing is, when I had this machine at the palace I had it set it up in a special way, to save me having to use fresh coins all the time. Normally you have to put a new coin in for each game, but the moonpennies are larger and heavier than the normal ones. If you put a moonpenny in, the machine spits it out again *here* at the end of the game. So you can use it again and again.'

I nodded. This was sounding increasingly bizarre.

'You pull back the plunger, here, and shoot a metal ball around the playfield. It falls down and hits a number of bumpers, some of which may shoot it back up again. When the ball reaches the bottom of the playfield, you try to shoot it back up again using the flippers, *here*. The longer you can keep your ball in play, the higher your score.'

Bumpers, flippers – what was the man talking about?

'Now, this is the thing. You must reach a score of 100,000 points. All of these lamps across the top must light up. If you don't make that score, put the coin back in and try again. When you reach that score, and *only then*, take this ...' – he handed me a tiny key – 'and open the locked drawer in the front, here. It can only be opened when you reach that score. It contains a small item. Take that and bring it to me.'

'Why on earth did you make it so complicated?'

'Well, originally I had a bottle of *akvavit* hidden in there. It was just a silly game I played with myself, to provide a little extra motivation. Being a king can be a tiresome business sometimes, let me tell you. On occasion I even sneaked out of the Rose Castle in disguise and went down to that gaming hall, just for a little diversion. No wonder monarchs start wars. They are bored to death.'

'But sire ... Rex, you are obviously experienced in this game. Would it not be easier for you to do this yourself?'

'Don't you think it would look a little suspicious if the Yule Father were to be seen playing at a machine in a gaming hall? And if I am discovered my life may well be forfeit, let me remind you.'

This was all starting to feel rather familiar. There was at least one game at which he was an expert.

Back out on the street, the late afternoon gloom was fast turning into night. Time was getting on – would I still be able to catch the last ferry back to Sandviken? If I had known the business was going to be this convoluted, I would never have agreed to come along.

Rex led me down another side street to a basement establishment with an entrance decorated in lurid colours. A sign above the doorway proclaimed the name *Hellfire*, alongside which was painted a large, demonic-looking clown face. This was not at all the kind of gaming hall I had imagined.

'A strange name,' I remarked, to cover my nervousness.

'Inspired by one of Kramer's speeches, I believe. The idiot said such places were the gateway to hell. Here is the moonpenny. I will wait for you here. Good luck!'

I walked down the steps, passing the traditional iron griffins that guard visitors to Kantarborg cellars from the perils of the underworld. He had said the underground would not be involved this time. Well, perhaps a cellar did not strictly count.

The door opened onto a long passageway, lit by oil lamps. The walls were painted dark red, and bore pictures of demonic and macabre scenes. From the far end, I could a low hum of talk and occasional laughter.

At the end of the hall was a counter and cloakroom, where a sign announced an admission charge of half a sovereign. But there was no-one there, and in any case the only money I had on me was the moonpenny, so I walked past.

I turned a corner and entered a large, dimly-lit room full of billiard tables. Not many customers were around at this hour of the day, but a few young men in waistcoats, some of them smoking pipes, observed me curiously. Nearby, a group of women sat on high stools, talking animatedly over glasses of rum. They fell silent as I passed by in my cloak and silken hat, then laughed. If the idea was not to attract attention, I was clearly failing badly. (Though admittedly I was probably doing better than the Yule Father in full regalia would have done.)

There was no sign of the machine the King had described. Perhaps it had been thrown away as a useless antique. But after a few moments I heard a raucous clangour of bells coming from the far end of the room, and when I rounded a corner, I found myself in an area full of exotic-looking machines in gaudy designs, mostly clockwork or passively mechanical, but some also lit up by small electric bottles that flashed in all the colours of the rainbow, while small bells rang noisily. A few youths were standing around and laughing as one of their number tried and failed to win a game. He cursed loudly and hit the machine with the flat of his hand. Some of the machines looked new, perhaps copies of ancient designs, while others were clearly antique, with dark, splintering wooden frames and worn paintwork. I finally found the one called Demon Fire in a corner, looking dusty and somewhat neglected. It was a dark yellow in colour, dowdier than the other machines and apparently rarely used. It bore a picture of a man firing some kind of weapon at a monster, with a pair of scantily-clad women standing admiringly on either side of him.

Glancing around to make sure I was unobserved, I produced the heavy moonpenny from my pocket and pushed it into the slot. The machine immediately gave a jerk and seemed to come to life, lighting up with small electric lamps. A metal ball-bearing dropped into position on the plunger, like a musket ball being loaded into the barrel of a gun. It was clearly a machine of some sophistication – hard to believe that it was used for such a trivial purpose as gaming. But the ancients, by reputation, possessed both great ingenuity and extraordinarily decadent tastes, so who could tell?

Cautiously, I drew back the spring-loaded plunger as the King had instructed me, and let it go. The ball-bearing shot away and arced swiftly around the board, hammering from one side to the other, before dropping uselessly into the hole at the bottom. The machine made a derisive noise, then spat out the moonpenny again, just as the King had promised it would.

Perhaps this device was designed to teach the user something about Newton's laws? Certainly impetus, mass and gravity seemed to be the governing principles. I tried again, using less force on the plunger this time, and began pressing the flippers at the bottom, as the King had told me to do, and thereby succeeded in hitting the ball-bearing up again once. 100 points. It was not going to be easy to score 100,000.

Half an hour later, I was growing a little better. The points seemed to leap up exponentially rather than linearly, so despite my limited skills, I was soon achieving scores in the tens of thousands. The first time I hit eighty thousand, I received a shock: a bell rang several times and something that looked like a line of blue gas jets ignited at the top of the board. A small flap folded up, revealing an illuminated text: *He smoulders! He smoulders!* It looked occult and sinister. I was so startled that I took a step back – and as I did so, I sensed a man watching me. I tried not to look directly at him; he was standing at the other side of the room, staring across at me.

I pushed the moonpenny back into the slot as discreetly as I could and tried again, this time achieving only a miserable score. From the corner of my eye I could see that the man was small but powerfully built, dressed in a black leather waistcoat like an Irdai tribesman. Probably the owner of the establishment. He was making no secret of his interest in me.

I tried again. 85 ... 90,000! Again the machine reacted. The small blue flames appeared again, and the flap opened, this time with another text: *He glows! He glows!*

The man began to walk slowly across the floor in my direction. I quickly pushed the moonpenny back into the slot and began a new game, ignoring him. The scores began to creep up ... 70,000 ... 80,000 ...

He was standing at the end of the row of machines now, looking straight at me. I glanced at him and continued, pretending to be absorbed in my game. The ball fell to the bottom, almost out, but I caught it and hit it back up again with the flippers. It shot about between the bumpers. The score mounted... 90,000 ... 95,000 ... 100,000!

The blue flames lit up, and the words *He burns! He burns!* came into view. Bells began to ring loudly and the whole machine flashed with lights. I tried to get the tiny key out of my pocket, fumbled it and dropped it. I found it with trembling hands on the floorboards, inserted it into the keyhole, and turned. A long drawer slid open to reveal the end of some kind of decorated metal rod. I swiftly drew it out and hid it beneath my cloak, closed the drawer, then turned and walked away – leaving the moonpenny behind in my haste.

'Hey you! Just a minute!' came a shout from behind me. A hand grabbed my shoulder – I shook it off and began to run – out of the gaming machine area and through the billiard room, holding the rod under my cloak. I overturned a chair behind me as I ran, and heard him stumble over it and curse.

Sprinting out into the hallway, I pushed my way through a group of people on their way in. They reacted predictably to the commotion, grumbling but not trying to apprehend me – it was someone else's problem. You can always rely on the indifference of Kantarborgans.

Once outside, I pulled the hood of my cloak up over my hat and simply walked away, not looking back. From behind, I would have looked like any other man in the street.

There was no sign of my companion anywhere. When I felt I was in safety, I took the object out from beneath my cloak and looked at it. It was about three feet long, and seemed to be made of gold. It was roughly tubular, though with some odd protuberances here and there. It bore a number of strange designs and markings that made it look as though it must be either from ancient times or from a distant country. Or both.

Further down the street, I thought I could hear Rex's voice raised in some kind of argument. I joined a small group of curious onlookers who had gathered round to laugh at the sight of the Yule Father in heated dispute with two members of the Watch.

'I assure you, officer, I was *not* begging, I was collecting for the poor! No, there is no law against that, my good man. Royal Proclamation number 438 of 3 June 2414 on Charitable Works and Yule Collections – third paragraph, if I remember rightly. Yes, of course I have a licence. Look – I have it right here, with the King's signature and seal! I *know* it's an old one, but I assure you, it's still perfectly valid! Well, go and get your superior officer then, if you don't believe me.'

The two Watchmen, perhaps sensing that they were slightly out of their depth, eventually wandered off – threatening to come back later, as they always do when they are at a loss. The crowd dispersed and I approached the fuming Yule Father.

'The effrontery, Karl! And they took the money I had collected. Why, that's nothing but blatant theft!'

'Is this what you wanted?' I opened my cloak and showed him the strange object.

'Ah yes, very good. Well done. Was it difficult?'

'It was damn nearly impossible. I had to make a run for it in the end. What is it, anyway?'

'It's a sceptre. A key to power. To be held by the reigning monarch only. I hid it there during the upheavals and the fools never found it.'

'Please don't tell me I've just helped you to steal the crown jewels of Kantarborg.'

'Oh, no. Well, only part of them. And anyway, how can I steal my own property? I am the reigning monarch of this kingdom, you know. I never abdicated!'

'You could have made it a bit easier to get hold of.'

'Ah, but I knew you'd come through. I put my faith in you, Karl!'

I sighed.

'So, what now? Where do we go?'

'Well, where does the Yule Father always go?' he asked with a smile.

'I'm not sure I follow you, sire.'

'We must find a chimney, of course! But a particular kind of chimney. It's in New Square.'

He led me back down High Street to where it opens out onto what had once been the stately plaza of New Square. Some of the buildings surrounding it were still in ruins, but I noticed that the Royal Theatre had been rebuilt since the bombardment. We crossed the street, threading our way through the bicycles and carriages, to the centre of the square, where a clump of naked trees and a few statues partly concealed a small group of odd-looking brick towers, about ten feet tall. I had never really noticed them before.

'Ventilation shafts,' said Rex. 'Built by the ancients. Everyone thought they were the remains of buildings until my knowledge miners opened them up again. They lead down to the underground.'

'But you assured me ..!' I protested.

'No, no, don't worry, you can stay here. I shall go down there myself and meet Lady Amalia.'

'She's down there?' I asked, astounded.

'She should be, with a bit of luck. Then I will deliver your work and collect your payment. And I will also collect the other items I mentioned. I won't be long. Give me your lamp.'

I took the torch from my inside pocket, wound it up and handed it to him.

'Now, your job is to stay here and collect the money,' he said. 'Take off your hat.'

'My hat?'

'We'll pretend it's a little show for Yule, if anyone asks. I'll be back shortly.'

He walked over to the nearest tower, took out the sceptre and seemed to insert the end of it into some kind of hole in the wall. Then he removed it again, pulled up the hood of his costume and began to climb up the tower with his sack slung over his shoulder, using some rusty metal rungs set in the side. A few mildly curious passers-by stopped to watch. Reaching the top, he lowered himself halfway into the shaft, then called out 'Ho, ho, ho!' loudly to the spectators, and vanished inside. The onlookers, mostly smartly-dressed young men and women on their way to the theatre, laughed and walked on. I held out my hat, but they passed me by without a glance – which was probably exactly what Rex had intended.

Half an hour passed, and he did not return. It was icy cold in the exposed square, with the wind blowing in from the nearby harbour. I decided I would give him until the Round Tower clock – my clock! – struck nine, but then I would have to hurry if I was going to catch the last train to the ferry. At the time, of course, I had no idea just how long this night was going to be.

CHAPTER TEN

'What in the name of all that's holy was Ekramer blethering on about?' asked Joe, as she and Christopher walked back up Woolmerchant Street. 'I had the feeling we were talking at cross purposes there.'

'Not at all, Joe. He's just scared of us, that's all.'

'Why would he be scared of us?'

'Why? Well, it's obvious, isn't it? We've got his number.'

'How's that?'

'Well, I don't know what the qualifications are for becoming prime minister of this kingdom, but I'd take a fair bet that being a citizen of the country would be one of them.'

'So?'

'But he's not from round here, is he, Joe? He's from another world! He's an alien! And we're the only ones who know it. No wonder he's scared. We could really queer his pitch here, if we wanted to.'

The evening streets were full of Yuletide bustle. Joe and Christopher bought some roast chestnuts from a stand – after some slightly fractious negotiations concerning the true value of Popish silver coinage – and stopped to watch a fire-eater. Despite the cold, the man was bare-chested and clad in leather and metal, like some kind of warrior. To the beat of a drum played by a young boy standing alongside him, he threw and spun the burning torches above his head and caught them nimbly, the flames lighting up the shop fronts behind him and hissing when they touched the snow. The climax of the act came when he appeared to spit out a jet of flame, making the crowd gasp and jump back.

'I used to be able to do that,' said Christopher, popping another hot nut into his mouth. 'Kept me alive a couple of times when I was down on my luck. I could spit the fire all right, but I wasn't much good at the juggling.'

'You should have kept it up,' said Joe. 'You would have had a good honest trade.'

'Heh, yeah. Waste of good alcohol if you don't make any money, though.'

Someone from the crowd approached the fire-eater and muttered something urgently to him. The man made a quick bow and hurriedly began to pack up.

'Looks like the Law's coming,' said Christopher. 'We'd better get along.'

The snow began to fall again as they went on their way. Joe took the key out of the hood of her habit, where she had been carrying it in lieu of a pocket, and pointed up ahead.

'Is it the tower we nearly crashed into? That looks like a right swanky den altogether.'

'Told you we'd get diplomatic privileges, Joe. We'll be living the life of Reilly here.'

'Yeah, well, don't get too used to it. If the King's not here, we'd better get home as soon as we can. We're not supposed to be helping them with their war effort.'

'Well, we don't have much of a choice, do we, Joe? We'll have to stay here for a while, till the airship's repaired. Anyway, the Lord moves in mysterious ways. He might have some purpose for us to fulfil here. It was his winds that gave us the hard landing out in the woods, after all.'

'That or your flying,' muttered Joe. 'What the heck's going on over there?'

Christopher followed Joe's gaze to a corner of the street, where a group of men in strange round helmets emblazoned with the letters CCCP seemed to be in the process of ejecting people from a basement café. The sound of breaking glass could be heard. A woman standing outside in fine clothes protested loudly, then screamed as one of the men gave her a blow on the arm with a baton. He shouted at her in Kantish.

'Bully boys,' said Christopher. 'Same all over the world.'

'What do those letters stand for?' asked Joe.

'What was it the minister said? Community of Celestial

Concord and Peace,' said Christopher. 'Otherwise known as the Moonies.'

'Infernal Discord and Trouble, more like,' said Joe. 'Wonder what they've got against that place?'

'They don't approve of alcohol, would be my guess,' said Christopher.

One of the helmeted men emerged from the café holding some bottles, which he cast down violently onto the street. From inside came the noise of what sounded like someone smashing a piano with a mallet.

'They don't seem to be great fans of music, either,' said Joe.

'True, not much of an ear, by the sound of it,' said Christopher. 'You go on ahead. I'll catch up with you in a second.'

'Don't you go getting involved now, boy,' said Joe. 'We've no dog in this fight.'

'I won't, I promise. Go on!'

Joe reluctantly began to walk up the street in the direction of the tower. After a minute, Christopher came hurrying up behind, holding his arms in under his cloak.

'So, what did you get?' asked Joe.

'Who says I got anything?'

Joe looked at him.

'All right, couple of bottles of gin,' said Christopher. 'No sense in it going to waste, is there?'

'That's theft, you black sinner.'

'Not at all. Sure you saw them throwing it away. The bottles would have smashed only for the snow. Like I said, Joe – the Lord moves in mysterious ways.'

Near the Round Tower was an open space, where a group of children were whooping and shouting, running and sliding about on what looked like some kind of skating rink.

'Now, who would put a pond there?' asked Joe. 'In the middle of the street?'

'Er, I think we did, Joe. That's our water ballast.'

They stopped at the foot of the tower beneath the clock

automaton, which was just striking nine, and watched in fascination as the procession of figures passed by above them.

'Wouldya look at that? A clockwork angel!'

'Hah! Look at that fella there! He looks just like you,' said Joe.

'That's a saint, Joe. Christopher Columbus, I think. The Moonies have a thing about him.'

'Same name as you and all, then. And he has tattoos as well.'

'Well he was a sailor, after all. Or do you think someone saw me and mistook me for him?' asked Christopher with a grin.

'No offence, CC, but it would take a right eejit to mistake you for a saint.'

When the clock had finished chiming, Joe inserted the large key into the lock of the heavy tower door and gave it a push. It creaked open.

'Jaze, look at this! Is it a spiral all the way up?'

'Looks like the Tower of Babel. I saw a picture of that one time.'

They began to ascend the walkway. Candles left in the window recesses lit the way.

'I don't know about you, Joe, but I'm finding this a touch creepy,' said Christopher.

'Arrah, not at all, boy. It's just like the cloisters at Kilkiernan. Only more ... round and about.'

Joe stepped ahead in sprightly fashion, while Christopher strode more deliberately behind, carrying the bottles of spirits with care. After five turns of the spiral, he stopped and leaned against the wall.

'How're you doing, Joe? Not feeling the strain?'

'Not at all. What about you?'

'No, I'm grand. I just need to get my breath back. How far up are we supposed to go?'

'All the way, said Tillonsen. It's an observatory as well as a mooring tower.'

'I suppose they'd need to get close to the stars, so.' He pointed to a doorway set in the wall of the tower. 'What's in here, I wonder?'

Alongside the door was a brass nameplate: *Marchas*.

'That'll be yer man the court painter,' said Joe. 'Tillonsen told me about him. He does the official portraits for the palace. All the ministers and things.'

'An artist? Well, it'll be nice to have a neighbour. Case we run out of milk or something.'

'Yeah, you wouldn't want to be running up and down this tower all the time.'

''Specially not in your condition.'

'Or yours.'

Near the top of the tower was another doorway. Joe inserted the key again and opened the door. Christopher was looking back the way they had come, down the walkway.

'What?'

'Nothing ... just thought I saw something.'

'What kind of thing?'

'Just a sort of a shadowy ... class of a thing. Moving. Along the wall.'

'Will you get in here and stop your nonsense. There's nothing there.'

They walked into the dark apartment. Christopher stumbled over something on the floor and picked it up.

'A wine bottle, flip's sake ... You'd think they tidy up a bit, if this place is for guests.'

Joe found a switch on the wall. The room flooded with yellow light.

'Electric lamps! Like in the palace. Not bad, eh?'

'Hmm. Think I'd prefer a lantern all the same.'

'Yeah, it's a bit flickery all right. I'll light a couple of candles.'

The apartment was spacious but gloomy. The furnishings were minimal and looked to be very old. A chess set with an unfinished game lay on a low table between two battered leather armchairs. More empty wine bottles lay alongside. In the kitchen, Joe found a wood stove and a tin bath.

'Ah now, this is the business. I'll be able to keep clean, at least.'

She took some kindling from the wood basket and began to stuff it into the stove. Christopher wandered into an adjacent room.

'Joe, come and look at this,' he called.

He was standing beside a set of bookshelves that stretched from wall to wall and up to the ceiling.

'Wow, there'll be some reading there,' said Joe. 'We won't get bored, anyway.'

Christopher pulled down a volume.

'*Diseases of the Dark Ages,*' he read.

'What's the date on it?'

'2148.'

'It can't be that old! Sure that's nearly back to the time of St Michael.'

'Reprint, I think. But it's old alright. The pages are falling apart.'

'Wouldn't be my choice of bedtime reading, anyway,' said Joe. 'This one's more like it – *Principles of Clockwork Engineering.* I'd love to know how they make those trains.'

Joe lit the stove, and the two exhausted brothers of St Michael settled down in the leather armchairs with their books and before long were dozing gently. Outside the window, the snow drifted steadily down.

CHAPTER ELEVEN

The Charmillion

No more trains today due to the situation. What situation? There was no explanation. I kept re-reading the sign stupidly, as though I expected it to change. The night was windy and icy cold, and snowflakes were swirling around the train stop near the royal palace. On the platform was a wooden shelter, open to the weather at the front, but with a bench inside for waiting passengers. I trudged over to it through the snow and sat down while I considered what to do. I had no more money, only my return ticket – and that would not buy me a carriage to the other end of Agaholm, where the ferry sailed from. To walk that distance would take all night, and in this weather I might not even be able to get through. It seemed that there was only one thing to do, which was to wait for the first train in the morning. Marieke would worry, but if I caught the first boat I could still be back before she woke.

The first hour passed achingly slowly. The shops and taverns closed one by one, and the streets gradually emptied. The only illumination now came from the upstairs windows of the houses on the other side of the canal. The wind seemed to go straight through my clothes, and although I tried getting up and walking up and down, I found I simply could not hold any warmth in my body. How on earth did vagrants survive? You could easily freeze to death here, within a few yards of the warmth of someone's living-room. I looked enviously across at the lighted windows. It was almost as though there were two worlds: Inside and Outside. And once you were Outside, it might very well be hard to get back in again. I thought, too, of the King, and of what he must have suffered while living on the street. No wonder he wanted to get back to Kantarborg, where he might at least have the chance of a life Inside, even at great risk. Anything was better than this.

Eventually I became too tired and cold to pace anymore, and sat down again, leaning back on the narrow bench with my eyes half closed, shivering, the snow blowing in upon me when it gusted. Every part of my body seemed to be in pain, first sharply, then slowly diffusing into a dull glow. I gradually fell into a half-doze.

The mind does strange things in such situations. As the hours passed, I saw the snowflakes begin dancing as though alive, creating patterns of occult significance in the night air. I began to see figures forming out of the mists above me. I saw the Ice Palace, and Queen Ulrika weaving at her loom. She looked at me and spoke some words in her own language, as though telling me something of great import, but I could not understand what she said. Then I saw shadows moving along the canal bank, like rats in an alley after dark. But these things were much bigger than rats. One of them suddenly loomed large before me.

'Charlie! There's one of 'em here. 'E's an Enzo[3], I betcha.'

'Drunk as a lord, anyhow. Snazzy hat, eh?'

A hand began to shake my stiff shoulder. My eyes were half open, but I found I could open them no further.

'Hey, friend! You can't sleep here.'

'Give 'im a drink.'

My lips were pushed apart by the neck of a bottle and some caustic liquid was forced between my teeth. I began to cough violently.

'Still alive, then.'

'Just about. Mate, you awake now?' His hand was still on my shoulder.

'Yes,' I gasped.

'Has he got any money?' asked the other one.

'Course 'e don't. Otherwise he wouldn't be here, would 'e? We got you just in time, friend. If you fall asleep, you're gonna

---

3 Kantish term for a vagabond of upper class origin who has lost all his money at cards.

freeze, and then you're gonna die. Got me? You can't stay here.'

As I emerged from unconsciousness, the pain in my body returned. I found I was shivering uncontrollably.

'Nowhere ... else ... to go,' I managed to stutter out. My lips were stiff.

'Well, go for a walk then. Don't stay still. Keep moving.'

'Leave 'im, Charlie. We gotta get along.'

'Can't let him freeze to death, can we? You go on. I'll be along later.'

'Please yourself ...'

My new companion hoisted me up, against my protestations, laid my arm around his shoulder, and began to march me along the canal bank. My legs were so stiff I could barely move them.

'Let us go then, you and I, when the evening is stretched out against the sky...' he declaimed suddenly, in Anglian. It was said in such a sonorous, cultivated voice that I glanced over at him in some surprise. He was younger than me, dark of complexion like the King, with a long pale scar across one cheek, and a grey woollen cap pulled down over his forehead. His eyes twinkled.

'Bet a gentleman like you didn't think I could quote poetry. I'll quote you some more along the way.'

'Where are we going?'

'Oh do not ask "What is it", let us go and make our visit.' Nighttown, mate. Other side of the bridge. There's a dosshouse there.'

When he switched from Kantish to Anglian, it was as though he became a completely different person. It was not just a question of accent; he acquired a whole new voice. He regarded me with knowing amusement.

'And yeah, to shorten the road, I'll tell you my story. I can see you're curious.'

We were approaching the long wooden drawbridge that spans the harbour inlet. The way narrowed here, and we had to tread carefully to avoid stumbling in the railway tracks that share the roadway. My legs were still stiff and painful, and I had to lean on my companion for support.

'I used to work around here, one time,' he said. 'King's service. Down at the grain docks.'

'My father, too,' I gasped. 'Merchant Nielsen.'

'Go on! Your dad was Corn Merchant Nielsen? I knew him. Well, sort of knew him. I saw him now and then. I was just a lad, working as a tallyman. Counting up the bottles and the sacks. Until I got the sack for the bottle, so to speak. See, they don't mind you taking a drop now and then, they all do it, you just keep quiet about it, but when you actually pass out on the job...' He laughed in his 'Anglian' voice: deep and reverberant.

'After that I went to sea for a bit. Signed on board an Anglian merchantman, working the West Sea back and forth. That's where I learned the lingo. Handy, that. We carried corn, rum, slaves, all sorts of stuff. Had to sell the slaves up north, though, you can't do that round here. Norn merchants, they'll give you a good price for them. We used to exchange them for barrels of pickled herring, we called it the herring run. That was all right, but I got the sack again for being drunk on duty. I had the wheel and nearly rammed an Alban man 'o' war. Could have got us blown out of the water, said the Master. Albans, they don't mess about.'

We had crossed the bridge and began to walk down the slope towards the labyrinthine district known as Nighttown. I knew it only by reputation; it was not a neighbourhood people with my background often entered – or not openly, at any rate. My companion stopped to light up a pipe. He offered me a pull, but I shook my head. We walked on.

'So after that I went to work at the Royal Theatre as a rigger. Bit of a change, you'd think, eh? But the thing is, sailors are in demand there, as stagehands. They know their ropes and their knots, see. And they're not scared of heights.'

'Nice easy work. Once you had a scene set, you could sit down with the boys and play a game of cards until the next change of scenery, unless they wanted a ghost to appear out of the stage or something. We knew all the lines in the scripts, heard them a thousand times. Used to sit there saying them along with the actors, laugh about it. But then one day, before a show, the theatre manager rushes backstage, "Who speaks Anglian here?" he says. And me like a gom, I sticks up me hand. It was Romeo and Juliet, and the Nurse had broken her leg. No stand-in. So they dresses me up in the whole gear, big flouncy dress and all, and pushes me out on stage. Well, like I said, I knew all the lines. Most of them, anyway. But the thing is, I had a drop of rum in me. Steady me nerves, like.' He laughed again.

'So there I am on the stage, and I'm hamming it up like mad, giving it all I've got. If I don't remember a line, I just make it up. And the audience loves me, they're pissing themselves laughing. Trouble is, in between my scenes, the boys are pouring even more rum into me. So by the time we get to the bit where she has to deliver the message to Mercutio, I'm practically paralytic. "My fan, Peter," says I, and don't I go and trip right over him? So there's me lying flat on me back on the stage, and the guy playing Mercutio, he walks over, picks up the fan, and puts it over my face. "Good Peter, to hide her face, for the fan's the fairer face," says he. Pandemonium! They had to bring the curtain down.'

We turned a corner. The streets grew narrower here, and the houses rapidly shabbier and more dilapidated, as we moved away from the main streets.

'So there I was, out of a job again. But this time I was an unemployed actor, and that's a better class of dosser, see? And my stage career had given me ideas. So me and a couple of the lads, we started a troupe of strolling players. Used to work the markets with plays and poetry readings. Practised the voice, like the actors I'd heard, very deep, very literary. We did all the classics: Shakespeare, Dickens, Disney. I gave it good as Marley's ghost: "Ebenezer Scrooge!" Course, we had to shorten them a bit. You have to hold your audience, dontcha? They love the sword-fighting and the romance and all the knockabout stuff, but you have to ditch the long speeches. 'Hamlet' would take half an hour, start to finish, tops – less, sometimes. *The rest is silence*, as they say. Then we'd give them a bit of a sing-song, and do a few magic tricks, and pass round the hat. On a good day, you'd make enough for a slap-up meal. I used to love that. Go into a posh place, hand the waiter a fat tip to get us a good table. They'd always take it, though they'd stare at us from the kitchen door, us all decked out in our costumes and all. We were living the life there for a while. But then comes the flipping revolution, and the elections, and next thing we know we have a Moonie for a prime minister, and doesn't he go and flipping well ban street entertainment? A source of drunkenness and disrespect, he says. So no more acting for me, curse him and all his kin. But with my actor's voice, I reckon I could still get a good job somewhere, don't you think? Maybe like a proclaimer or a Yule Father, something like that. *Ho ho ho!*'

We turned another corner.

'It's down this street. It's a handy thing, being an actor. See, someone like you, sir, no offence, but anyone can see you're a gentleman. You're cut to fit your coat, as the saying goes. You can't be no-one else. But me, I can be anyone I like. I'm a char-million, I am. I have a million faces. That's why they call me Charlie. This is the place.'

He pushed open a nondescript door. It might once have been the entrance to a shop, but the front windows had long since been boarded over. A rank, ripe smell wafted out of the dark interior, together with the sound of animated conversation. I hesitated.

'Come on, you won't come to no harm. I'll look after you.'

Inside, when my eyes got used to the gloom, I saw a group of twenty or thirty men, sitting on benches around an iron stove. At a table, another man was serving soup. At first glance, with his long dark hair and brown eyes, he bore a startling resemblance to the King – but my mind was addled, and I was still hallucinating. Charlie misunderstood my stare.

'Hungry, are yer? I'll stand you a bowl.'

He took a couple of coins out of his pocket and paid for two bowls of soup and a small piece of bread. We sat on a bench, holding the warm bowls close. I found I was indeed ravenously hungry, and ate quickly.

'Enjoying that, are yer?'

'Yes. Thank you.'

'And the story I told you, was that a good 'un?'

'Yes, very good.'

'Worth some modicum of recompense, you reckon?'

'I'm sorry ... I have no money.'

'I know that, otherwise you wouldn't be out in this weather. But what you do have, what you *do* have, my friend, is a very nice hat.'

Well, he might well have saved my life, after all. I took off the hat and gave it to him. He tried it on for size and looked around him.

'What d'yer think, lads?'

There was jeering and laughter in response.

'Oh, I'm quite the gentleman now! They'll be calling me Charlie the Charmer in this get-up.'

The banter continued for a while, in a backstreet argot, faster than I could follow. My eyelids began to grow heavy in the warmth of the room, so Charlie gave the man another coin and took me upstairs to an attic, where straw pallets had been laid out on the floor.

'You can doss down here. I've some business to attend to downstairs. Sleep well. And when you get back to your gentleman's life, remember Charlie, won't you?'

I thanked him, took off my boots and lay down on the straw, drawing my cloak around me for a blanket, and I was asleep in an instant.

I dreamed of Erika. She was standing by the city ramparts, with two of the town gates behind her. She looked at me and said, 'Karl, you can go through this gate and find one life, or you can go through the other gate and find another. But you cannot go through both gates at once. If you try, you will disappear.' Make of that what you will.

I awoke abruptly to the sound of something smashing into pieces, and raised voices downstairs. Some grey dawn light was insinuating itself through a cracked skylight in the roof. Somewhere nearby, church bells were ringing. It was Sunday. I sat up on the pallet, and reached for my boots to pull them on. They were gone. I looked around, but there was no sign of Charlie among the sleeping men.

I made my way down the staircase. The stove had long since gone out and the air was frigid, my breath coming out in clouds. In the lower room, the dark-haired man was serving up steaming bowls of warm porridge for a penny each to the few early risers. I tried to explain my predicament to him. He was sympathetic but shrugged.

'Never take your boots off. That's the first rule of dossing, my friend.'

'But I can't go out in the snow with no footwear!'

'Gentleman, are yer?'

But he took pity on me and gave me a bowl of porridge for nothing while he asked around. No-one, of course, knew anything about any boots. He found a few rags in the back room and handed them to me.

'Wrap these around your feet, they'll keep the worst of it out.'

I tried to work out what I could do. There could be no question of trying to walk all the way to the train terminus without shoes, in this weather. There was Johansson's house, though – it was about a twenty-minute walk away, as I remembered. I could perhaps manage that. But he was Minister for Defence now, I had heard. Could I really just go and knock on his door? Still, he was an old friend – and what choice did I really have?

The day was sunny but painfully cold as I stumbled through the snowy streets. The rags were soon soaked through and frozen stiff, so I discarded them and walked barefoot. With my numbed feet, I found myself treading upon sharp stones which left them bleeding. The cuffs of my trousers grew wet from the snow and then froze, scraping stiffly against my shins. Eventually, I was moving so slowly and stiffly that when I crossed the road my life was in peril from the carts and their impatient drivers. Slightly to my surprise, I attracted little attention from passers-by – a shambling, barefoot beggar, even in a fine cloak, was clearly not an unusual sight in the city these days. And as I said, you can always rely on the indifference of Kantarborgans.

In the event it took me more than an hour to reach Johansson's house. It was a detached townhouse – a rarity in Kantarborg – in the southernmost suburbs of the city, surrounded by what I remembered had been a small, pleasant garden in the summer months. Now just a few withered shrubs remained, poking up above the snow. I opened the squeaking iron gate, made my limping way down the path and up the steps to the front door, and pulled the doorbell. The servant girl who opened the door recoiled involuntarily at the sight of the barefoot, hatless, unshaven man with the smell of the dosshouse upon him.

'Who is it?' came the call from within.

'It's a tramp, sir. He says he knows you.'

Johansson came out, pipe in hand, and seemed about to slam the door in my face. But then he stared at me and burst out laughing.

'Dear God, it's Nielsen! But look at the state of you, man! Come inside to the fire.'

I have never known greater relief in my life, I think, than being invited *inside* once again.

Over tea and toast I explained my story to Johansson, who was greatly amused. (I left out the part played by the King, of course, and said only that I had heard about some jazz records for sale in the city.)

'And you went through all this just for a few dance tunes! I would say that was a poor bargain, Karl.'

'Indeed. And now all I want to do is get back home again as

soon as possible.'

His expression changed.

'Ah, well now, I'm afraid that might be a little bit difficult at the moment. You haven't heard? We're under blockade. The Northlanders are rather upset about the re-imposition of the tolls, especially now with a hungry winter on the way, so they are letting no ships in or out of our harbours. Their navy is at anchor in the Sound, just beyond range of our shore cannon. Our military is on high alert, of course, but we are not at war. Not yet, anyway.'

'But I *must* get back, Kaare. Marieke will be frantic with worry!'

'Well, you're not the only one in this situation, you know, Karl. Lots of merchants and traders have been caught on the wrong side of the Sound. We have more than a hundred foreign citizens here right now without food or shelter. We are trying to accommodate them, but we have little enough food ourselves. We might be able to negotiate with the Northlanders to allow us to send some boats of civilians across. You will just have to be patient.'

I put my hand to my brow in frustration. Damn the King and all his schemes! Did he know this was in the air? Was that why he was in such a hurry to get back here?

'But what about Marieke?'

'I wouldn't worry too much. Your wife, if I remember rightly, Karl, is quite the independent type.'

He looked at me, deliberately. How much did he know?

'I suppose so,' I said carefully.

'And she is fed and housed, which is more than we can say for some of the other poor wretches caught out by this. So everything will be all right. You'll see.'

He was probably right. I began to feel a little reassured.

We talked for a while of this and that. I congratulated him on his new position. According to him, the appointment had come as a complete surprise. That seemed a little ingenuous to me; Kramer would have been very foolish indeed not to give an important post to the officer who, rumour had it, was chiefly responsible for the overthrow of the King. He laughed when I asked him what it was like to serve under such a man.

'Well, you know Kramer. He's a political novice, a religious zealot. Although he is learning fast, I must say. He mainly relies upon the advice of those of us who are... more experienced.'

'Just a figurehead, then?'

'I wouldn't go that far. He's very popular in some circles as a religious leader. We must not underestimate him and his faction.'

'Is it true that the Moonies tried to get all mineral products banned?'

'Yes, they tried. And I had to explain to them that you cannot defend a country with wooden swords.'

'But Kramer was on my team when we worked on the locomotive! He should know better than that.'

'Well indeed, but he's seen the light, hasn't he? Ever since his trip to the moon. Everything from the underground is evil or dangerous. Anyway, the compromise is that we have banned all mining here in the Kingdom, but we can quite happily import iron from abroad.'

'But there have never been any mines in Kantarborg!'

'Exactly.'

'So isn't that just blatant hypocrisy?'

'Of course it is, Karl, it's politics. But a side effect is that our archaeological excavations have also been closed down, sadly. No more intriguing artefacts to be brought up from the Irrational Layer, and so nothing to challenge the fairy tales told by the Church about the past. Very convenient for them. Not so convenient for me, because I was hoping to open up more of the ancient tunnels. But that is the bargain we have struck. For now, at least.'

'Between you and me, though,' he continued, 'it's damned inconvenient, this business with the Northlanders, for someone of my background.'

It took me a second to realise what he meant. I was so used to thinking of Johansson as a Kantarborgan that I had quite forgotten that he was from a Northlander family.

'Surely no-one cares about that!'

'You'd be surprised. Though I've been taking elocution lessons, so now at least I don't sound quite so foreign anymore. More suitable for a minister in the Kantarborgan government.'

I sipped my tea and looked around me at the living-room. It was an average-sized house for a senior military officer, but quite opulently decorated. Silk coverings and carved furniture. Paintings on the wall. And a fire lit, even at this hour. Johansson was doing well for himself. It would make a good family home.

'What about your personal life, Kaare?' I smiled. 'No wife yet?'

Wrong question. For a moment I saw a shadow, as of anger or pain, pass across his face. It lasted just a second, and then he was his genial self again.

'No, not yet. I haven't been very lucky on that score, I'm afraid.'

It was hard to imagine Johansson being unlucky with women. I didn't really know what to say. There was an awkward silence.

He glanced up at the clock on the mantelpiece.

'You will have to excuse me, Karl, I must be getting on. We have an emergency cabinet meeting this morning about the blockade. I will raise the question of the stranded civilians with the Prime Minister. Perhaps I will be able to bring you some better news later. Of course you can stay here as long as necessary.'

'That is very kind of you.'

'Not at all. Just tell Martha if you need anything. I will tell her to bring you a pair of my shoes.'

He left, and I began to relax a little after my ordeal. Everything would be all right now. I was a personal friend of the Minister of Defence, after all. Kaare would work something out. I lay back in the armchair, stretched out my sore feet in front of the fire, and, in my exhaustion, fell asleep. And I was still lying there an hour later when the militia came and arrested me.

CHAPTER TWELVE

Joe and Christopher were eating their morning porridge.

'So, what's the story today?' asked Christopher.

'I'm to report to Tillonsen.'

'On a Sunday?'

'It's an emergency. Because of the blockade.'

'Just you?'

'That's what they said.'

'They're after your underwater boat, I bet.'

'Course they are,' said Joe. 'They're under siege. It makes sense.'

'Sure by the time you have one built we'll all have starved to death.'

'They already have a prototype, apparently. But they're having problems with the buoyancy. They want me to help them solve it.'

'And are you going to?'

'I dunno. Depends on what they want to use it for. I'm not going to help them blow people up, if that's what they think.'

'But then how will we get our airship back?'

'That's the thing. I'll have to think about it. And by the way, that's the last of the oats. It won't be easy to get food now. Apparently they imported most of it from across the Sound, and now that's all stopped.'

'Speaking of which, is there any milk?' asked Christopher. 'Or were the cows all Northlanders, too?'

'There might be a drop out in the scullery. Or else yer man the artist might have some down in the studio.'

Christopher disappeared into the scullery.

'I don't know how we're going to buy stuff,' Joe called after him. 'We don't have much silver left. We were only supposed to be away a short while.'

'Maybe I could go down on the street and do my fire-breathing act, so.'

'Yeah, you never know your luck. They might throw some tomatoes at you.'

Christopher returned with a jug and poured the last of the milk on his porridge.

'But they have to feed their soldiers, though, don't they?' he said. 'And we're working for the military.'

'So?'

'So why not ask if we can be put on military rations?'

'You think they'll agree to that?'

'They'll have to. Otherwise, no underwater boat. If we starve to death a couple of dead monks won't be much use to them.'

'I suppose it might be worth a go.'

'Give it a try. Oh, and er, in the navy, they get a daily ration of rum, too, you know.'

'You can blow fire for that one, boy.'

The bowls and spoons on the table began to vibrate as the tower clock prepared to strike eight.

'I'd better be off,' said Joe. 'I'm supposed to be there now. They start work early in this kingdom.'

'You mind yourself out there, now.'

'I will. And see if you can find us something to eat for this evening.'

The first bong of the clock resounded through the tower, rendering further conversation impossible.

CHAPTER THIRTEEN

Twelve drummers drumming

The first thing I heard was a violent banging on the door, then some kind of argument in the hallway. The next moment, a group of militiamen in red and white uniforms burst into the parlour, bayonets fixed to their muskets.

'Clockmaker Nielsen! You are under arrest!' shouted the commanding officer.

This was more like the Kantarborg I knew. I sighed, stood up and put on my cloak and Johansson's shoes.

They led me out of the house and put me in the back of a covered military wagon. I was not placed in shackles – perhaps they thought the presence of armed soldiers would be enough to quell any thought of escape. They were right about that.

By now I had acquired a certain amount of experience in the business of being arrested, so I had learned some of the tricks of the old hands: *Don't resist. Stay silent. Do what they tell you. Don't look them in the eye.* It would do no good in any case, right now, to protest that I was a personal friend of the Minister of Defence. They had their orders, and it would make no difference. Save that for later.

We set off, and from what I could see out of the back of the wagon, we were heading for King's Harbour. That meant the military barracks there, with the splendid cannons outside – the ones that I had so often admired as a child. In those days I had often wished I could go into the barracks and see what was inside. Well, no doubt now I would have my chance.

The wagon halted at the barracks gate for the militiamen to present their papers, then clattered under the archway. We drew up at the far end of the parade ground, and they lowered the tail gate. One of the militiaman jumped down, and the other one poked me in the ribs.

'Right. Out you get.'

They led me into a long, low stone building. Inside was a desk manned by a sergeant. I knew the routine – empty your pockets. All that was in mine was my ticket to Sandviken, which the officer examined with a smirk.

'Thinking of doing a runner, were you?'

I said nothing.

'All right. Name?'

'Karl Nielsen.'

'Occupation?'

'Clockmaker.'

He looked up at that, as though he vaguely remembered me from somewhere.

'Put him in number one.' He handed the keys to a guard.

'May I ask what I am charged with?'

'No you may not, sunny Jim. You'll find out soon enough.'

He probably didn't even know. But whatever my offence was, it must have been in some special category, since it was the militia that had arrested me rather than the Watch. This could be serious. I tried to push the apprehensive thoughts away as the guard led me down the corridor. *Don't panic. Concentrate on the details.* It was a short corridor with just a few cells. Not a prison, then. More like some kind of jail. Perhaps the punishment block for the barracks. There were no other prisoners, as far as I could see.

Facing the corridor, the walls of each cell consisted only of bars, like a cage. All they otherwise contained was a bench and a latrine bucket. The guard opened up one of the cells and locked me inside.

I sat down. Now the waiting begins. You always have to wait. The wheels of justice grind slow, but they grind fine, as they say. I tried to maintain my calm by reciting fragments of songs, poems, tables of equivalents, anything to occupy my mind and dull the anxiety. But the unsettling thought kept returning: *What if they've found him?*

After a couple of hours I heard people talking animatedly in the reception area, and to my intense relief, I heard Johansson's voice among them. He must have come to get me released. Surely it had all been a misunderstanding?

'Kaare!' I called out. 'Kaare, is that you?'

There was a brief silence, then I heard footsteps approaching and Johansson appeared. He looked furious.

'Karl, what have you done?'

'Done? I haven't done anything! Can you get me out of here?'

'You lied to me.'

'What are you talking about?'

From his pocket, he produced the moonpenny.

'*You were seen!*'

'So I cheated on a gaming machine. Hardly a heinous offence.'

'Using a coin that you had previously purchased from a shop in Draper's Alley. Which you visited in the company of a man dressed as the Yule Father. A man with brown eyes, who spoke aristocratic Anglian. Who was he?'

I found I could make no answer.

'I cannot save you this time, Karl. You tried to use me. You are a traitor and a conspirator against the state. And you came to *my house*! You compromised me and gave my enemies material to use against me. I suppose that was all part of the plan?'

'Why didn't you just let me go, Kaare?' I asked wearily. 'No-one would have been any the wiser.'

'And when it was discovered? The Minister of Defence, a *Northlander*, gives shelter to a conspirator against the state, and says nothing? I would have been hanged, you fool! My only hope now is to find your friend before he does any damage. That way I may be able to salvage something from this disaster. You will not bring me down with you!'

I looked into his eyes.

'So finally you are forthright with me,' I said.

'What?'

'In all the years I've known you, I don't think you've ever

really spoken frankly to me. Now you have. Thank you for that.'

He stared at me for a moment, then turned and left.

All right, now was the time to worry. I still did not know if the King was in custody or not, but witnesses had seen him with me. Clearly the government thought there was some subversive plot afoot to restore him to the throne. And perhaps they were right. But in that case, why would the King try to enter the Kingdom alone, without support or protection? On the face of it, it did not make sense. Then again, with the King, who could tell? He had told me that he had a plan – and I had dismissed it, as the pathetic fantasies of yesterday's man. The authorities here, though, were clearly taking him a lot more seriously than I had.

So now I was, once again, a traitor. And as usual, I had no-one but myself to blame. I had let myself be drawn into this for the sake of a few jazz records and a toy train. All right, not just for that – for the sake of a friend. I simply had not thought it through. But now, one way and another, I had plenty to think about.

I received nothing to eat or drink at first, but in the afternoon I was given a bowl of gruel and a cup of water. However, I had not even had time to finish it before I heard the sound of a cart drawing up outside, and orders being shouted in peremptory Anglian. The guard came down and unlocked my cell door.

'What's happening?' I asked.

'You're for the high jump, lad,' he said with a smug expression.

In the reception area stood a man in a startlingly fine red military uniform. He wore white gloves, dark spectacles, an officer's tasselled cap and a silk scarf around his neck.

'This is the prisoner?' he asked.

'The only one we have, sir.'

'You are Karl Nielsen, Clockmaker?'

I nodded. He took out a document from an inner pocket and read it aloud.

'Clockmaker Nielsen, the Special Military Court of the

Kingdom of Kantarborg has found you guilty of the crime of treason. The sentence of the court is death by hanging, to be carried out immediately on Gallows Hill. May God have mercy upon your soul.'

The shock swept over me, then anger. I had expected at least a trial. Was I really such a danger to the state that they would put me down like a dog?

'Put some shackles on him.'

'We don't have any, sir,' said the sergeant.

'Then tie his wrists! What kind of establishment are you running here, man?'

The sergeant nodded to the guard, who went off to look for a length of rope.

'You'll be needing a cart, I suppose, sir?'

'We'll use the wagon. But get me a driver.'

'And some guards?'

'No need. I'll guard him myself.'

'It *is* normal procedure, sir.'

'A couple of cavalrymen, then. They can ride behind us and make sure he doesn't get up to any funny business.'

'Very good, sir.'

Once my wrists were tied I was led out to the covered military wagon, and we set off. Gallows Hill lay beyond West Gate, so we would have to pass through the city centre. The officer sat opposite me, his sabre resting on his lap, checking his pocket watch anxiously. By law, I remembered, executions had to be performed before the sun went down. It was unusual to have one on a Sunday, though. They must want to get rid of me very fast. I stared numbly out of the back of the wagon at the guards riding behind. The streets were busy at this hour, full of carts, bicycles and livestock. I took my last look at the citizens of my home city; children, peasants, drovers, merchants – all oblivious to the fate of Clockmaker Nielsen. Curiously, I felt no fear as such – just a deep sense of unreality. Perhaps the story would be in The Journal tomorrow. The merchant families would read about it over breakfast. *Did you see that about Karl Nielsen? The fellow who made the Moon Clock? Can't say I'm surprised. He was always mixed up in one thing or another. A good thing his father's not around to see it, he was such a nice man.*

Near the Foundry Street canal, the wagon came to a halt.

'What's the delay now?' shouted the officer angrily.

'Boom's down, sir,' called the driver from in front. 'Must be a train coming.'

So the trains from the foundry were still running. For the military, no doubt. The officer gave a sigh of exasperation, got up – and then, to my surprise, took his sabre, inserted the blade of it into the planking of the cart floor, and levered up the edge of some kind of hatch. Opening this, he poked his head through it and looked at the roadway underneath. Apparently satisfied, he came over to me, sabre in hand. I drew back my head, but instead of cutting my throat he quickly cut through my ropes, then went back and lowered himself down through the hatch and down onto the road. He gestured to me. When I hesitated, he whispered urgently: *'Quickly!'*

I slid along the bench seat of the wagon, keeping out of the sightline of the cavalrymen behind, and squeezed down through the narrow aperture. Beneath the wagon was just the cobbled road surface, but slightly off to one side the squatting officer was trying to lift a manhole cover with the aid of two metal implements.

'Where's that bloody train?' said the driver to himself, above us.

Unable to shift the heavy lid alone, the officer beckoned to me and handed me one of the tools. We inserted them into two small holes and heaved. It was difficult to work in a crouching position underneath the cart, but between us we managed to lift the manhole cover and drag it to one side. It made a loud scraping sound, and the horses clopped their hooves nervously. The driver, his attention elsewhere, seemed not to notice.

The officer gestured to me to enter the manhole, and I

climbed down the iron rungs some ten feet or so. At the bottom, the drain was knee-deep in foul, stinking water. Above me, the officer dragged the manhole back into place, then climbed down after me, holding a wind-up lamp. Reaching the bottom, he held up the lamp to reveal a narrow tunnel, just wide enough for a man.

'I can't go down there,' I said.

'You prefer to die?'

Then he set off, sloshing unperturbed through the fetid stream. I followed unwillingly, my body stiff and – despite my desperate situation – almost paralysed with the instinctive terror that Kantarborgans always feel for the underground world.

We had been walking for perhaps a quarter of an hour – by which time the cold had almost put me beyond my fear – when we reached an intersection which, by the light of the officer's lamp, I could see was a much larger tunnel, containing a dark, rushing watercourse, perhaps five yards in breadth, fringed here and there with grey ice. A narrow ledge was provided alongside, presumably for the use of maintenance workers.

'The River Kant,' said the officer, shining his lamp down on the torrent. 'Culverted over in ancient times, and now rarely seen by Kantarborgans. Most of them don't even know it exists.'

He took the silk scarf from around his neck and began to wipe his face. In the lamplight, the cloth came away covered in white.

'Greasepaint,' he said in Kantish, *in a completely different voice*. 'Not the first time I've had to white up for a role. Didn't recognise me, didya? I told you I had a million faces.'

CHAPTER FOURTEEN

Eleven pipers piping

Christopher was setting out the evening meal.

'Got a bit of cabbage and some leeks in the market. And some spuds. It's not much.'

'It'll be grand,' said Joe. 'Anything warm. It's flipping freezing out there.'

'It's not a whole lot better in here,' said Christopher. 'That stove doesn't help much. Some luxury kip this turned out to be.'

'Yeah, it's like an old castle.'

'Probably was, once.'

'No, apparently it's always been an astronomical tower,' said Joe. 'So says Tillonsen, anyway. That's why there's all these spyglasses and scientific instruments lying around. He told me he helped the royal clockmaker build the clock.'

'That thing! Chiming all fecking day. Drives you nuts. How did you get on with him, anyway?'

'Can't tell you. I'm sworn to secrecy.'

'Oh come on, Joe! You're my ... I'm your ... the ... well, I'm something. We're a team, you and me.'

'Well, I'll tell you this much. Them Kantarborgan fellas are half cracked. I mean Tillonsen, he calls himself an engineer, but he has no notion of equilibrium. He should have stuck to his flipping clocks.'

'Why, what are they up to? I mean, they want your underwater boat design, right?'

'Yeah, but they want to ... I'm not supposed to say this, all right? But they want to use it to attack the Northlander ships out in the Sound. To end the blockade.'

'What, like, creep up underneath them? And then what?'

'That's the mad part. They want to put a cannon on the boat.'

Christopher gave a contemptuous snort.

'And how are they going to light the powder underwater?'

'They want to light it from inside the boat. With some kind of valve in the barrel to keep the water out.'

'And fire cannonballs out of it?'

'Grapeshot. Fire it straight up, smash holes in the Northlander hulls. But it won't work. It shifts the whole centre of gravity, for one thing. And with that kind of weight on board, the buoyancy tanks would have to be huge.'

''Twould be a big yoke alright.'

'They want to mount a surprise attack, so the Northlanders won't know what hit them. Sink one ship after the other, all in one go. But I told them you'd have to get right up under the hull of each ship, almost touching it, otherwise the ordnance will lose all its momentum in the water. But that would take quite some manoeuvring, and you know what it's like trying to steer a boat like that.'

'And they'd have to pedal the thing all the way out there in the Sound. That's a fair distance. And if it's submerged they'll have all the water resistance against them, too.'

'They don't need pedals. They have a clockwork motor.'

'Clockwork? How do they wind it up?'

'They use the windmills, same as with the trains. They wind up the springs and load them into special tanks, Hansen pods they call them. Quite clever, really.'

'So what are you going to do? You said you didn't want to help them in their war effort.'

'Well, what can I do? We have to get out of here somehow. And they won't repair our airship unless we do something for them. So I suppose I'll have to go along with it for now. But I told him, I said, Tillonsen, I won't be held responsible if it doesn't work. On yeer own heads be it. But he says it's their only chance. They can't take the Northlanders on in a straight fight, they lost nearly all their warships years ago in the bombardment, and they haven't had the cash to build more. Things are pretty bad, apparently. They're trying to keep it quiet. It was a bad harvest and there isn't much grain in the storehouses. They have a couple of airships, but they can't bring in much. The city will starve if the blockade goes on more than a week or so.'

'And we'll starve along with them.'

'Right. So what I'm thinking is, we need to get their submersible working as fast as possible and get our airship back. I just hope they keep their side of the bargain.'

'They will,' said Christopher. 'They respect an agreement, the Kantarborgans. *Nugget for nugget*, you know.'

'Well, I flipping well hope so. We need to get out of here before it all goes tits up. Because it will, you know. They haven't a prayer. Seriously. '

CHAPTER FIFTEEN

In the dark garden, Marieke is digging. 'Work done in haste is seldom done well,' her mother used to say, but there is no time to exercise any more care. This has to be done in one evening. She has chosen a spot at the end of the garden, close to the solitary apple tree, where she has dragged the heavy wooden chest. She is wearing her woollen gardening clothes against the night air, and her clogs to get a better purchase on the spade.

She keeps an eye on the nearby apartments to make sure that none of the neighbours are watching. It is not unusual to dig your garden at this time of year, ready for the winter frosts after the crops have been pulled, but it would be very strange to do so after dark. She has not taken a lamp with her; instead, she has placed one in the kitchen window, where it illuminates the garden like faint moonlight – just enough to let her see what she is doing.

She chops at the earth with the spade. The ground is already hard, so that at first it is more like hammering than digging, but after an hour she has dug a rectangular hole a yard deep, into which she drags the chest. It contains their marriage certificate, the deeds to the apartment, most of their gold coins, and as many of Karl's tools and precious discs as she could fit inside. She refills the hole, making sure to spread all the extra soil well away from it, and covers it with some clumps of grass. It will have to do.

There are tears in her eyes as she walks back to the house. But she wipes them away – the sentimental do not survive times like these. And she is determined to survive.

Back in the kitchen, she packs some food for herself, then sits by the fire, waiting for midnight. Beside the fireplace, her shoulder bag is ready – the one with the embroidered border that Karl brought her from Kantarborg – with her purse, some clothing, and the knife she had used to kill Hapgaard, in its leather sheath. Nothing suspicious – the knife would surely be considered normal for a woman travelling alone in times like this. She has no identity papers. She has never needed them before.

She has already selected the rowing-boat. It belongs to Eriksson the toolmaker, but he uses it rarely and does not depend on it for his living. She knows where he keeps the oars – in the wooden hut by the harbour.

It is not certain that she will survive the crossing. Few people attempt to row across here, where the Sound is at its widest and the currents are strong. But there is no time to journey to a better spot – she will have to go tonight.

She closes her eyes, trying to get some rest. She is sitting in the kitchen armchair, by the heavy oak table where Karl used to draw his designs. Their furniture is good, some of the best in town, but there is nowhere to hide it. Perhaps someone will get a good price for it. If they don't just burn it all when they burn the house. As now they surely would.

It had begun, as these things always do, with a rumour. After the bad harvest, food was growing scarce in the town. No-one was starving yet, but it was on everybody's minds. *You have food, we don't.* You could feel it in the wind, in the looks people gave you on the street on your way to market, in the silence as you passed. *Potato pigs*, they whispered. Marieke's father said he hadn't heard that since the Schisms. Then one day in the Cat and Crown, Petúr Jansson had begun shouting that the Lowlanders were behind it all, that they were hoarding food to push the prices up. But Petúr Jansson was crazy and no-one ever paid any attention to him.

Of course the Lowlanders were better fed than most – they had grown the food themselves, after all. And they ate the root vegetables that Northlanders fed only to animals. And yes, they were selling very little, anxious to keep enough back for their families for the winter. Prices in the marketplace were steep and growing steeper.

But then Petúr Jansson disappeared. His body turned up after a week, in the woods outside the town. It was much decomposed and had partly been devoured by wild boars, but some people said he had been tortured. There were marks of a ritual sacrifice, they said: foreign symbols carved into his flesh. That night, the Lowlander chapel was torched and burned to the ground. Several members of their community, who had sought refuge there, burned to death inside. There were plenty of their neighbours standing around. No-one tried to put out the fire.

Marieke and her sister and father had watched the blaze from Trollberget, the troll mountain, above the town. Distant shouts and jeers reached them on the wind.

'What do they want from us?' asked Gertrude.

'They want what they have always wanted,' said their father. 'They want our land. And they will have it.'

'It's more than that, this time,' said Marieke. 'It's like some kind of madness. I saw Marga Berntsdatter raving in the market square, screaming about the end of days and how wolves and demons were coming to devour us all.'

'They called me a witch,' said Gertrude. 'They said I had the mark of the Beast on me. I had to run to get away from them.'

'We will soon have to go where they are afraid to follow,' said Hendrik. 'You won't come with us?'

Marieke had shaken her head.

Now Marieke grips the oars, hauls back with all her strength. She does not know how many hours she has been rowing. Her hair is matted with salt water, she is shivering in her damp clothes. Her hands are already blistered and bleeding, and she is not even halfway across yet. She can see the towers of Kantarborg, but the current is carrying her the wrong way, too far south. She may miss the far shore completely and be dragged out to the open sea.

'Damn you, Karl Nielsen!' she shouts into the night. 'Damn you and all your secrets!'

The anger gives her strength. She gasps as the cold wind cuts into her again. She is glad of the pain. Glad to be alive.

CHAPTER SIXTEEN

'Perhaps you would walk with me a little, my lord Commander?' said Brorsen. 'Somewhere away from prying eyes and ears? I do not entirely trust the palace walls.'

Lord Commander, thought Johansson. That had a nice ring to it.

'It would be my honour, Astronomer. If the day is not too cold? Where shall we go?'

'I thought perhaps the ramparts. I am familiar with them, and they have changed little since I was a young man.'

Once outside the palace, an easy intimacy settled over the two men. Johansson offered his arm for support as Brorsen struggled up the wooden steps to the top of the bastion. Two musketmen followed them at a discreet distance.

'Obliged to you, Johansson. The steps get a little slippery in winter.'

He weighs nothing, thought Johansson, wondering at the light touch. *And yet he is of such moment.*

On top of the snow-covered bank, they could look out across the Sound. The distant masts of the Northlander fleet could just about be made out in the mist. The frigid sea air made Johansson shiver, but the older man seemed not to regard it.

'Unusually cold for the time of year, is it not, Astronomer?'

'Yes, but not unprecedented. There are records going back to before the Cataclysm that suggest that winters here used to be much colder. In fact, did you know, on a few occasions it is recorded that the sea froze solid, right across the Sound, all the way from here to Northland?'

Johansson looked out across the grey waters to the distant Northland shoreline. *If that happened again*, he thought, *it would change everything.* They walked along the top of the ramparts, following the sentry path that had been cleared in the snow.

'I trust you are settling in all right?' asked Johansson. 'I'm sorry we cannot offer you your old apartment in the Round

Tower.'

'Believe me, Lord Commander, at my age, I am quite grateful for that. I would be quite incapable of climbing that spiral. My lodgings in the Regence are more than satisfactory.'

'So, do you have any news for me?'

'Well, I'm afraid the only news I have is no news. I have trained my best instruments on the opposite shore, but of the events that have so terrified the Northlander flightings, I could see nothing. My own suspicion is that it is just hysteria and rumours. You know what happens in time of war and crisis.'

'There's another one,' said Johansson.

As the two men watched, a small fishing-boat with a single sail made its way into the harbour. It was listing somewhat to one side, overloaded with men, women and children. Soldiers in red and white uniforms hurried along the quay to detain them.

'More and more of them are coming over, and they refuse to be sent back,' said Johansson. 'They would rather die, they say. They talk of phantom wolves and monsters coming out of the north. The Northlander warships make no attempt to stop them. Which makes me think that it may be some tactic to put pressure on us.'

'It is possible, though a little convoluted, even for the Northlanders. One would think that the blockade is exerting pressure enough as it is.'

The people on board, some carrying children, scrambled desperately up the stone steps on the harbour wall as though pursued by an enemy. The boat, forgotten and unmoored, slowly drifted back out into the harbour.

'Or else they are infected with some pestilence that the Northlanders hope to spread among us,' said Johansson. 'Look at them. They seem almost deranged.'

'Where are you putting them?'

'We're sending all the Northlanders to Sythorn. Both the merchants who were caught on this side by the blockade, and the new arrivals. They are enemy nationals now, after all.'

Brorsen nodded his approval.

'A good choice. If they are disease-ridden, we need to keep them isolated. And in any case, some of them are bound to be spies or saboteurs. You don't want them running around in the city. Even in the Citadel, they would be certain to see something of our military.'

'Kramer wants us to attack the Northlander fleet now, before we are completely overrun by these civilians,' said Johansson. 'He says God will stand by us.'

'The man is a fool. We don't have the ships or the manpower to sustain a war now. Can't you talk sense into him?'

'Well I am Minister of Defence, it's my job to advise him. Though of course I must afford him all due deference. He still thinks he is in charge, you see.'

'Hah! Long may he continue to believe so. Then he will remain harmless.'

'He is not being quite harmless at the moment, I would have to say.'

'He's making trouble for you?'

'His followers are. His gangs have been going around smashing up taverns.'

'And no-one stops him?'

'He says it's nothing to do with him. But he makes no effort to condemn them.'

Brorsen looked pensively at the group of Northlander flightings, now being herded into the back of a large military cart by the soldiers.

'Tell me, how is he financing this private campaign?' he asked.

'Well, not every drinking establishment is targeted.'

'Ah, let me guess ... only the ones that don't pay?'

'Precisely. Some taverns can escape trouble by making an unofficial contribution to the Community of Celestial Concord and Peace. I believe five percent is the going rate. They call it a sin tax.'

'Which will eventually put Kramer's crew in charge of the liquor trade throughout the city. That will be quite a powerful position, won't it? And all in the name of morality.'

'Yes. They are also condemning immodest clothing. And music, for some reason.'

'And pictures, no doubt?'

Johansson glanced at the astronomer in surprise.

'Yes. You'd heard?'

'No. But it's always the same story.'

'Pictures are an abomination to the Lord, apparently. I was able to get word to the National Gallery. They managed to get most of their paintings hidden away in a cellar, where the gangs are loath to go. But Kramer's men broke in and burned the rest. They held a bonfire of them outside, beside the lake.'

'And you're sure it was Kramer's men?'

'They made no secret of it. They were even wearing CCCP helmets.'

Brorsen laughed scornfully.

'Were they, indeed? Well in that case, my lord Commander, it would appear that the prime minister has handed you a Yule gift. Now you know how to control them.'

'How so? These men are a private militia. They have nothing to do with the state.'

'Well, precisely! And so when people are attacked and abused by these thugs, who will they turn to for protection?'

'So you think I should arrest them?'

'No, of course not! You should ignore them.'

'But how will that discourage the gangs?'

'Discourage them? You don't want to *discourage* them, Commander! You must encourage them! Tell Kramer privately that you are entirely on his side, although, as you must explain to him, you very unfortunately cannot say so publicly. But assure him that he has your total support. Let them form dozens of these gangs and run amok, close down every tavern in town, put out every candle of merriment. They will soon lose any support they ever had. And then, of course, when things are completely out of control, and Kramer's men are universally hated...'

'I step in.'

'Exactly. You sort things out. Arrest all the gangs. Write a good speech, Johansson, and make sure it is printed in The Journal. The need to restore public order. The law must be respected by all parties, no matter who they are. Et cetera, et cetera. You know the sort of thing. You will be the hero of the hour.'

'But Kramer is a popular man in the city. He won the election easily.'

'Trust me, by the time you've finished helping him achieve his objectives, not even his own mother would vote for him.'

'You are a clever man, Astronomer.'

'It is how I have achieved my great age, lord Commander.'

CHAPTER SEVENTEEN

Nine ladies dancing

In Marchas' studio in the Round Tower, the Grumfel laid back his long furry ears to show his displeasure.

'Looks nothing like me,' he said.

'I always try to make my subjects look better than they are,' said the painter.

'You are making of me a mickery.'

'A mockery,' said the painter. 'And it's not supposed to look like you. Not exactly like you. You are a figment of my imagination. I am just using you as inspiration.'

'Mickery, mockery, hickory, dockery,' said the Grumfel.

Marchas wiped his brush with a cloth, and adjusted the easel to better catch the morning light. He took a sip of green liquid straight from the bottle. The Grumfel, standing beside him on a footstool, leaned forward and peered at the canvas. The painting showed a woman in fine clothing sitting in an armchair, reading a letter. The Grumfel was depicted standing alongside the chair, looking at her – his expression, as usual, simultaneously disgruntled, curious and sceptical.

'What those machines?'

'The Duchess wishes to be painted in the style of the ancient past. This is the kind of thing they had back then.'

'Nothing like that,' sniffed the Grumfel. 'Nothing like that, no no. What hat that?'

'The hat? It's the kind of headgear I imagine women wore in the ancient world.'

'If she fell over, she couldn't get up.'

'I think the Duchess will like it.'

'She couldn't wear it. The painter is a fool.'

'Well, she doesn't *have* to wear it, does she? It's only a painting. All that matters is how it looks. And she's coming in to model for me this morning, so don't disturb us.'

The Grumfel pointed at the picture.

'I know who the letter from.'

'No you don't, and if you do, keep it to yourself. That is between me and the Duchess.'

'And her lover. You know who.'

'Sshh! Get lost! Now!'

The Grumfel faded slowly and disappeared. The painter sighed. It was getting harder and harder to dismiss him these days. Sometimes he almost seemed real.

'One day he will be around for good,' he said, lifting the bottle to his lips. 'And then it will be time to lock you up, Marchas.'

'Sorry, do you have company?'

Startled, the painter looked up. A woman had poked her head around the door.

'I did knock, but there was no answer.'

'Duchess! No, no, I was just muttering to myself.' He quickly hid the bottle beneath some cleaning rags. 'Please, come in.'

The Duchess entered, bowing her head to cross the low lintel. A servant followed her, took her cloak, and left again to wait below in the carriage. She was wearing a dark blue, high-collared dress with intricate embroidery.

'I have my best portrait clothes on. So, how's it coming along?'

'I have made good progress. Your fine robe has come out well, I think. You look just like a lady of ancient times.'

'May I see?'

Without waiting for an answer, the Duchess walked around the easel and regarded the portrait. There was a protracted silence.

'Well, I like the hat,' she said at last.

'I thought you might, Duchess.'

'And the brocade is beautiful. Very becoming. But what *is* that peculiar creature?'

Marchas glanced nervously around, but the Grumfel was still out of sight.

'Ladies of the time often kept pet animals, Duchess.'

'But I thought they were dogs and cats and suchlike?'

'For ordinary people, yes. But a lady such as yourself would have had something more exotic. Nothing so common as a dog or a cat!'

'How clever you are, painter! You know just how to flatter a girl. I suppose it does look rather sweet, whatever it is. So – what do you need me to do today?'

'Well, today I would like to get started on the face, if it pleases you, my lady. So if you would just take a seat here ... I will find a piece of paper for you to hold, to stand in for the letter ... there's one somewhere here ...'

The painter drew back a curtain that hung in front of an alcove. The Grumfel, standing behind it, helpfully held out a sheet of paper. The painter took it and hastily pulled the curtain back across. To his consternation, the Grumfel's furry feet could still be seen poking out at the bottom.

'*Go away!*' he hissed.

'I beg your pardon?' said the Duchess.

'Forgive me, Duchess, I am getting old. I have developed a habit of talking to myself. It is quite unconscious, until someone points it out. Rather embarrassing.'

'Poor you, all alone here in the tower, and you do so love to talk! But today you must talk to me, Marchas. I hope you have lots of juicy gossip for me.'

The painter gently guided the Duchess's arms and face into the correct position in the high-backed armchair, and walked back to his easel.

'I will do my best, my lady. Well, I'm not all alone here anymore, for a start. I have a couple of visitors. From Birmingham.'

'From Birmingham! Good heavens. You mean from the Pope?'

'Keep looking in that direction, Duchess, if you please. Yes, a couple of monks. I don't really know what they are doing here. Some official business. They won't tell me.'

'How fascinating. Makes one wonder what Commander Johansson is up to now.'

'He was in last week, for his official portrait. But of course he is rather a dull chap, he says nothing at all.'

'Oh, I know! He's become such a dry stick. He used to be much more fun, when he was younger.'

'On the other hand, his secretary is an old friend of mine, and he had quite a few stories to tell. You've heard that they caught Clockmaker Nielsen trying to smuggle the Young King back into the Kingdom?'

'Well of course I know that, that is old news.'

'But did you hear he escaped again?'

'What? Really? How?'

'Apparently he vanished into thin air. He was in a guarded wagon, on his way to execution on Gallows Hill, and then suddenly he was gone. They say he may have used witchcraft. Or some magic clockwork device.'

'How extraordinary! And the Young King escaped, too?'

'Yes, he gave them the slip. Apparently he was disguised as the Yule Father. Please try to keep still, Duchess.'

'Oh I'm sorry, that is just too funny! As the Yule Father!'

'Yes, the street urchins have been going around pulling the beards of all the Yule Fathers in town, to see if they can find the Young King and claim a reward.'

'Well, that must really contribute to the seasonal cheer!'

'Indeed. There are a lot of very grumpy Yule Fathers around this year.'

'Oh Marchas, you are wonderful,' laughed the Duchess. 'I really don't know what I would do for entertainment without you.'

The Grumfel emerged from behind the curtain and took up a satirical stance behind the Duchess's armchair, posing like a ballerina. The painter glared at him.

'Are you all right, Marchas?'

'Oh ... sorry, Duchess. Just distracted for a moment. So – how are you managing with the blockade?'

'Well, not too bad so far, though the price of tea has gone through the roof. And our cook cannot find good cabbages for love or money.'

'Yes, well, the Northlanders practically ran the market, didn't they? Someone must be profiting from these high prices, that's for sure.'

'Well, my husband says he heard a rumour that Johansson invented this whole crisis. That he engineered it to drive up the price of Northlandish produce. He doesn't believe that, of course.'

Marchas come over to adjust the Duchess's pose slightly, pointedly ignoring the creature now standing beside the armchair.

'No. But you would wonder, wouldn't you, my lady? Him being a Northlander and all. Although he tries to disguise it. Your finger against your chin, like last time. That's it. Perfect.'

'But tell me this,' she asked tartly, 'has our military really grown so incompetent under Johansson that they cannot hold a single prisoner without losing him?'

'It does seem strange, doesn't it? Mind you, there are evil tongues with theories of their own about that.'

'Such as what? Do tell, Marchas!'

The painter returned to his easel, lifted his palette, and applied some paint to his brush.

'Well you see, they say Johansson and Nielsen are old friends.'

'Really? I didn't know that.'

'Oh yes, they go back a long way, those two. They were both on the Young King's expedition to the north, that time he sold out the country. So somehow I doubt that this miraculous escape came as a complete surprise to our Commander Johansson.'

'How interesting. How very interesting. You have such a wealth of good gossip, Marchas. I don't know what I'd do without you.'

'I aim to please, my Lady.'

The Grumfel gave Marchas a sardonic look, and slowly faded into the air.

CHAPTER EIGHTEEN

Standing in front of Johansson's desk, the woman looked tired and bedraggled. Her clothes, once perhaps of reasonably fine quality, were soiled and torn. Johansson felt a moment of pity. But greater things were at stake here than the suffering of some foolish peasant woman.

'Mrs Nielsen, I am so sorry for what you have had to endure,' he said in formal Northlandish. 'I got you out of the cells as soon as I heard. In times like these, our guards are inclined to suspect every Northlander of being a spy. They even suspect me, I think, sometimes. My sincere apologies.'

She said nothing, but simply stared at him. She had very direct look. He found himself glancing away involuntarily, to his own irritation.

'So, purely as a formality, perhaps you can tell me what you were doing in Kantarborg? Were you fleeing some demons from the north, like your compatriots?'

'You know very well what I was doing here. I was looking for Karl.'

'You were looking for your husband, yes of course. Quite understandable. But we are under blockade by your country. No ferry has sailed for days. So how did you get across the Sound?'

'I rowed. At night.'

'Forgive me, Mrs Nielsen, but you know that is impossible. You must have had help.'

'How is it impossible, Johansson?'

'*Commander* Johansson!' interrupted the officer standing behind her. Johansson gestured to him to ignore the impertinence.

'Please don't insult my intelligence, Mrs Nielsen,' said Johansson. 'I am a naval officer, I know the Sound. A woman could not possibly row that distance alone.'

'You would be surprised what a woman is capable of.'

He looked at her. Her hard expression. It was said she had

killed a Kantish agent with her bare hands.

'Indeed. Well, perhaps in your case anything is possible. But I'm afraid I must tell you that your husband has disappeared. It seems he was involved in a conspiracy to destabilise the government of this kingdom. We arrested him, but he made his escape, with help from the other plotters.'

'What utter nonsense. Karl doesn't have a political bone in his body, as you well know! He despises all that kind of thing.'

'I don't know that I know him, and I don't know that I know you!' snapped Johansson, his temper rising.

He let the implication sink in.

'Johansson, you were friends,' she said at last. 'He admired you. What happened?'

'I cannot allow our past acquaintance to interfere with this case, Mrs Nielsen. I have a job to do. The security of this kingdom is more important than any one of us.'

She looked into his eyes.

'What could drive such a wedge between old friends? What is really going on?'

'What? What are you talking about?'

She caught his expression.

'This is about a woman, isn't it? Who is she?'

'Madam, I am the Minister of Defence of the Kingdom of Kantarborg, not some lovelorn adolescent. If you have no more to say, I think we can terminate this interview.'

He gestured to the guards.

'*Who is she?*' she shouted as they hauled her away, her body bucking under their arms. The door slammed behind them. Johansson exhaled to regain his composure. Blasted woman. The officer was looking at him curiously. He would have to say something.

'Who can understand the female sex, Ottesen? Nielsen tried to smuggle the *King* back into Kantarborg, and she thinks I have a grudge against the man because of some woman!'

'You used to know the clockmaker, sir?'

'At university,' said Johansson casually. 'And later at court, when he became the King's favourite. I saw him then, of course.'

'It seems that she knew you, as well?'

'I met her once, in Sandviken. She was all smiles then, but I saw through her. The woman's a fanatic. Where did you find her? Was she up to something?'

'She was picked up out on Agaholm, walking towards the city. She didn't have any papers on her, and seeing as she was a Northlander ...'

'A Lowlander, actually,' said Johansson. 'If I remember rightly. We'll need to keep her in custody. What can we charge her with?'

'Well, she hasn't actually done anything illegal, other than being without papers.'

'Was she carrying anything incriminating?'

'No, just some food. And a knife.'

'A knife! Well, there you are. She was obviously planning some mischief. Any valuables?'

'She had a few sovereigns in her purse. And some jewellery.'

'Excellent, it will help pay for her keep. Confiscate those and charge her with terrorism. No – attempted espionage. That will keep the Watch out of it. Spies are a military matter.'

'Yes, sir.'

'And for God's sake, put her somewhere secure this time. I want no more fiascos! Send her to Sythorn with the other flightings.'

'Yes, sir.'

'Then put the word about that we have her. If I know the clockmaker, it will draw him out. And if we can get hold of Nielsen, we can probably find *him*, too.'

The officer saluted and made to leave.

'And ... Ottesen? One more thing.'

'Sir?'

'They were in on this together, so she probably knows where Nielsen is hiding. Get it out of her.'

'If you think it necessary, Commander ...'

'Of course it's necessary, man, this is not some game we're playing. She is a spy and a murderer. But don't kill her, we will need her later. I understand you have some interrogation techniques that leave no permanent damage?'

'There's the water method. Perfected by the ancients. I've seen some of the toughest subversives crack under it.'

'If I get to hear that you have used methods like that on her, I will be extremely displeased. I'm telling you that officially.'

'Yes, sir.'

'If I get to hear of it.'

'I understand, sir.'

The officer left. Johansson got up, walked over to the window of his office, and looked out at the busy plaza beneath.

'So, Karl,' he said to himself, 'what you will do now, I wonder?'

CHAPTER NINETEEN

'You led us quite a merry dance, Karl,' said the King. 'Not that I will be dancing the gavotte for a while.'

He was seated on a makeshift throne – a large armchair, upholstered in red velvet, with carved, scrolling arms. Probably the most royal thing they could find around here. He was still wearing the Yule Father costume, but his beard had been trimmed and his hair cut. He was holding the sceptre in one hand, its end resting on the floor. His right foot, in bandages, was propped up on a footstool.

I had not been invited to sit. He was now, once again, the King.

'What happened to you, Majesty?'

'I slipped on the ladder, going down the chimney. My boots were wet with snow and I ended up having quite a violent encounter with the tunnel floor. It is just a sprained ankle, but it does rather impede one. But tell me this, scientist, what is the force that propels all men towards the centre of the earth?'

I am an engineer, not a scientist. He was playing with me. But I might as well play along.

'Why ... the force of gravity, sire. As described by Newton, and others.'

'And it acts upon all men equally? King and commoner alike?'

'It acts equally on all men and on all objects, sire.'

'Then that would be the proof that all such forces emanate from God, would it not?'

'I'm ... not sure that I follow, sire.'

'Because we are all equal before them. And because we can all stumble from time to time.'

He smiled at his own wit.

'Indeed so, Majesty. A most subtle observation.'

Abruptly, he seemed to tire of the game.

'Anyway, incapacitated as I was, I sent Charlie to find you.

But he was followed. Our friend in the coin shop must have talked to the Watch – they knew something was going on. So we had to be discreet. Here is your footwear. My apologies.'

He gestured to Charlie, who stepped forward and placed my old boots in front of me. I was still wearing Johansson's shoes, which were of better quality, but too big for me.

'Steal a man's boots in the dosshouse, that's the lowest of the low, that is,' said Charlie. 'I wouldn't have done it, only I was under orders, see. You were supposed to stay where you were till I came to get you next day, not go walkabout in your bare feet, a gentleman like you.'

He was still wearing my hat, though.

'Why didn't you just *tell* me?' I asked in exasperation.

Charlie just shrugged and smiled. *(You know why. That's not the ways things are done at court, my friend.)*

It occurred to me that I was probably expected to show some sign of gratitude.

'It was a most remarkable rescue, Majesty.'

'Yes, well, we had a plan in place in case one of our number should fall into their hands. We could only play that card once, of course, but you are a valuable member of our team.'

I'm not on anyone's damned team, I wanted to say, but now was clearly not the time.

'I am most grateful to Your Majesty. And to you, Charlie.'

'One of my better performances, if I say so myself,' he said, bowing.

So you're playing Charlie now? Who are you really?

The air in the hall was frigid, barely a degree or two warmer than it must have been outside. There were no windows to be seen, only row upon row of bookshelves, some of them accessible only by ladder. A few electrical bottles gave out a little flickering light. Where was the power coming from? Above, the ceiling was out of sight in the darkness. I could hear a low buzz of urgent conversation on all sides, and the sound of heavy objects being moved. There were clearly quite a number of people here, murmuring in the darkness, though I could not see them. Hand-written notices warning people to be quiet had been placed around the walls.

'What is this place, Majesty? Some kind of library?'

'Indeed it is. Of a kind. It is where I found the discs I told you about. There are many fascinating things here. But I fear it would take a lifetime to explore them all, and we have very little time available to us. We must move on quickly.'

'Why is that?'

'This place may well be known to them. Johansson was busy mapping out the subterranean networks of the city at one point, though we tried to put a stop to that.'

'I thought it was the Moonies who banned going underground?'

'With a little encouragement from us. It suits us well not to have anyone poking around down here while we are still in Kantarborg.'

'So we are within the city walls?'

The King smiled.

'You were always quick with your wits, Nielsen. Well, let's see if we can hold on to you a little longer this time before we start telling you our exact location, shall we? I don't want you ending up in Johansson's interrogation chamber.'

No wonder they had rescued me so promptly – but perhaps the thought was unworthy?

'I will set you a little riddle, though,' the King continued. He was playing with me again. He reached into his pocket and drew out what looked like a gaming dice, though it was made of silver, and had strange symbols on each of its sides – I saw a crown, and an anchor, and some kind of beast. The King held the item in the palm of his hand.

'Imagine a fortress shaped like a cube. All of its walls are impenetrable. The four outer walls, the ceiling and the floor, like this. Six sides in all. But it can be breached through the seventh wall. Where is that?'

'I have no idea, Majesty. I don't have much aptitude with riddles.'

Or patience with them, I thought.

'Well, I will let you ponder that. And if you can work it out, you will know where we are. Charlie, find him a bed. He looks dead on his feet.'

Given the events of the day, the phrase was unfortunate but apt. I was utterly exhausted. I had no idea what time it was, but it must surely be late at night by now. Charlie showed me to a cubby hole between the bookshelves where there was a military-looking folding bed and a couple of grey blankets.

'And I reckon you can safely take your boots off this time,' he smiled as he left – still wearing my hat.

I lay down on the bunk with my hands behind my head. So – here I was, still alive. It all felt almost too confusing to make sense of. How could I get a message to Marieke to tell her I was all right? All communication across the Sound had no doubt been cut off. But there must surely be a way. If I only I could work it out.

The King's riddle was going round in my head. A fortress with six sides. Where was the seventh wall? My conscious mind could make no sense of it, but as I slipped into oblivion, I could feel the seventh wall gently dissolving. It was, indeed, most porous.

CHAPTER TWENTY

'Hello Valdemar.'

'Hello.'

'Do you know who I am?'

'Yes. You're the Yule Father.'

'That's right, Valdemar. Bit of a mouthful, that name of yours, isn't it? What do your friends call you? Valda?'

'I don't have any friends.'

'That's a shame, Valda. Are there no other children in the palace for you to play with?'

'No.'

'Well, I can be your friend if you like.'

'All right. What happened to your foot?'

'I had a bit of an accident. Going down a chimney. Have you decided yet what you want for Yule?'

'No.'

'But I bet you like toys, don't you?'

'Yes.'

'What kind of toys do you like best?'

'Toys that can do things.'

'They're the best kind, Valda. I like those, too. Do you like trains?'

'Yes.'

'You know the train that passes by the palace? Do you like that one?'

'Yes. I like that train a lot. It goes past every day. And it rings a bell.'

'Would you like to have a toy like that?'

'Yes. Yes, I would.'

'Well, do you know what, if you are a *very* good boy, I think I could bring you a toy train of your very own. And you would be the only child in the kingdom to have one. Would you like that?'

'Yes.'

'And if I promise to bring you that, do you think you could promise to do something for me, too?'

'What?'

'I just want you to give someone a very important message. That's all. But it has to be our secret, you and me. Because if you tell the grown-ups I've been here, they'll be cross with you. They don't believe in me, you see. Only children can see me. So it's just between us two. Is that all right?'

'Yes. All right.'

'Good boy.'

'Be careful in the chimney this time.'

'I will.'

CHAPTER TWENTY-ONE

'And I'm telling you I saw it. Little furry thing. It looked round the door at me. I went after it, but it was gone.'

'Sure it wasn't a rat or something?' asked Joe, shaking out the folds of her habit to dislodge the snow that had collected there.

'Joe, did you ever see a rat this big?' Christopher held out his hand at waist level. 'And it opened the flipping door!'

'And you haven't been at the gin while I was out?'

'At this hour of the day? But jaze, I wouldn't mind a glass now, I can tell you. That fecking thing put the heart crossways in me. The way it looked at me!'

'I'll make us a cup of tea, that'll have to do you.'

'Not that Kantarborgan stuff, that's not real tea.'

'I'll use the last of the black. There's some left out in *Stella Maris*, too, if the weather hasn't gotten to it by now.'

Joe began to fill the very sooty kettle from the pail and placed it on the wood stove.

'I'll tell you something, though,' she called back. 'You said you saw something creepy today. Well, so did I, boy.'

'Where was that?'

Joe returned and poured some milk from the jug into their mugs, and sat down in an armchair.

'Out in the palace. I was just after meeting Tillonsen, to give him the new drawings. I went out into the corridor and got a bit lost. I must've gone the wrong way, all those halls look the same. Anyway, next thing I see is this little boy.'

'A boy?'

'About seven or eight years old. Pure white-blond hair and blue eyes. He must have been someone special, because he was dressed in some fancy silk clothes, poor kid. You can't play much in that get-up.'

'The Crown Prince, probably. So what's creepy about that?'

'Wait till I tell you. So he seems to be wandering about all on his own, like, and I'm wondering if anyone's looking after him, you know? So I ask him, "Are you all right young fella? Are you lost?" And do you know what he says? He looks me straight in the face, cool as you like, and says "We are all lost!"'

'In Anglian, like?'

'Of course Anglian.'

Christopher laughed. 'Well he might be right, at that.'

'Then he asks me if I've come from the Pope. And I say yes. But do you know what he says then? He says, "The seventh wall has been breached. The Yule Father wants to meet you behind the fireplace."'

'What? Ah sure, he must have been playing some kind of a game. Great imagination, kids.'

'Not the way he said it. Deadly serious. And looking straight at me, with those scary blue eyes. Like he was saying something really important. I'm telling ya, it gave me the heebie-jeebies.'

'The seventh wall, heh. So then what happened?'

'Well then this old fella turned up and, like, bundled him away. Like no-one was supposed to see him or something.'

'He might have something wrong with him. They'd have to keep that quiet, him being the heir to the throne and all.'

'It looked more like he was flipping possessed or something.'

Joe took the water off the stove and poured it into the teapot. Christopher sighed and looked out of the window.

'You know what, Joe, it's like there's something creepy about this whole kingdom.'

'You're telling me. You'd wonder would they have some kind of a curse on them or something.'

'I've been thinking. Do you know what might be the cause of it? You know the bottom of the spiral walkway in this tower? I think it used to go down right into the ground. It's blocked off now, but you can see that it used to continue on down.'

'So?'

'So I reckon they've been messing about with the underground. And you know what happens when you do that. They've been stirring things up. That thing I saw today – I bet you it came from down there. From the underground devils.'

'You'd want to get the holy water out, so.'

'You're right there. Sprinkle a bit around here. It'd do no harm.'

CHAPTER TWENTY-TWO

Eight maids a-milking

'Whores and cutpurses! Time to go!' The guard marched down the corridor, opening the cell doors. Marieke shifted her stiff body into an upright position on the wooden bench where she had spent an uncomfortable night.

The remand jail was known as St Breda's Well – a strangely attractive name for a vile place, stinking and damp. Marieke had heard weeping and protests during the night, occasional screams. The guard unlocked the door of her cell and slammed it back.

'Out!'

Marieke stood up and walked unsteadily to the door. The guard grabbed her by the shoulder and pushed her through.

'Hurry it up, your ladyship! Your carriage is waiting.'

Other women prisoners were standing outside in the corridor. She followed them out to a high-walled courtyard, where a row of wagons on rails stood waiting. Each had a central sliding door. The door of one had been slid back and a low wooden stepladder had been placed in front of it. She mounted the steps, and as she lowered her head to enter the wagon, one of the guards gave her a push from behind, making her stumble. The guards laughed. 'That's the last bit of ass you'll be getting for a while, Frederiksen!' said one.

The floor of the wagon was covered in straw. When her eyes had got used to the gloom, she could see some other women sitting or squatting around the walls. She found a space and hunkered down, too. Outside, she could hear male prisoners being herded on board the other trucks. Then after a few minutes the wagon gave a jerk, and with a metallic screech the train began to move.

So this was Karl's invention. It didn't look much like that model he'd been making. He'd been so proud of it, she had thought it must be a very fine conveyance, fit for princes. She hadn't expected this. It was freezing cold and damp in the wagon, and the only light came from gaps in the wooden planking around the walls, and from a small hole in the centre of the floor.

Two women sitting on her left were talking animatedly. They were dressed, thought Marieke, as though they were on their way to a party of some kind. One was dark, while the other had frizzy red hair that didn't look entirely natural. The red-haired one produced a small bottle from somewhere in her voluminous skirts and handed it to the other.

'Drink up dearie, they'll only take it off me when we get there.'

The other woman took a gulp from the bottle and handed it back. 'I need to piss,' she said. She moved across to the hole in the floor, hoisted up her skirts and urinated into it, holding onto a post. As she did so, she looked up at the ventilation hatch in the roof.

'You know, if you were smart you could probably find a way to get out of here.'

'If you were smart, you wouldn't be in here, sweetheart,' laughed the red-haired woman. 'You can always run away when you get to the workfarm, they won't bother stopping you. There's nowhere to go except the wildwoods, and you won't last long there.'

'What's it like?'

'The workfarm? It's all right. You get your food. And what they don't give you, you can steal. Or ...'

She gestured with her thumb and forefinger.

'Get assigned to the milking shed if you can, you'll be out of the weather. Those'll be no use to you in there, though,' she continued, pointing at the other's knee-length, lace-up boots. 'Tell you what you do. When you get there, find someone who's your size and about to be released, and swap those for a pair of decent work boots. Otherwise they'll just give you clogs to wear, like her.'

She pointed at Marieke.

'No offence, dear,' she said, leaning across to Marieke. 'What are you in for?'

Marieke understood Kantish fairly well, but could not speak it. In the shop she had always left the Kantish customers to Karl.

'*Undskyld*,' she said, and pointed to her mouth.

'Oh, you're a Northlander!' said the other woman.

'*Nej*,' said Marieke. '*Nederlander*.'

'What's that?'

Marieke made a sideways motion with her hand.

'Low land ...'

'She means she makes her living on her back!' said the dark-haired woman, and they laughed raucously. 'So what did you do to end up in here?'

Marieke wanted to say 'Nothing!', but she knew she would not be believed. Then she remembered the knife that had been in her bag when she was arrested. She made a stabbing motion with her hand. Like when she killed Hapgaard.

'Oh, right! Customer, was he?'

Marieke did not understand. The woman made an 'O' with her mouth and gestured with her thumb and forefinger again.

'Yes,' said Marieke. Well, it was partly true after all. She had done her best to distract him before killing him.

'Good for you, dear. Hope you gave him what for. And did you rob him?' She mimed taking a purse.

'Yes.' Well, that was true, too. In a way. All that gold that had been diverted into her pockets instead of his.

The women laughed. 'Ooh, she's a bad one! Give her a drink!'

Marieke accepted the bottle, took a burning mouthful and handed it back, trying not to cough.

The women fell silent again.

Two days ago, I was a respectable shopkeeper, thought Marieke. *Now I have just confessed to being a murderess, a whore and a thief.*

They were going faster now, to judge by the rocking. Much faster than a horse and cart. Through chinks in the plank walls, shadows flicked past at speed. It felt very unsafe. She already felt nauseous with the movements of the wagon, and the liquor made her feel worse. If this was the mode of transport of the future, they could keep it. It was not fit for the beasts of the fields. She would tell Karl that when she saw him again, she certainly would. She leaned her head back and gradually fell into a doze.

After an hour or so, the train began to slow, then stopped. The wagon door was abruptly slid back.

'Third class passengers out!' said the guard sarcastically.

The women rose and began to exit the wagon. Marieke rose and followed them, but when she got to the door, the guard held up his truncheon and stopped her.

'Not you. You're first class.'

The other women laughed as they climbed down from the wagon.

'Cheerio, darling. Good luck!'

The guard slid the door closed again, leaving her alone inside. She wondered what kind of special treatment they had singled out for her. The wagon gave a jerk and the train moved off again, into the gathering darkness.

CHAPTER TWENTY-THREE

'Majesty, that riddle you set me ...'

We were walking between the rows of shelves, looking for the jazz records the King had promised me. They hardly seemed relevant now, after I had first almost lost and then regained my life, but he insisted on showing them to me – perhaps to demonstrate that he had not just been telling me some fancy story. He was walking much better now, I noticed. The rooms were dark, but illuminated by a few electric bottles strung from the ceiling here and there. We passed by several groups of armed guards. There were many more people here than I had at first thought – a whole militia, it seemed. Though still hardly enough to make the King's ambition to regain his throne seem in any way realistic.

'You said the fortress had six sides, all impenetrable.'

'Yes? Have you worked it out?' The King smiled at me. A little too readily, perhaps.

'I think I know what the seventh wall is. It's the mind, isn't it? Our thoughts and assumptions.'

'Excellent, Karl! And what do you deduce from that about our location?'

'We don't penetrate any of the six walls. We're already inside.'

'Precisely. Well done.'

'So we're in the Royal Palace? In some kind of cellar?'

'Yes. Or rather, just alongside it. We are in the vaults of what was once the Palace Library, before the Cataclysm. Most of what is above ground here was destroyed and later built upon. But I always knew of the existence of these catacombs.'

'Surely we can easily be discovered here?'

'Not as long as the Kingdom is run by those dreadful religious fanatics. There is little danger of them venturing underground, thankfully. It's forbidden for them.'

'And the lighting is electric? Where is the power coming from?'

'From the Great Windmill. We have borrowed a little electricity from the Palace. They won't notice. I think this is the place.'

He stopped by a long line of shelves that seemed to be full of old cardboard files. I ran my finger across their spines and drew one down. It contained a black disc. All these shelves contained old recordings – hundreds of them. Enough here to keep my business going for many years.

'Quite a collection, isn't it?' said the King. 'There is a story that they were left behind by an invading army in ancient times. I don't know if that is true or not, but the labels are in neither Anglian nor Kantish.'

I slipped the disc out of its cardboard sheath and looked at it. The label was indeed quite indecipherable.

'A lot of them are sentimental melodies in foreign tongues, many of them a bit dreary to be honest, but there are quite a few good lively jazz tunes among them,' said the King.

'It's certainly a treasure trove, Majesty,' I said, replacing the disc.

'Well, it's the property of the Crown, or at any rate it used to be in ancient times, so I am its lawful owner and I can gift the collection to you. I'm sure you will make good use of it.'

You're not buying my services again, if that's what you think.

'I am most grateful, sire. It will be of great benefit to me when I get back home. Hopefully this crisis will not last much longer.'

'Ah. Yes. Now, there is something I need to talk to you about.'

I felt my chest beginning to tighten. I *knew* there was something. He turned and fixed his brown eyes upon me.

'Karl, there is no easy way to tell you this. I'm afraid your wife is no longer in Sandviken. She is here, in Kantarborg.'

'Here!'

'She was arrested out on Agaholm, heading for the city. She has been charged with espionage.'

'Marieke! But that's preposterous!'

'On Johansson's personal orders, as I understand it.'

'Where is she now?'

'They've taken her to Sythorn, I've heard. I'm sorry.'

The idea of my Marieke in a cell in that place was a shock, but it was followed by an even more horrific thought.

'Espionage, you said! Is she being interrogated?'

'I don't know. But of course that is a possibility.'

'But this is insane! Johansson knows her, he's met her. He can't possibly believe ...'

'Karl, listen to me. Listen to me very carefully. I'm sure Johansson knows perfectly well she is innocent of any crime. So you must ask yourself: Why is he doing this?'

'Why? I don't know why! Because he has lost his reason?' I was shouting now. A guard turned towards me, saw I was with the King, and turned away again.

'You know Johansson,' said the King urgently. 'Perhaps better than any of us. Does he seem to you like the kind of man who would act irrationally? Think, Karl!'

'I don't know, and I don't care! Marieke has nothing to do with any of this, or with any of you! Damn you all and your schemes! I will go up there now and kill him myself.'

The King took hold of my sleeve.

'You are upset, of course. But for Marieke's sake, you must try to think clearly. We must not do anything rash. There is more at stake here than just...'

He left the sentence unfinished. I looked at him.

'Than what? Than just a clockmaker's wife? Is that it?'

'It's not that. Of course Johansson knows she is innocent. He wants you to show yourself. He thinks that if he can get you, he can get me, and then our whole enterprise.'

'I would tell them nothing.'

'Ah, but you would, Karl. You would. They have torture methods that no-one can withstand. And then they would hang you for treason. And how would that help your wife?'

I took a deep breath. He was right, of course. Damn the

man.

'Then what do you suggest?'

'Karl, we can get your wife out of Sythorn and get you both back home. I have a plan. One that will help both you and me.'

I sighed. He always had a plan.

'And when can it be put into effect?'

'Within a couple of weeks, at most.'

'A couple of *weeks*?'

'Patience, Karl! These things take time to arrange. But you will not be kept idle in the meantime. I have some work for you.'

CHAPTER TWENTY-FOUR

'Joe! Take a look at this!' Christopher stood in the doorway to the tower apartment.

'Don't be disturbing me now, I'm working,' said Joe, sitting at the desk by the window with her calculations. She looked up and put down her pencil. 'What in the name of all that's holy is that?'

Christopher was holding a very peculiar contraption in his arms. It looked like some kind of musical instrument: a wooden box with a curving brass trumpet emerging from it.

'It was down in Marchas' studio. He gave me the loan of it. Wait till you see. It's brilliant altogether.'

He put the device down on the table and produced some discs from under his arm. Joe came over and sniffed at him.

'You've been at the gin.'

'I have not. It was just some hooch Marchas had. Green stuff. Just a couple of glasses. He's a nice fellow, Marchas. Very friendly.'

'Obviously.'

'He told me it's a copy of a machine from ancient times. Apparently they found the original in pieces here in the tower, and the royal clockmaker put it together.'

'Are you sure it's safe?'

'It's only clockwork. But wait till you see what it can do.'

Christopher put a disc on the turntable and wound the handle. As it began to revolve, he lifted the arm and placed it gently on the edge of the disc, as Marchas had shown him.

A braying, jaunty melody burst suddenly forth from the trumpet. Startled, Joe stepped back with her hands up.

'Sacred heart of God! Make it stop!'

Christopher laughed.

'Sure it's only music. Are you up for a dance, Joe?' He gave a couple of steps on the spot.

'How'd they do that? It sounds like there's a whole flipping orchestra in there.'

'I know. Isn't it amazing?'

'What kind of weird music is that at all?'

'Ancient dance music. Same kind of stuff as they play in the cafés around here.'

'Then for feck's sake turn it off before you bring the bully boys up here.'

'All right, all right. No more music. But wait till you hear this...'

He lifted the turntable arm and the music stopped. Then he replaced the disc with another, and a rushing, whistling noise filled the room.

'What the heck's that?'

'Windy night,' said Christopher. 'Theatrical Effects, volume III. It's got all kinds of different sounds: footsteps, people talking, thunderstorms, doors creaking, horses trotting, you name it.'

'What would you want that for?'

'Handy if you're putting on a play, like.'

'If you don't mind the audience running away screaming.'

'Oh, I'd say they'd be used to it in ancient times. It was probably normal to them, back then.'

'Well, I think it's creepy.'

The noise stopped as Christopher lifted the needle.

There was a sudden loud, echoing report from outside, like a cannon. Or an explosion.

'Holy God, what was that?' asked Christopher.

Joe looked up at the clock.

'Crap. I think I can guess.'

'Looks like we're in for a bollocking,' said Christopher, as they walked up the palace staircase. He pointed at the messenger boy in front of them. 'That fellow sounded like the voice of doom. *You are to attend the Prime Minister immediately.*'

'They can't blame me. I *told* them it wouldn't work,' said Joe.

'There's something different around here ... where have all the paintings gone?' asked Christopher.

There were pale rectangles to be seen on the walls all along the corridors.

'Maybe they took them down for cleaning or something,' said Joe.

They arrived at the door, and the boy announced them to the Prime Minister's secretary. They entered the outer office and sat down to wait. Opposite them, the secretary was busy with papers at his desk.

'So was it the underwater boat that made that bang, you reckon?' Christopher murmured.

'Must have been. They said they were going to test the cannon today. Twelve o'clock.'

'What do you think went wrong?'

'Simple physics. If you shoot straight up, the recoil has nowhere to go except straight down.'

'So they shot the boat straight to the bottom of the harbour, is that what you're telling me?'

'Probably, yeah.'

Christopher glanced curiously at his partner's face. Joe stared straight ahead.

'Well, that's a little bit odd, isn't, Joe? I mean, you're a pretty good engineer.'

'Why thank you kindly, Brother C!'

'So ... this problem with the recoil. Are you telling me there are no solutions to that? Like a gun carriage or something?'

'There's no such thing as a vertical gun carriage. It can't be done.'

'What about spring-loaded cannons, like the Albans have?'

'You'd have the same problem.'

'No, you wouldn't. It'd be like a catapult. Or a bow and arrow. Much less recoil than with gunpowder. Even I know that.'

'So what are you saying? That I made a mistake?'

'No. The thing is, you don't make mistakes like that. That's what makes me wonder, like.'

'I did what I did, OK? I had to fulfil the contract.'

'Jayzus, Joe, don't tell me you sabotaged their weapon!'

'Keep your voice down, for feck's sake.'

'Why the heck couldn't you just do what they asked?'

'And who was it said *thou shalt not kill*?'

'What about the men on board, then?'

'Better than killing two thousand on those ships.'

'I suppose. If you put it like that. But jeeze, Joe ...'

A bell rang in the other room. The secretary opened the door to Kramer's office and looked in, then returned.

'The Prime Minister will see you now.'

They stood up and entered the inner office. There were not invited to sit. Kramer looked at Joe.

'You are a saboteur!'

'Well, you see, Prime Minister,' Joe began, 'there's something called the laws of motion. To every action, there is an equal but opposite reaction...'

'Your science talk does not interest me. You are the designer, you are responsible! You sank this boat!'

'Indeed I did not, Prime Minister!'

'Then who did?'

'Feck's sake ... Isaac Newton!'

'And who is he? One of your accomplices?'

'In a manner of speaking.'

'Then we will have him arrested!' He glanced over at Christopher. 'What are you laughing at?'

'Ah, sorry, Prime Minister, Joe's just having a little joke.'

'I see nothing amusing here. We nearly lost two men. Let's see if you are still laughing when you are charged with sabotage!'

'Now just a minute, Ekramer ...'

'Chris, leave it,' said Joe. But it was too late. Christopher's fuse had been lit.

'Do you know what? Do you know what, you ungrateful, misbegotten little ... *alien*? I'm sorry we saved your miserable life! We should have left you to drown where we found you.'

'You are imposters!' retorted the Prime Minister. 'We have never met before. Never! You are not who you pretend to be. Who really sent you?'

'Excuse me, your Prime Ministership, but *we're* imposters? Aren't you getting things the wrong way round? How are we imposters?'

'You are no saint!' said Kramer.

Joe guffawed.

'That fella a saint! Are you joking me?'

Kramer turned to Joe.

'And you! You are no angel, either!'

'Sure I never said I was. If I'd a been an angel I wouldn't be sticking out a mile, would I?'

The Prime Minister looked confused.

'Perhaps now, Ekramer, before you start getting yourself all riled up, you might just remember one thing,' said Christopher. '*We know your secret.* And how long do you think you'd last as prime minister here if that got out, hey?'

'Are you threatening me, false saint?'

'Well now, it sounds to me more like you're threatening *us*. So I'm just telling you. We had an agreement. And it seems to me that Joe here has delivered her side of it. She did exactly what she was asked to do. It wasn't her fault it went wrong. And we expect you to do the same. So here's the deal. We want our airship back in airworthy condition, delivered to the top of the Round Tower, by the end of this month. And then we'll be on our way, and no-one will be any the wiser about you. But if that doesn't happen, then we start to get nasty. And you do not want to tangle with the Brothers of St Michael. And now, if you don't mind, we'll be going.'

'You shouldn't go saying things like that to him, he's a dangerous man,' muttered Joe as they made their way back down the broad palace staircase.

'He started it, he fecking threatened us.'

'I know, I know. But the thing is, CC, he's got power. And we haven't. I mean, what would be the easiest way for him to solve his problem with us right now? Have you thought about that?'

Christopher thought about that.

'You may be right there. Maybe we should start making a few preparations.'

CHAPTER TWENTY-FIVE

Six geese a-laying

Johansson and Brorsen were walking the ramparts, in what had become their daily routine. It was a grey universe up here, thought Johansson: grey sky, grey sea. Nothing clear, nothing defined. When had the world become so amorphous? The waters shifted restlessly. Some sea ice was beginning to form along the shoreline, down where the trunks of black naked trees hung out over the banks.

'So, are you still a believer in mob rule, Johansson?'

The question startled him out of his private thoughts.

'Well ... yes. I'm still a democrat, if that's what you mean. But I admit I had not foreseen the practical difficulties.'

'Such as what?'

'I had not realised that being a moderate was such a radical choice. It would be so much easier to be an extremist.'

The older man laughed.

'The hardest position of all to maintain. Any fool can wave a flag and shout revolution. But if you stand in the middle of the road, you are likely to get run down by the traffic going in both directions.'

'My former comrades are out for my blood. They say I betrayed the revolution.'

'You oversaw the peaceful transition of this country from the old regime to a constitutional monarchy, Johansson. For that, of course, they will never forgive you.'

'They wanted a republic. But without my firm hand, there would have been no democracy, only civil war or brutal dictatorship. And yet some of them still brand me with the name of traitor.'

'Well, if they know your name, one might say you are already in trouble.'

'I thought I could escape that fate. But this kingdom is too small. Everyone knows who is really in charge.'

'Everyone but Kramer, it seems.'

Johansson laughed.

'Yes, everyone but him. Do you know he burst into my office today and ordered me to "do something" about those two foreign monks? As though his private vendettas were of the slightest interest to me! He is convinced that they are fakes, that they are really spies. But for whom? The Church? That wouldn't make any sense.'

'If Kramer is afraid of them, it might be worthwhile finding out why. Knowledge is power, and knowledge of other people's secrets is its most refined form. Those monks could be useful to you.'

'They are useful to me as they are. They're skilled in foreign methods of warfare. Their knowledge may help us break the blockade.'

'You're not putting all your eggs in one basket, I hope?'

'I only have one basket, Brorsen. The storehouses are running low. A few foreign merchants are still getting through to the North Gate. They will not accept silver coinage, so we must give them gold, and their prices are high. But the roads through the wildwoods are plagued by bandits, and little enough can come in by that route. We need ships. We must break the blockade now, or the city will soon be starving.'

They walked on, passing a windmill, its blades still on the windless day. The path began to curve back towards the city.

'I hear the Mad Monarch was seen in town?' asked Brorsen.

'The Pretender? Yes, dressed up as the Yule Father, so the rumour goes. He was apparently seen with Clockmaker Nielsen, before he turned up at my house. We get these stories from time to time, but this time it seems there may be something in it. Unfortunately Nielsen escaped before I could interrogate him.'

'And you think the King was behind it?'

'Who else would rescue the clockmaker?'

'True. But what is he up to, do you think? It makes little

sense him coming back here.'

'Well, it's obviously co-ordinated with the blockade. He must have made some kind of bargain with the Northlanders. I also think he may have an arrangement with those two monks. They claim to have a message for the King, but they will not tell me what it is.'

'Can't you find out?'

'I cannot interrogate emissaries from the Pope, sadly. Or throw them in prison. Anyway, we need their expertise. But I can keep a close eye on them. They may lead me to him. He always has some plan.'

'He's not just acting out of desperation, then?'

'I doubt it. He may seem like a buffoon, but we must not underestimate him. In the old days, at court, he was my equal on the chessboard, often better. Rescuing Nielsen was clever – but getting the finger of suspicion to point at me? That was genius, Brorsen! He knows how to use my background against me.'

They had reached a set of wooden steps leading back down off the ramparts. The astronomer looked at Johansson.

'Is that a problem for you? Your ... background?'

'Under these circumstances? Of course it is. It's common knowledge that my family were Northlanders.'

'Then you know what you must do.'

'Do I? What must I do?'

'Johansson, if you will hear my opinion, your democracy is all very well in comfortable times. When things are going well, every man is a democrat. Lazy, affable, agreeable, willing to accommodate fellow human beings of every colour and creed. But when life grows hard – and it certainly is that now – human beings become like savage dogs. Then their code is: first me, then my family, then my class – and only then, my kingdom. In that situation, there is only one way for you to survive as a man of power. You must become more Kantarborgan than the Kantarborgans. You must show utter ruthlessness to the Northlanders and to every subdivision and segment of the Kingdom that is not of the purest Kantarborgan blood. That is what you must do.'

'Is there really no other way?'

'Of course there is. You could resign your position and flee.'

Johansson gave a bitter laugh.

'That would just confirm the suspicions about me. I would be hunted down and killed by one side or the other.'

'Then you have no choice, do you?'

'It would seem not.'

'So – what are you going to do about the flightings?' asked Brorsen.

'Well, what can I do? We cannot feed them, and they refuse to go back.'

'Then they have brought the consequences upon themselves.'

Johansson turned away and leaned on the wooden parapet, looking out towards the distant Northlander ships.

'Once, when I was first officer on board *Redemption* during the Attrition, we ran into fog in the West Sea and came upon a Northlander frigate, laying to. They had twice as many guns as us, but we fired first – a lucky shot from our side hit their magazine and the whole ship went up in an inferno. Every man of theirs who could, jumped overboard. There were hundreds of men in the water, all swimming for our vessel. *Redemption* was a corvette, the smallest ship of the line. The captain ordered us about, and we left them there to drown like rats. I was just a young man. I was shocked at the time, but now ...'

'Now you don't see what else he could have done.'

'We killed a lot of Northlanders that day. From a military point of view, I suppose it was a highly successful engagement.'

'But there are ... other points of view?'

Johansson made no reply.

They descended the steps carefully, the younger man supporting the elder on his arm, and began to make their way back towards the palace.

'How is the boy, by the way?' asked Johansson.

'He is well. He is making good progress in mathematics and languages.'

'You don't find him ... a little unusual?'

'He's a bit of a dreamer, certainly. He seems to live a lot in his imagination. The other day he told me he'd had a visit from the Yule Father. He said he came out of the fireplace in his nursery.'

'I don't remember seeing a fireplace in the nursery?'

'That's just it. There isn't one. The royal apartments at the palace have been heated by hot water since ancient times. Unlike the rest of the building, sadly!'

'So it's all in his imagination?'

'All children have an active imagination. The problem is that he seems unable to distinguish between that and reality. To be entirely candid, I am not sure that he will ever be a capable monarch.'

'A capable monarch is the last thing we need, Brorsen. What we need, when he gains his majority, is a legitimate heir to the throne who will sign the laws and do what he's damn well told. A simpleton would be ideal. '

'He is not that. To tell you the truth, I'm not quite sure what he is, Commander. You may need to keep an eye on him.'

They arrived at a small but heavy-looking wooden door at the rear of the palace. Johansson heaved it open and held it for the older man.

'Indeed so. That offer I once made you ... you would make a good regent, you know.'

Brorsen waved the compliment away.

'I make a good astronomer. And a passable tutor, I hope. That is quite the limit of my ambition. Besides, Kramer would never agree to it, and he would have to sign the order.'

'So you would not consider ...'

'I gave you my answer then, and I will not alter that opinion. Look at me, Johansson! I'm an old man. I lack for nothing.

What would you offer me? Gold? Land?'

'Power,' said Johansson.

'Ah well, when it comes to power, my lord Commander, I learned a lesson a long time ago. And I think you may have learned it, too. Power is something best exercised in secret.'

The door closed behind them.

CHAPTER TWENTY-SIX

'Northlanders outside!' barked the guard.

So now, finally, I am a Northlander, thought Marieke. *Here in a foreign land. How ironic!* The guards in Sythorn had no interest in the finer distinctions among the people from across the Sound; as far as they were concerned, they were all just Northlander flightings.

Marieke, wearing a long grey prison dress, followed the others outside. The cold air hit her as she walked out through the door, and she shivered, tucking her hands in under her arms for warmth. The day was overcast, the wind bitter even in this walled courtyard. But thankfully, they would not be out here for long – just while the guards searched the cells, as they did every day.

As the inmates filed out, they formed two distinct groups in the courtyard, standing among the piles of wet slush that had been swept up into the corners. At one end stood the Lowlander merchants, perhaps fifty of them, murmuring to each other in their soft secret tongue. At the other end were a hundred or so Northlander flightings, who said nothing at all, but simply stared around them with blank expressions.

'Boot's on the other foot now,' said Berendina Jansen to Marieke, nodding towards the group at the opposite end of the yard. 'Just look at the frightened little weasels.'

Marieke looked at them. They seemed more stunned than scared, she thought.

'You think it's us they're frightened of?' asked Marieke.

'Oh it's us, all right. Don't believe all that other nonsense. They can't even get their own stories straight. No two of them can agree on what it was that was supposed to have come out of the north. Monsters and ghouls and the Lord knows what.'

'Have any more of our own people come over?'

'I haven't seen any new faces since last Thursday. I'm sorry, Marieke.'

Marieke nodded.

'My father has been through this before. He will know what to do, where to hide.'

'I know. They'll have enough food, at least. The storehouses have been full since the blockade started. They can wait it out.'

'And perhaps now their persecutors have other things to think about than to go looking for them.'

'From your lips to God's ear, my dear.'

There was a sudden commotion at the other end of the yard as a big Lowlander man stepped forward and dragged one of the Northlanders from the group. No-one from either side intervened as he began to beat and kick him. The Northlander fell to the ground.

Marieke saw the face of the man, twisted in pain. She ran over to his attacker and grasped his arm.

'Jacob, stop! That's Magnus Petersson. This man is our neighbour. He had nothing to do with it!'

The Lowlander pushed her away and pointed at the man on the ground.

'You stay out of this! I saw him! I saw him at the chapel!'

The Northlander man struggled to his feet, his hand to his bleeding mouth.

'I was not there,' he said. 'You are mistaken, Jacob Dreyer.'

'You were there!' Dreyer kicked him again.

'Jacob, please! We've had enough fighting,' said Marieke. The man looked at her with a sneer.

'Oh really? You've decided that, have you, clockmaker's wife? It's not like you don't have blood on your own hands, is it?'

She held his gaze.

'I don't know what you're talking about.'

'Really? Well, no doubt your high-born Kantarborgan husband will come along and rescue you from this hellhole one of these days. But the rest of us, we're all going to die now, aren't we? So by God, I'm going to take one of these bastards with me!'

A pair of guards who had been watching without much interest now strode over and drove the men apart with truncheon blows, as though they were recalcitrant cattle. Dreyer strode angrily back to the Lowlander group.

'I saw the beast!' shouted the Northlander man. 'The beast of the underworld, who speaks with tongues of fire and wears the visage of a wolf!'

'Oh, here we go,' said Berendina. 'They're off again.'

Marieke looked at the raving man. Magnus Petersson was a ship's chandler, not some religious zealot. He must have seen *something*.

'What did Jacob mean? About us all going to die?' Marieke asked.

'They've no more food in Kantarborg,' said Berendina. 'They can't even feed themselves, let alone us. If we're going to starve anyway, they might decide to shorten the process.'

'They will not kill me,' said Marieke. 'Not yet.'

Berendina looked at her questioningly.

'Why's that?'

'They think I know something.'

The other woman said nothing for a few moments.

'I hear it's bad,' she said at last.

Marieke nodded. 'It's indescribable. You think you're going to die. But there's nothing I can tell them. If Karl was mixed up in some plot against the state, he said nothing of it to me.'

'Have you had any news of him?'

'No. They told me he was dead. I'm sure they're lying. They want me to think I have nothing left to hope for. They think that will break me.'

The older woman smiled.

'They don't know you very well, do they?'

The bell rang the quarter hour, and the guards shouted at them to get back to their cells. The Northlanders went in first, herded in with a few more blows from the truncheons.

'It's like they don't care,' said Berendina, looking at the lethargic expressions. 'Like they've given up. It doesn't take much. We were always stronger than them.'

Marieke entered last, as she had been instructed to do. Inside, an officer placed her in shackles and led her along the corridor to the women's wing and up a spiral staircase. Her cell was on the third floor, separate from the others. 'We'll give you the room for our special guests,' the governor had said sarcastically, when she was admitted. Yesterday she had found the name 'K. Nielsen' carved into the window casement. A common enough name, but it comforted her to think that it might perhaps be the same cell in which Karl had been held, years ago. She knew he had been a prisoner here, though he rarely spoke of it. She had scratched the letters 'MH' alongside: Marieke Hendriksdatter. At least they would be together here, if nowhere else.

The guard removed her shackles and opened the cell door. Marieke went inside and sat down on the bunk in the tiny space. There was something under the blanket. She placed her hand on it without looking down. It was flat and rectangular. The guard locked the door and walked away. Marieke waited until she heard the footsteps disappear down the corridor. Then she slipped her hand under the blanket and drew the object out. It was a sheaf of papers. On the first sheet, in Northlandish, was written: *Your husband lives. If you wish to see him again, this is what you must tell them.*

CHAPTER TWENTY-SEVEN

'Anyone home?'

Christopher, holding the music box, knocked on the open door of the artist's studio. Inside, he caught sight of Marchas sitting slumped in an armchair, a bottle open on the floor beside him.

'Hello there! I was just bringing your machine back ... holy moley, what's after happening here?'

Christopher put the music box down and looked around. The place looked like a shipwreck. The furniture had been overturned, the sheets and canvases torn – even the painter's brushes had been snapped in two. All of the portraits were gone, including the one of the fine lady that Marchas had been working on.

'Who did this?'

'Can't you guess?'

'Was it the bully boys? The roundheads?'

'I was out. When I came back, this is what it looked like.'

'But what have they got against you?'

'It seems that God does not like pictures. Paintings and drawings are to be forbidden. They are burning all the artworks in town. They are even tearing down the St Nicholas banners. Look at what they wrote.' He pointed at some graffiti scrawled in black paint on the wall.

'It's in Kantish,' said Christopher. 'I can't read it.'

'It says something like "You must not make pictures".'

'*You shall not make for yourself an image in the form of anything in heaven above or on the earth beneath*,' said Christopher. 'Exodus twenty, verse four.'

He sat down on a stool opposite the painter.

'Jaze, Marchas ... I don't know what to say. I'm just so sorry. I mean, I'm a monk of the Anglian church, we're supposed to be devout and all that, but we'd never go in for anything like this. The Pope himself would be shocked. He's commissioned loads of paintings.'

'These people don't care about the Church. They go their

own way. They do what suits them. Their God is just an excuse.'

'What will you do now?'

The painter held up his hands, a touch theatrically.

'What can I do? I can't stay here. If portraits are forbidden, I have no more work. I am ruined. Perhaps Lady Amalia will give me shelter.'

Christopher thought for a moment.

'Would you do me one favour, Marchas? Would you stay on here a little while longer? I think I might have a bit of an idea.'

CHAPTER TWENTY-EIGHT

Reptilicus redux

It was an antechamber of the dead. A half-world of shuffling, mumbling figures made grey by the dim light of the electric bottles. Soldiers with grey uniforms, grey beards. The dust was everywhere: on our clothes, in our hair, in our mouths. Every step you took raised a small cloud. You would wake up with a fine layer of the stuff covering the blankets on the bunk. Brush it off, and it would be back again ten minutes later. The stuff of nightmares – or perhaps rather one of those frustrating dreams where nothing makes sense and all your efforts are in vain. Truly, the subterranean world is no place for human beings.

For our meals, we gathered in a central hall. The food was mostly just gruel, though sometimes the frustrated cook tried to spice it up with a few berries and herbs – which I noticed most of the men simply picked out and discarded. We were well supplied with beer, though.

One evening – I presume it was evening, though I had no way of knowing – I was invited by the King to dine at what he was pleased to call his High Table, although all the tables were merely boards set upon trestles.

The King took up his customary place at the table end, and, to my surprise and slight embarrassment, indicated I should sit at his right-hand side, the place of greatest honour. Opposite me sat an aristocratic-looking woman whose face looked familiar, but whom I could not immediately place. Her smart and pristine blue dress suggested someone who did not spend her days and nights in this dungeon.

'Nice to see you at our table once again, Clockmaker,' she said. 'I have not seen you since the Rose Castle.'

Then I recognised her. Lady Amalia – my customer for the toy train. Belatedly remembering my courtly manners, I stood and bowed.

'Duchess.'

As I sat down again, a boy appeared and poured us out some wine – good God, did the King have servants even here? And wine?

'I hope the model was to your satisfaction, my Lady,' I said.

She glanced at the King, who gave a slight nod.

'It was quite perfect, Clockmaker,' she said. 'A wonderful piece of work. I will see to it that you are paid the balance immediately.'

Why is it that the nobles always seem to think that money is the sole preoccupation of the merchant classes?

'Who is it for, if I may ask?'

'I'm afraid that's a bit of a secret for now, Clockmaker. Wouldn't want the word to get around. You understand, I'm sure.'

It is not your concern, tradesman. Irritated, I looked around at the small gathering; perhaps a hundred men and women, some in patched and worn royalist uniforms, others in civilian clothes with just an armband in the colours of the King. It struck me that they seemed quite unperturbed at being underground – whereas I had to fight to put on a civilised front, with a constant, desperate fear gnawing at my insides, as though I were drowning. I am a Kantarborgan, after all, born and bred.

The King caught my glance.

'Marvellous, aren't they? And, as you can see, completely impervious to fear of the subterranean spaces.'

'Perhaps they are not from the Kingdom, Majesty?'

'See, Duchess? I told you he was clever.'

'I was just wondering why I was hearing so little Kantish.'

'No, no, you're quite right Nielsen, most of them are from the southern lands. Anglian is their common tongue. Sailors, circus riggers, former miners.'

'So they're not actually ... soldiers, sire?'

'Not before they joined us, most of them. I know what you're thinking, Karl: a ragbag force like this could barely start a fracas on Palace Square, let alone do more useful military work. But there are more ways than one to win a campaign, you know.'

'His Majesty has everything in hand, Mr Nielsen. You will see.'

Lady Amalia looked warmly at the King, and an intimate glance passed between them. *Well and good for him*, I thought, a little bitterly, as I spooned my gruel without enthusiasm. The King took his spoon and held it up.

'Give me a lever and a place on which to stand, and I will move the whole world,' he said. 'You know who said that? Archimedes. Ancient man of science. What you see around you here, Nielsen, is just the lever. And I am about to give the King-dom of Kantarborg a damn good shake!'

Lady Amalia laughed and lifted her glass to him. 'Cheers to that!'

'And where do you intend to stand to do that, Majesty?' I asked.

'Well, not here, Clockmaker. That's all I can say for now. Not here. But all will become clear very soon.'

The meal over, the King took his leave of the Duchess and asked me to accompany him to what he called his office. He leaned on my arm and hobbled along, using his sceptre as a walking-stick, as we walked along another of the long passages between shelves of books. I was completely disoriented by now, and wondered that the King could find his way around the labyrinth in the gloom. But he seemed very familiar with the layout of the place.

'You mentioned that we would be moving on from here shortly, sire?' I asked. I had no desire to spend even one more day in this crypt.

'Yes, as soon as we can,' said the King. 'Though I really wish we could stay longer. Just think – these vaults hold the records of centuries of human progress, spared by happy chance from the fires of the Cataclysm. Think of what we could achieve here, Karl! Think of the machines you could build!'

He stopped and began with difficulty to limp up a spiral staircase made of metal. I gave him my arm to lean on.

'And no-one knows it's here?' I asked.

'No. Or perhaps they do, but they don't care. What good would it be to them? Hundreds of dusty books on incomprehensible subjects. Anything that is not in the Bible is superfluous, or of the devil, they think.'

At the top, he stopped on the gantry and leaned on the railing, looking out across the hall.

'This is what happens to knowledge, Karl,' he said, nodding at the rows of shelves below. 'A thousand years of scientific learning can be blown out like a candle, when the times change. All the secrets of the ancients are concealed here, somewhere. I used to sneak down here alone, when I was a boy. Nobody knew. I could happily have spent my whole life studying and deciphering these documents. Had the times been different, I should have liked to have been known as the Scholar King. But wars and religious conflicts were the ruin of my good intentions, just as they have been for so many monarchs before me. I hope history will exonerate me.'

'I am sure that it will, sire,' I said – though in truth, I was far from sure of that. A king who had bankrupted, sold and then bombarded his own kingdom? His chances of salvaging his reputation for posterity seemed slight. But then again, barely a week ago he had been a beggar on the streets, so who could tell?

His makeshift office was further along the gantry: an airless little room containing only a desk, two chairs, and a few shelves. An electrical bottle hanging from the ceiling gave off some yellow light. He had hung a map of Kantarborg on the wall. His bunk, identical to my own, was folded up and stowed along one wall.

I helped the King climb up onto a chair, and he began to hunt among the boxes and files on the top shelf. As I stood waiting, I noticed an odd little object on his desk. I picked it up. It was a tiny figure of a man, rather stylised, but it seemed to be made of small blocks of some shiny, smooth material in grey and yellow colours.

'What is this, Majesty?'

The King looked over his shoulder.

'Hm? Oh, that. Never seen one before? It's a laygod. We found thousands of them during the excavations. I used to have one in my nursery when I was a child. I thought it was a toy.'

'Is it not?'

'No, no, they were sacred objects for the ancients. Hence the name.'

'Sacred!'

'Yes. Do you know, when we were clearing the forest for the railway lines we found a whole city in miniature, full of figurines like that. Clearly of religious significance. It must have been the burial place of some ancient chieftain. He took all his servants and warriors to the next world with him in tiny replicas, apparently.'

'I have never seen such a material before.'

'No, it doesn't exist anymore.'

'Why not?'

The King retrieved a cardboard tube from the shelf and climbed down.

'It's all gone. Did you ever meet Gregersen, from the University's history department? Clever fellow. He had a theory about that. He believed that a rock from the outer void had fallen onto the earth in ancient times and brought this material with it. Since it had fallen from the sky, the ancients naturally thought it had come from the gods, so they used it to make sacred objects. Until the Cataclysm came and it all melted. Gregersen predicted that we should be able to find a thin layer of the material under the ground, covering the whole earth. Couldn't publish the idea, of course, that would have been heresy at the time. But then when we began our excavations, sure enough, we found the Gregersen layer: a slender stratum of this substance, mostly blackened and burned. And we found relics like this embedded in it. Extraordinary, isn't it?'

I looked at the figure. It had an alien and occult appearance, with a rather disturbing smile. It was hard to imagine what religion it could be a part of, but it was surely a brutal one.

'Now, this is what I wanted to show you,' continued the King, taking a large sheet of paper out of the cardboard tube and spreading it out on his desk. 'Can you see what it is?'

The paper was clearly very old, brown and crumbling at the edges as though it had been exposed to great heat, but I could make out a drawing of some kind. The overall outline was a familiar shape.

'It would appear to be some kind of map of Kantarborg, sire.'

'That's exactly what it is. But one that is rather unusual.'

I studied the document. Long, curving lines, drawn in blue, snaked out from the city centre to the city walls, and even beyond.

'Are these rivers, sire?'

'No. Sadly, our capital city has never been so plentifully supplied with watercourses. Not even in ancient times. Water supply has always been a bit of a problem. But look: you have been here before. This was where we first went in search of the Unconscious, remember?'

He pointed to a line that ran parallel to the North Gate ramparts, not far from the Rose Castle. It was where he had shown me the underground station, all those years ago.

'Then these lines must be railway tunnels? But ... on such a scale?'

'That's it, Nielsen. Ancient railway tunnels. A truly vast network, much bigger than we ever imagined. They criss-cross the entire city, although many of them are flooded now, and others seem to have collapsed with the passage of time.'

'But why build them underground? Surely it would be much easier to build such lines on the surface?'

'Well, exactly. They must have had some good reason for doing all this. It would have been a colossal engineering project, one that would have taken many years of labour – even in those days, when they had machines to do much of the hard work. I think it was probably because of the Cold War.'

'The what?'

'The ancients could control the weather, Nielsen. So they had hot wars and cold wars between their kingdoms. The Great Cold War lasted thirty years, can you imagine that? They had to burrow beneath the ground to stay warm. This whole kingdom is simply riddled with secret tunnels and underground shelters that date from that time. But of course, you know what happens when you build tunnels like that, piercing the Irrational Layer.'

'They would have let loose monsters...'

'Yes. Or demons. Perhaps that was the reason for their downfall in the end. Let us hope that the same does not happen to us. You've heard the rumours coming from the north?'

'No, Majesty?'

'It seems the Northlanders may have the same problem. Since they reopened the iron mines. We don't quite know what's happening yet, but they are very scared. There is panic and hysteria among the population. Many of them are trying to flee across the Sound, like your wife.'

Was that really why Marieke had tried to follow me? It did not sound like her to flee from anything. She would have fought the monsters first.

'But there are no mines in Kantarborg, sire, and no mention of monsters in our sagas, as far as I know.'

'Well actually, Karl, that's not quite true. We found something here. In the archives, hidden away – as though no-one wanted to be reminded of it.'

From a drawer in his desk, he produced a sheet of luridly-coloured paper, like a poster. A headline of some kind was scrawled diagonally across it. Underneath were images of terrified people, running away from a hideous, dragon-like creature with huge teeth. It bore an undeniable resemblance to the monster we had encountered on our journey north, years earlier.

'What word is that, Majesty?' I asked, pointing to the head-line.

'*Reptilicus*? It's the name of that beast, I think. Ancient scientists used the old Roman language to name animal species, so this was no doubt taken from some kind of scientific publication. But of course, it's just possible that it might be an illustration from one of their more imaginative sagas. They had so many of them, it's not always easy to tell what is true and what isn't. But look here ...'

He pointed to one of the buildings in the background.

'That looks like the clock tower – in our town hall!' I said, amazed.

'It does, doesn't it? And if you look carefully, you can see other buildings in our city that have survived since ancient times. I believe this is Kantarborg, Karl, as it then was. As for the beast itself, you can see that it greatly resembles the dead one we found in the Westlands, though on a much larger scale. So to my mind, the conclusion is inescapable. This was a real monster – one that the ancient Kantarborgans accidentally set loose from the Irrational Layer. Probably as a result of their tunnelling activities.'

I stared at the garishly-drawn picture.

'You're wondering whether such creatures still exist down there,' said the King, reading my thoughts in his usual irritatingly accurate manner. 'Well of course we can't rule it out, but so far we have encountered nothing untoward.'

'And I suppose your plan involves these tunnels?'

'To some extent, yes. I'm sorry, Karl, there's no way around that, I'm afraid, now that things have taken the turn they have. But don't worry, for once it will not involve battle.'

He still apparently harboured the notion that I was afraid of combat. *Of all the things I could be afraid of in this situation*, I thought to myself, *that would surely be the last of them.*

'You once made an ingenious device for me, a clockwork singing bird,' he continued. 'It was a gift for a visiting diplomat.

Do you remember?'

'Yes, in fact there were several, Majesty. Of various sizes and varieties.'

'It was most realistic. If you scaled it up, do you think you could make something that sounded like that monster? Something like Reptilicus?'

'A monster, Majesty? What would that sound like?'

'Oh, I suppose like a walrus or something.'

'A what?'

'It's a sea creature that lives in the North. Or a lion, whatever. A roar of some kind. Use your imagination, Karl!'

'But sire, I have no tools here.'

'Andreasen the swordsmith has some tools. He will help you. They're not the sort of tools you're used to, of course, but I imagine this device would have to be on a fairly large scale anyway.'

'Well ... I can try, sire.'

'Good man. And it's not just for my own amusement, you know. This is important. In fact I would say it's an essential part of my plan. I cannot reveal the details to you yet, but if all goes as I expect, your Marieke will be returned to you.'

That, of course, was his trump card. So, although I had no idea what it could possibly achieve, there was nothing to do but to set to work.

Andreasen, who had been a smith in civilian life, was a tubby, genial fellow with a long black beard. He gave me some tongs, a soldering iron and a hammer, and directed me to the only place a fire was permitted in our underground hideaway – the kitchen. This was positioned some distance from the main body of the library, the reason being that here it was directly below the palace itself; the smoke from the stove could then rise through the palace chimneys and blend with the smoke from the other fireplaces, thereby concealing its origin.

For my first attempts at creating a monster's roar, I used the same principle as I had done to create the singing birds, namely a bellows. But this bellows would obviously have to be a lot larger.

I persuaded the cook to let me have a bellows from the kitchen stove, onto which I soldered various copper mouthpieces that could vibrate and produce noise. The results were not impressive. I have no idea what a monster sounds like, but I feel sure it does not sound like a honking goose. To get a deeper note, I tried pushing the bellows very slowly.

'Does that sound like a monster?' I asked.

'Maybe if it farted,' said the cook, to much hilarity among the kitchen staff.

I decided I had better rethink my methods. I was pondering the problem at dinner the next day when a soldier opened the iron door to a cellar room that had once perhaps been a strong-room of some sort, and now served as our armoury. I heard the eerie creaking of the hinges, and it gave me an idea.

The master of arms was very loath to let me remove the door of the armoury – because, he said, of the risk of explosion. But as the King pointed out, if an explosion were to occur in such a small space, it would be better to have an open door than a closed one – otherwise you would in essence have created a very powerful bomb that would likely kill us all. So, rather reluctantly, the officer let me dismantle it.

Thankfully, it was not necessary to use the whole thing. The part that made the uncanny noise was the lower hinge, which was attached to a metal arm that supported the door.

My work with music boxes had taught me something about acoustics and amplification, which in essence boiled down to this: If you want to produce a loud sound, you must vibrate a large surface. The string of a musical instrument, whether it is plucked, bowed or hammered, is barely audible in itself. If we are to hear it, it must be connected to a sounding-board of some sort, like the body of a guitar or violin. The same goes for the needle of a music box.

So the metal arm needed a sounding-board – preferably one made of wood, which is a material that vibrates very well. I tried drilling a hole in an empty beer barrel and setting up the device in that, but it was rather unstable and kept toppling over.

Finally, I found a solution in a wooden tea chest, with the metal arm and hinge bolted to a post in the centre. Although I hardly dared to test it very much because of the restrictions on noise, when the arm was turned slowly it made a loud and quite blood-curdling sound.

I showed the King my handiwork.

'Most ingenious, Karl. To quote one of my ancestors, "I don't know what effect it will have on the enemy, but by God, it frightens me." But of course it will have to be automated.'

'Automated, sire?'

'Yes, with some kind of clockwork mechanism. It will be placed in the tunnels, and it must be able to work when no-one is around.'

'Majesty, I fear that that would be quite beyond me with the resources available to me here.'

'Oh, you'll think of something, Karl. I put my faith in you.'

I did at times grow weary of the King's boundless confidence in my skills. This time, however, I really could see no feasible solution to his request. To move something that heavy would require an enormous clockwork mechanism, and I no longer had a whole workshop and a team of workers at my disposal, as in the days of the clockwork locomotive. All I had now were a few ironworking tools and a kitchen fire. But if this bizarre contraption was to play a part in getting Marieke released, I had better come up with something.

I was lying on my bunk early one morning when I heard a door that had been left open slam somewhere, followed by hissed curses at the person responsible – and the answer came to me. The tunnels below ground had always been draughty places – perhaps that could provide enough power to turn a metal arm?

A mere draught will not of course shift a large piece of metal on its own. I would need to equip it with a sail, set out on a long arm so that it could exploit the power of leverage. *Give me a lever and a place on which to stand, and I will move the whole world.* If I then attached a couple of fairly strong springs to the base of the arm, one on either side, it should in theory return to its place of origin after being deflected by the air current. It was worth a try.

A day's work saw the strange device fitted with a long wooden arm like the spar of a sailing-ship, with a makeshift sail made of cast-off dishcloths, and a brick counterweight on the other side to balance it. I could not test it fully, but I was pleased to see that a fairly light touch on the tip of the arm would cause it to move and emit a deep bellow.

The King was delighted.

'You never let me down, Karl. I will see that you are rewarded for your loyal service when I am returned to the throne.'

'My only wish is to see my wife returned to me, sire. That is all I ask.'

'Well, I'm quite sure that can be done. It's time to reveal to you the next part of the plan. Come with me.'

We returned to the King's office, where he once again took out the map of the underground railway lines.

'Now, this map was one I found in the Rose Castle in the old days, and put aside. I have shown it to no-one but you, so Johansson has not seen it, although he has probably seen other maps of the ancient railway networks. But this one is a little special. I don't know if you noticed, but it has a tunnel on it that is not marked on any of the others I have seen.'

He pointed at a line that was shown in a different colour – in faded red ink.

'First of all, do you see, that line's as straight as an arrow – not writhing about like the others. And secondly, it leads from the palace *here* and straight out of the city, right underneath the city walls, and has no marked stopping places at all. Not even at New Square, even though it passes directly beneath it. And that is a little odd, you might think, if it is intended to serve as a means of transport. The lettering is hard to make out now, but it appears to say 'Royal Road' in old Kantish. It is also much longer than the others. As you can see, it leads right off the edge of the map.'

'The Royal Road? You once mentioned...?'

'The Royal Road to the Unconscious, yes exactly! Isn't that intriguing?' The King began to remove another document from the tube. 'And that was all we knew. Until recently, when we found this in the library here.'

We? He had been out of the Kingdom for a long time. How long had this plan been in the making?

He placed the second piece of paper beside the first. They seemed to align perfectly. The red line continued from one to the other.

'This is the lost other half of the map.'

The route marked on the second map showed the line leading straight out of the city to a destination well beyond the city walls, in a dark complex marked in Kantish lettering: *Regan Øst.*

'Regan? What does that mean?'

'I don't know,' he smiled, 'but where there is a Regan, I think there's a fair chance we may one day encounter Gonorrhoea and Chlamydia as well.'

I had no idea what he was talking about.

'Three daughters of an ancient king,' he explained. 'I suspect this ... complex is named after one of them. Which would imply that there are two more, somewhere.'

'But it must be several leagues away! To build a tunnel that long would surely be impossible, Majesty.'

'Many things were possible for the ancients, Nielsen. Did you know that in America, they had an underground railroad that led right from the south of that country to the north? It's very well attested in the sagas. But they had to close it because their slaves kept escaping through it.'

'But why would the ancients build such a thing here, in Kantarborg?'

'Ah. Let me show you a little secret.'

The King rolled up the maps and replaced them in the tube. Taking his wind-up lamp from the desk, he led me back out onto the metal gantry and began to limp rapidly along it, leaning on the sceptre. Even with a sprained ankle, he always seemed to be in a hurry. I followed behind, struggling as usual to keep up.

'In any kingdom, ancient or modern, it is important to protect the children of the monarch,' he said over his shoulder. 'If your enemies can kill not only the ruler but also the heirs to the throne, they can break the line of succession, and thereby remove any chance that a defeated royal line might rise again. So certain measures must be taken in time of conflict to protect the royal family.'

He stopped and shone the lamp upwards. Above us was a square hatch, like a trapdoor, from which an electrical cable emerged and was suspended along the ceiling. Protruding a couple of feet from the opening of the hatch was the start of an iron ladder.

'We are directly beneath the palace here,' said the King. 'This is where we tap the power from the Great Windmill. That shaft leads up to my old nursery. It was meant to be the escape route for my brother and I, in case some enemy of my father breached the palace defences. It was a secret passed down through generations of my family. No-one else knew about it, not even the servants. It was also how I got down here without being seen, when I was a boy. Though of course I did not tell my father that.'

He clicked off the lamp and looked at me.

'My father knew about the shaft to the basement of the Palace Library, but what he did not know is that the escape route does not end here. When I saw that map, and the 'Royal Road' marked on it, I had a moment of enlightenment. I realised that the ancients must have built an underground railroad from the palace here to some safe place where their own royal family might survive an overhanging calamity. But to keep it secret, they would have to ensure that only the monarch and his immediate entourage could gain access to it. And they did that in a way that was rather clever.'

He held up the sceptre.

'They did it with this. It's a key. Of sorts. There's only one, and only the reigning monarch may hold it. So if there are upheavals or war, the King and his family, together with his ministers, can seek shelter in the secret hideaway. And the government of the country can continue.'

'A key? How does it work? Is it electrical?'

'Not at all. I suspect they were worried that an electrical device might not work in a crisis situation. No, it is entirely mechanical, though of cunning contrivance.'

'And you're sure it still works?'

'Oh yes, it works. Come with me, I'll show you.'

We descended the spiral staircase and walked over to a bookcase that looked like any other in the library. But beside it, in the wall, was a small round aperture. The King took the sceptre, inserted the end of it into the hole, and turned part of the shaft. The bookcase slid back, revealing concrete steps leading downwards into darkness.

'The entrance to the underground railroad,' he said. He clicked his lamp on and started down the steps. I followed, in some trepidation. Visits to the Irrational Layer with the King rarely ended well.

The steps led downwards a good thirty metres. When we reached the bottom, the King held up his lamp, to reveal a subterranean railway station like the one at North Gate. But this one was quite small – barely more than a large grotto. The platform, such as it was, could hold perhaps thirty people. I looked down at the tracks. They appeared to be the usual gauge.

'It's not nearly as big as the one at North Gate, of course,' said the King. 'Or as grand. It was only meant to be used in time of war and crisis, not for religious or ceremonial purposes, so the design is rather perfunctory. Not much decoration.'

'The rails look in remarkably good condition, Majesty.

Considering their age.'

'Yes, aren't they? I suspect that they were made of something other than the usual iron or steel. They had to remain useable for decades, you see, with minimal maintenance. And that was another reason to put the whole thing underground, away from wind and weather.'

'There doesn't seem to be much in the way of draughts here, compared to North Gate.'

'You're thinking of your invention? I wouldn't worry. Right now, this line is blocked at this end. It used to connect to the main network, but at some time in the past, the route was cut off. So now we need to unblock it, so that we can get a train in here. Knock a wall down and extend the line. I'll need you to take charge of that.'

'Me, Majesty?'

'Yes. Well, you're an engineer, aren't you?'

'A horological engineer, sire. A clockmaker. I have never worked with civil engineering.'

'Nonsense, you designed a moonship for me that worked perfectly well. Not to mention the locomotive. Besides, it's all the same thing basically, isn't it? Forces and resistance. Just scale it up. I will make sure you have plenty of people to help you.'

'Forgive me, sire – I am having trouble seeing how all this fits into your plan.'

By which I meant, of course, *How on earth is all this supposed to help release Marieke?*

'All will be revealed in good time, Nielsen. The mechanism has been wound up, and it has already been set in motion.'

CHAPTER TWENTY-NINE

'She said all this?'

Johansson flicked through the sheaf of papers on his desk.

'It was the third session that broke her,' said Ottesen. 'Although I must say I almost despaired that we would ever get anything useful out of her. But they always crack in the end.'

'So it seems. Did she reveal the whereabouts of the Pretender?'

'She clearly doesn't know, or else she would have said. But she did give up the details of the plot against us.'

Johansson studied one of the final pages of the report.

'Extraordinary. You know, I was convinced all along that the King must be in league with the Northlanders, but it's good to get confirmation. So that's why he took such a chance coming here! He's a cunning bastard, I must say. The consequences would have been more devastating than any bombardment. Without gold, we would not have been able to buy any more food from outside. It might well have brought about our surrender. And this was all planned to take place when?'

'Four days from now.'

'On the Yule holiday?'

'Yes. When we would have been off our guard.'

'Indeed. Many of our men would have been with their families, and the rest might well have had a drop or two taken. It would have been easy pickings for the Northlanders, even without help from the Pretender's bandits.'

'According to the prisoner's account, the royalists planned to open the city gates and the main door to the Treasury. It is believed that the Pretender may be in possession of a key. Then the Northlander raiding party would simply have sailed into the harbour under cover of darkness and taken the entire contents.'

Johansson exhaled.

'We have clearly had a very lucky escape. You know, I'm sorry to have to say it, but this just proves the usefulness of such interrogation methods, even in a democratic society such as ours. We have clearly been in a ticking bomb situation. You did well, Ottesen.'

'Thank you, sir. I take it you will be cancelling Yule leave now?'

'No, we will act completely as normal. We must not arouse suspicions. Our great advantage, right now, is that they don't know that we know. But the contents of the Treasury will obviously have to be moved.'

'Yes sir. At once?'

'No, wait until the last moment. The night before the raid. And then we will give them a welcome they weren't expecting.'

CHAPTER THIRTY

Christopher and Joe had been taking turns to keep watch at night, but inevitably, it was while they were off their guard that the moment came. It was six in the evening, and dark outside. Christopher had been to the market and had come back rather triumphantly with half a cabbage, a few thin slices of bacon, and some small potatoes. Together with some spices they found in the kitchen, it made an almost acceptable stew.

'It's not what you might call a feast, but it will do us,' he said proudly as he tucked in.

'It's delicious,' said Joe, rather spoiling it by adding, 'and hunger is the best sauce, they say.'

'Worth waiting for,' said Christopher. 'It took me flipping ages to put the barricades back again.'

But they had eaten rather less than half their repast when the sound of thumping and angry shouts came from the street outside. They looked at each other.

'Showtime, do you think?' asked Joe.

Christopher opened a window and looked down.

'Yep. Roundheads. They're trying to batter down the door. Amateurs! They should have used a ladder to the lowest window. If you want to assassinate someone, you don't go barging in like an elephant at a tea party.'

Shaking his head, Christopher disappeared into the bedroom and came back with the chamber-pot.

'I'll just give them a little encouragement.'

'Chris, no!'

There was a splash and a roar of fury from outside.

'C'mon boys, the hooley's up here! Put your backs into it!' Christopher yelled down.

'Right. That's them warmed up. Time to get Marchas up here.'

The door to the Round Tower was robust and held for another five minutes before it splintered and gave way to the battering-ram. Seven men, carrying clubs and wearing the round white helmets of the Community of Celestial Concord and Peace, came charging up the spiral gangway, baying for blood. By the fifth turn, however, they were already beginning to lose steam, and their shouts were a touch less belligerent. Here they encountered a barricade made of the wreckage from Marchas' studio: broken tables and chairs, poles and planks, and the remains of an easel, blocking the walkway from one side to the other. They set to work removing the obstacles in a fury. It took them several minutes to clear a passage. Another turn of the spiral gangway, and another barricade awaited them: yet more flotsam from the ruined workshop. They were beginning to grow a little tired now, though no less determined. Finally they broke through and charged up around the next bend of the passage.

But then, something strange happened. All at once, seemingly from nowhere, they heard the sound of hideous laughter, reverberating strangely as though from the bottom of a well. In the echoing acoustics of the dark tower, the noise seemed to be all around them at once. The men faltered slightly, but their captain shouted at them, to stiffen their resolve.

'Devilry and witchcraft! Burn the sorcerers!'

The men took up the cry: 'Burn them! Burn them!' and advanced in a steady pace up the tower. The strange sounds continued: a galloping horse could be heard, rainfall and loud thunder, a baby crying, and, most disconcertingly of all, laughter and loud applause.

One by one, the Moonies ceased their ascent and stared around them in wild-eyed confusion. The noises suddenly stopped.

And then two monks came down around the spiral bend to meet them. Their hoods were drawn down over their eyes, and they were carrying burning torches. They stopped just a few yards from the gang, and in a loud, ringing voice, one of them began to declaim:

'From all sin, from your wrath, from sudden and unprovided death, from the snares of the devil, from anger, hatred, and all ill will, from all lewdness, from lightning and tempest, from the scourge of the Albans, from plague, famine, and war, from everlasting death, deliver us, oh Lord!'

'Deliver us, oh Lord!' said the other monk.

'For haughty men have risen up against me, and fierce men seek my life; they set not God before their eyes. Therefore I command you, every unclean spirit, every spectre from hell, every satanic power, *depart from me, ye accursed, into the everlasting fire which has been prepared for the devil and his angels!'*

The monk turned away for a moment, then turned back and breathed a jet of living fire out of his mouth. The flames shot out in a roar and lit up the whole gangway.

The men gasped and stepped back, though they did not yet run. But then a small, monstrous, furry devil with long, pointed ears suddenly appeared behind the monks, running back and forth and taking up martial arts poses. At that, the gang lost all remaining composure and fled in terror, stumbling over the barricades and each other as they made pell-mell for the tower entrance. They were pursued by more ghostly laughter, which gradually descended in pitch, ending in a hideous rumble.

Marchas emerged from the arched recess where he had been hiding with the music box. Brother Christopher brushed his hands together in satisfaction.

'And that, Joe, is how you deal with a bunch of ignorant rapscallions. Show them something they do not understand.'

'Well done, Chris,' said Joe, throwing back her hood. 'Though to be honest it looked more like they were scared of something behind us.'

'Behind us? Must have been the shadows, Joe. From the flames.'

'Must have been. I suppose.'

'They will be back, you know,' said Marchas.

'Probably,' agreed Christopher. 'I think it's time we had a

little word with Johansson.'

CHAPTER THIRTY-ONE

Five gold rings

'Now I am going to make robbers of you all,' said the King with a wink.

Charlie and I were standing with the King in his office. The map of Kantarborg, showing the underground railway lines, was spread out on his desk.

'Our spies tell us that Johansson is about to move all the gold reserves of Kantarborg out of the national treasury, because he fears a seaborne attack by the Northlanders. He needs to get the gold away from the harbour and find a safe place to put it. So, Nielsen, if you were him, what would you do?'

'Me? I suppose I would put the gold in a fortress, Majesty. Perhaps Alsina?'

'Too isolated. The Northlanders could easily cut the railway line along the coast, separate Kantarborg from its own money. Same goes for the Old Capital.'

'The Citadel?' suggested Charlie.

'Better, but he cannot risk moving such riches openly, on wagons and the like. The population is growing desperate, and he can no longer trust even his own troops.'

'He'd use the tunnels, I bet,' said Charlie.

'Yes, I think you're right. Johansson knows the tunnels, or at least some of them. And my information is that he has been planning for this very contingency. He has already connected the line for the clockwork railway to the tracks leading to the ancient station at North Gate.'

'But surely Kantarborgans would never enter the underground! They'd be terrified.' I objected.

'Well *precisely*, Nielsen! So why would he do that, hmm? If it isn't for the sake of the populace?'

'Well, to find somewhere to hide the gold.'

'Yes, but where? Remember he has to be able to access it,

too.'

'The Rose Castle!' I said.

'Exactly! He'll try to take the gold by train beneath the ground to North Gate, and thence via the secret passage to the cellar of the Rose Castle, where he no doubt believes it can be kept safely guarded behind the walls and moat. But unfortunately the consignment will never arrive, because we will intercept it *here*.'

The King pointed to the map.

'This is where the Royal Road used to connect to the rest of the network. It is currently blocked by a wall. Your job, Nielsen, will be to supervise the removal of that wall and install some bridging track. We must do this on the same night that Johansson moves the gold. They will expect it to be safe underground, so the train will have a minimal guard, perhaps five or six men at most, plus the driver. We can easily overcome them. Charlie will command the attack. Nielsen, you will instruct him in how to drive the train. Then he will divert it and bring it here, to the secret station beneath the palace. Once we have the gold, we will present the regime with our demands. One of which will of course be the immediate release of your wife.'

I felt both relieved and a little irritated that I was to play no part in the actual robbery. It was a little puzzling, though – driving the train was my area of expertise, after all.

'The other demands will be my reinstatement as monarch of Kantarborg and the recognition of my claim to the three crowns,' said the King, as though that were a mere afterthought.

'No negotiations. They can take it or leave it. And if Johansson refuses to parley, I also have a plan B in reserve.'

'But when Johansson knows we're down here, he'll send his whole army into the tunnels after us,' Charlie objected.

'No, he won't. I have my own ideas on how to prevent that. Nielsen, would you excuse us one moment?'

'Of course, Majesty.'

I stepped outside to the gantry, a little perplexed. Did the

King still not trust me? What part of his plans was he not willing to reveal to me? But that was typical of him: never tell anyone the whole truth. It's *the way things are done.*

I did not know whether or not he was going to call me in again, so I waited outside – at a discreet distance, so as not look as though I were eavesdropping. But I could hardly help overhearing what happened next.

'No! I did not sign up for this!' I heard Charlie shout from inside. The door flew open, and Charlie emerged and pushed past me, looking furious. The King came out onto the gantry and shouted after him.

'You signed up for the King's Men, that's what you signed up for! This is not some children's game we're playing!'

'Damn boy needs to learn to do as he's told,' the King muttered to me, watching Charlie walk away.

'He did seem a little ... impassioned.'

'Apparently he finds my plan for the attack on the train inappropriate.'

'Perhaps he is a little inexperienced in combat, sire? I mean, someone with his background?'

'What background?'

'Well, as a sailor. And an actor.'

The King looked at me, suddenly amused.

'Been spinning you a tale, has he? Don't let the proletarian act fool you. He's a noble through and through. He's actually one of the few men I have with solid military experience. He's a good enough soldier, but as an actor he's bloody difficult and won't take direction.'

CHAPTER THIRTY-TWO

Commander Johansson had seen a great deal in his career. He had encountered witches, demons and monsters in the cold north. He had endured and survived the skulduggery and machinations of court intrigues. He had even – it was whispered – organised a revolution. But nothing in his previous experience had prepared him for this latest turn of events. He was, to his profound surprise, surprised.

'The Prime Minister is an *alien*? What on earth makes you think that?'

'He told us so himself,' said Christopher. 'He said he was an ambassador from another world.'

'And you say you found him floating at sea? Do you have any proof of that?'

'I gave him a St Christopher medal,' said Joe. 'Did you see it?'

Johansson stared at Joe in shock.

'That medal! Then ... you are the *angel*?'

She pointed to her midriff.

'Do I look like a flipping angel? I'm a lay brother of St Michael! I may have sinned, but that wasn't my fault. I was a woman at the time. Or so *he* said.' She shot Christopher a look.

Johansson looked bewildered.

'The Minister doesn't need to know all that, Joe,' said Christopher. 'Sure you're only confusing the poor man. The point is that Ekramer is a fake. He's not a citizen of this kingdom. He wasn't born here. He's probably not even a human being. I don't know how he ended up being prime minister, but that must be all part of the plan. I wouldn't be surprised if he starts inviting his alien friends to join him down here on Earth soon. "C'mon over, lads, the women are gorgeous and the men are gullible." Er, no offence, your Ministership.'

'None taken,' said Johansson faintly. He sat for a few moments in silence, a variety of reactions crossing his face and being suppressed in turn.

'Well, this is most interesting intelligence that you have brought me,' he said at last. 'Most interesting. I will have to give it some thought to see how we can best deal with the situation.'

'But, er, if you could in the meantime see your way to placing us under armed protection, we would be most grateful,' said Christopher. 'His gang came close to bumping us off last night, and we might not be so lucky next time. You can see why he might want us out of the way.'

'Of course. That will be taken care of. We must make every effort to ensure that you can continue your important work here without inconvenience or harassment.'

Christopher caught the look.

'Ah, that's right, your Ministership. And we look forward to, er ... continuing our fruitful collaboration. *Nugget for nugget,* right?'

'Indeed.'

Johansson stood up and shook hands solemnly with the two monks. As they closed the door behind them, he sat down heavily at his desk, an expression of incredulity on his face. And then he laughed. And laughed. And laughed.

CHAPTER THIRTY-THREE

It was the noises that were the worst. Not the sound of the men working. That was almost reassuring – just the routine clamour of hammers, saws and pick-axes that I knew so well. But whenever they left off for a moment, passing their smoking-pipes around – then the dripping sounds returned, the unidentifiable creaking, the sighing of underground winds that seemed to carry the voices of the ancient dead. Perhaps my problem is that I have too much imagination. Or, on the contrary – that I simply knew too much about the real risks down there.

Just getting there had been trying enough. An hour's walk along passages bitter with darkness and damp, dragging timber sleepers and the long pieces of iron rail that Charlie's men had stolen from the Royal Foundry. Moving from one tunnel to the next in silence, arguing in hushed voices over the map by lamp-light, our boots slipping in the wet, the men hissing curses at each other at the sound of a rattling tool in someone's belt. To finally arrive at a concrete wall that blocked the tunnel firmly from side to side.

I was shivering with cold, yet sweating at the same time. I dried the back of my neck irritably, then held my hand out to steady myself. The tunnel wall was damp, like the wall of a cave. Or a tomb.

Even after an hour, the pick-axes were making only slow progress – the wall looked to be several yards thick. We would have to break through soon – if the King's information on the train's movements was reliable, it would be coming past in less than an hour. Reluctantly, I took the decision to use gunpowder. The men asked me where to lay the charges – as though I were some kind of expert! But with a piece of chalk, I drew some circles on the wall where I hoped the explosives would weaken the foundations without bringing the whole tunnel roof down on top of us.

Then we sat down to wait while the sappers got to work. The lamps occasionally ran down and had to be wound up again. At one point all of them went out at once, and the darkness seemed to me to be alive, teeming and seething with nightmarish forms. I involuntarily clutched the arm of the man beside me, who in turn started in alarm. *Get a grip on yourself, Nielsen.* Showing fear in front of the men was not a good idea.

When the sappers were finished, we retired to what they told us was a safe distance. The officers drew their sabres.

The men looked at me. I was the one who had to give the order. My first military command.

'Light the charges!'

The sappers lit the fuses. We turned away and covered our ears, as we had been instructed to do. There were a few seconds of silence, then the universe burst apart. The blast almost knocked me off my feet, and I staggered forward a few paces. A shower of gravel hit my back. When I turned around, most of the wall was gone. Choking, acrid smoke and dust was every-where. The hole was huge, much bigger than we had anticipated. One man, hit by flying debris, lay groaning on the tunnel floor. A medic hurried over to him. Time for my next order, and my last – after that, command was to pass to Charlie.

'Officers and men ... into the breach,' I coughed.

'Officers and men into the breach!' repeated Charlie, more loudly. Holding what looked like some kind of garden rake, he crawled up onto the pile of rubble and led the way through the gap. The rest of the armed men and women followed. They dis-appeared down through the tunnel, while I and the designated labourers set to work, clearing the line of debris and getting the new rails ready to drag into place. It took us just half an hour to cut the line on the far side and install the temporary track that would take the train into the tunnel that led to the palace. Then we began to walk back along the line to the secret station, leaving the scene to Charlie and his warriors. My ears were still ringing from the blast.

CHAPTER THIRTY-FOUR

The tower clock was striking six in the evening as Johansson strode down the palace corridor. Two members of Kramer's personal guard, wearing their CCCP helmets, were standing outside the office of the Prime Minister. They saluted him as he approached. Johansson ignored them, knocked on the door, and opened it.

Kramer looked up from his papers in irritation as Johansson entered.

'Johansson, if you wish to see me, I would appreciate it if you would make an appointment like anyone else.'

'My apologies, Prime Minister. It's just some documents that urgently need your signature before you go home. It won't take a moment.'

Johansson dumped a hefty pile of papers onto Kramer's desk. Kramer stared at them. His command of written Anglian was limited. *Trying to wrong-foot me again*, he thought. *Typical bloody officer. Always playing these stupid games.*

'I don't have time to look through all these now. What do they deal with?'

'Well, the most important of them is probably this one, Prime Minister. With your permission, I am ordering the garrison at Alsina to be evacuated. It has little defensive value in the current situation, and we need all the militia we can get in the city right now, in case the Northlanders decide to attack.'

'But what about the prison?'

'We will keep the staff there for the time being. It may be that we can find some other solution regarding the prisoners.'

Kramer picked up his pen and signed the document.

'Very well. Anything else?'

'The rest are just administrative matters, Prime Minister, I won't take up any more of your time. If you could just sign here ... and here. Thank you.'

Johansson actually bowed as he took the papers. Kramer

watched him with distaste as he left the office. *Smarmy worm, always so obsequious. Smile to your face, knife behind your back. Looks down his nose at me because I don't have his education. Doesn't think I'm fit to be Prime Minister of the kingdom. Him and Brorsen, thick as thieves, always with their heads together. Plotting, no doubt. Well, we'll see about that. The people elected me, Johansson, not you. They chose a man of God, not a godless noble. And I decide who serves the people.*

CHAPTER THIRTY-FIVE

Two workers were walking down one of the palace corridors in the early morning. One of them was a middle-aged woman, her dark blond hair tied back in a scarf. She was carrying a brown leather tool bag. The other was a young man, rather pale and thin. Both were dressed in dark blue, dusty overalls.

'So I threw the switch and the whole tree lit up all at once, top to bottom, lovely,' said the woman. 'But the old man went plain spare, thought demons had descended on his house. Terrified, he was. Calling for the priest and everything. And the young master tried to explain to him that it was just the new science, safer than candles, but he wasn't having none of it. Electrickery is devil's work, he says! So I had to go and take it all down again.'

Sarah Kaldur laughed quietly to herself.

'So did they pay you?' her assistant enquired.

'Paid me to put it up, and paid me to take it down again. A good day's work, I call that, Frederik.'

'Shame, though. About the lights. It's a good idea. Instead of candles.'

'Yeah, well, it'll catch on eventually. Lots of the big families are doing it now. Stops them burning their precious houses down. Long as ...'

She glanced around and lowered her voice.

'Long as our friends here don't go and ban it.'

'Why would they do that? It's no harm to anyone.'

'Well, they've banned every other flipping thing. They don't even allow music now, you know? I got thrown out of a café last weekend, just because someone was playing the piano there. If they think it's fun, they'll ban it, you can bet your life on it ... now, here we are. Look at that.'

She pointed at the electric bulb installed in what had once been an ornate oil lamp above the corridor.

'That ought to be twice as bright. You can hardly see where

you're going, these winter mornings. No wonder they're complaining.'

She stopped in front of a door that had once had a picture of some exotic animal painted on it, now much faded.

'This is the old nursery. It's directly underneath where we were before. Mind how you go, there are toys all over the floor, if I remember rightly.'

She opened the door, and they walked into what turned out to be a remarkably orderly space.

'Someone's been tidying up,' said Kaldur, looking around at the shelves with their neatly arranged clockwork devices. 'Or else he puts his toys away afterwards. But whoever heard of a child who did that?'

'I hear he's a bit odd,' said Frederik.

'Shh, Fredo, walls have ears. Now ... it must be around here that the voltage drops off. You'd expect some drop with the cable resistance, but not that much. It's like half the power of the windmill is disappearing along the way. You see that cable there, along the ceiling? It goes over to ...'

She pointed to where the wire disappeared through a small hole in a large wall cabinet.

'I reckon the problem must be in there somewhere. It's not marked on the wiring diagrams, and we've checked everywhere else.'

Frederik tried the cabinet door.

'Locked. Can we get hold of the key?'

'God knows where that might be. I bet it hasn't been opened in years. Hang on, I'll jemmy it open.'

Kaldur took a screwdriver from the tool bag, inserted it between the cabinet doors, and rocked it violently back and forth with both hands. Dust and a few bits of plaster fell from the ceiling. Frederik looked on worriedly.

'Steady on, boss.'

'Don't worry, Fredo. It's our job, we're allowed. Nearly there...'

With a creak and a snap, the old lock gave way and the door

opened.

'Well, well! Look at this!'

Behind the cabinet doors was what had once been a grand marble fireplace. The cable could be seen disappearing into it and through a large iron hatch at the back of the grate. Kaldur gripped the cable and gave it a tug. The iron door creaked and swung out towards them.

Kaldur got down on her hands and knees, crawled inside the fireplace, and stuck her head through the hatch. Then she gave a low whistle.

'My saints. Take a look at this.'

She crawled out and made way for Frederik to look inside.

'Mind how you go, it's a bit of a drop.'

'It's a shaft,' said Frederik. 'And I can see some kind of ladder down there.'

Frederik withdrew and Kaldur unhooked a torch from her tool belt, wound it up and shone it down into the depths. The cable continued on down into the seemingly bottomless hole. Iron rungs could be seen protruding from the wall.

'Well, I think we've found the source of the problem, Frederik. I reckon we've got rats.'

'Rats? You mean, like, chewing on the cables?'

Kaldur crawled out again.

'Not that kind of rat. The human kind. The kind that steal other people's electricity.'

She hooked the torch back onto her belt.

'We'd better go and tell the Commander.'

CHAPTER THIRTY-SIX

Once I got back to the library I had planned to rest in preparation for my mission next morning, but I found myself lying on my bunk unable to sleep, worrying about how Charlie's train robbery was proceeding. There were so many unknown factors: whether the temporary tracks we had put in place would hold, whether Charlie would be able to bring the train back here, and not least, whether the King's plan to prevent Johansson's men pursuing it – whatever that was – would work.

At the appointed hour in the early morning I went up to the gantry. The raiding party for the palace was assembled beneath the hatch in the library ceiling. Four men and three women, holding a motley collection of old weapons. Privately, I thought they looked more like pirates than men at arms. To my relief, I saw Charlie among them. He was wearing the uniform of the Kantarborgan militia, with shoulder epaulettes, and had again lightened his dark complexion with stage make-up, which made him look somewhat less aristocratic.

'What do you think of the get-up?' he asked. 'I'm a lieutenant now.' He gave a slightly nervous laugh.

'No cap?'

'I'm not a hat-stand, you know,' he grinned.[4] The humour seemed forced. Had something gone wrong?

Over his shoulder, he was carrying a coil of rope. He unwound a few yards of it and began to tie it around my waist.

'How did it go?' I asked him, quietly. 'Do we have the gold?'

He nodded.

'And you were able to manage the controls?'

'I'll never be a train driver, but it went OK. I got it here all right.'

'What about the prisoners? The train crew and the guards?'

'No problem. They were outnumbered. There were only six

---

4 A reference to the Kantarborgan army marching song *The Recruiting Sergeant*. See Chap. 40.

of them.'

'Did they put up a fight?'

But Charlie was unwilling to say any more. He turned and addressed the group.

'Right. Me and Clockmaker Nielsen first, then the rest of you. Not a word or a sound on the way up.'

He gave an athletic leap, grasped the lowest rungs of the iron ladder in the hatch, and swung himself up. The rope tautened and I was dragged forward a few steps.

'Give the gentleman a leg up!' Charlie called down.

Grinning, the soldiers linked hands and hoisted me up until I could reach the ladder. I caught hold of the rungs and scrambled up.

'All right. Up we go,' said Charlie.

To my surprise the shaft was not completely dark, but was illuminated by a faint greyish light, as though it were open to the sky somewhere high above. It must have been an old chimney that had been repurposed at some stage. It was sooty, cold and damp. The electrical cable, which we had been warned not to disturb, hung down alongside us. Strangely, I felt no fear as we climbed, although I am not good with heights; but with Charlie above me and the others below, it was quite impossible to see how high up we were.

We had been ascending for no more than a few minutes when Charlie signalled to me to stop. I passed on the sign to those below. Above me I heard the creaking of what sounded like a metal door.

We emerged, one by one, out of what turned out to be the fireplace of the royal nursery – a room I had not seen since the day I met the King for the first time, all those years ago. But it was almost unrecognisable now. Back then, it had been full of clockwork toys, covering the furniture and floor, while now it was almost bare. In the torchlight, a gloomy, musty atmosphere clung to it. The few playthings that remained had been neatly stacked up onto the shelves.

'The cabinet door was open,' murmured Charlie to me, so that the others would not hear. 'The lock's been broken. Not good.'

We checked the corridor outside, and then Charlie led his group, pistols and sabres drawn, swiftly down the varnished halls. I hurried after them as best I could, still out of breath after the climb. It was the Yule holiday and there was almost no-one about, although the dim electric lighting had been turned on. But Johansson, we had been told, started work early every day, no exceptions.

The men stopped outside Johansson's office. Charlie looked at me to confirm it was the right one. I nodded, then they burst through the door. I remained outside, as arranged. After a few moments, Charlie returned and beckoned to me to come inside. Not a word had been spoken.

I walked through the secretary's room, which, as we had expected, was empty, and entered the inner office to find Johansson sitting trussed to his chair, still behind his desk. His sabre had been removed from its scabbard and placed on the desk in front of him. He looked contemptuous, almost bored.

'Well, just like a bad penny. Welcome back, Karl.'

Outside in the city, the Round Tower clock began to chime the hour. Seven o'clock.

'You know why I'm here,' I said.

'I think I can probably guess.'

'We have the gold. All of it.'

'Well done.'

'I want her released. Immediately.'

Charlie looked at me. I was already departing from the script, but I could not help myself.

'Never mind what *you* want,' said Johansson dismissively. 'What does *he* want?'

That put me on the back foot. This was not how it was supposed to go.

'He wants to be acknowledged as the rightful king of

Kantarborg, defender of the Anglian faith and holder of the three crowns. Then the gold will be returned.'

'I see. So for the sake of his own vanity, he wants Kantarborg to break the terms of the treaty that we signed. Even if it means the probable destruction of the Kingdom?'

'Those are the terms.'

Johansson glanced around at the rest of the group.

'Nielsen, if this is to be a negotiation, I won't do it in public. Let's do things properly. Just you and me. Man to man.'

I hesitated.

'Well, I can hardly do you any injury while I'm tied to this blasted chair, can I?' he asked irritably.

I nodded to Charlie, who led the group out to the secretary's office in the adjacent room. Johansson waited until the door was safely closed, then he looked at me.

'How did you get in here?' he asked.

I was prepared for the question.

'The palace is old, Johansson. It's like a sponge. There are tunnels and passages to the underground everywhere. You cannot find them all. And your men are afraid to go down there.'

'Especially not after what you've done. Very clever.'

I didn't know what he meant. He regarded me for a moment.

'Your father was a grain merchant, was he not?'

I nodded. 'And my brother, after him.'

'Then you know the public storehouses. How much they contain. Enough for a few months. If we're lucky, it gets us through the winter. But this year they are almost empty, and winter has only just begun. The blockade has cut off our imports of food from Northland, and if the gold is not returned, we can buy no more food supplies from anywhere else. This city will starve. Men, women and children. Your own people. That doesn't bother you at all?'

'It is within your power to change that.'

'Karl, you are a rational man. For God's sake think about this. What he is asking for is impossible. We signed a treaty.'

'That treaty was illegal, as you well know. The King never abdicated. He is still the rightful ruler of Kantarborg. All he wants is for you to acknowledge it. I'm sure you could come to some accommodation. Spurn the Witch's child and put the Young King back on the throne. What difference would it make? You could keep your power and your position, if that's what you want.'

'You don't understand what you're dealing with here,' said Johansson. 'The boy is our insurance. If we lose him, we lose everything.'

'Don't be ridiculous, Johansson. His mother is a witch from a tribe of nomads. What possible threat could she pose to the kingdom of Kantarborg?'

'Nomads? *Ulrika?* Ask him! He knows! He knows exactly what she is. Ask him about the wolf winter!'

'You are making no sense.'

'He hasn't told you anything, has he? Good God, Karl, do you really not see what he is doing? He's using you, man, like he uses everyone! Just like he used your wife.'

'My wife? What are you talking about?'

'Come here. Open the drawer in my desk. The right-hand one.'

I hesitated.

'Go on, do it. Take out the top document.'

Reluctantly, I walked around his desk and opened the drawer by his knee. There was a folder of papers lying there bound up in red twine, perhaps ten pages in all, with a date on the cardboard cover. I undid the twine and leafed through it briefly. It was written in Northlandish, with occasional marginal notes in Kantish. *The prisoner speaks an unknown name. The interrogation continues. The prisoner faints.*

'Look at the signature,' he said. 'On the last page.'

I did so. It was Marieke's. I felt the blood leave my head.

'What have you done, Johansson? Did you force her to sign this?'

'Take it with you, read it. And think about it. And when you have thought about it, come back here and tell me where to find him. That is when I will release her, not before. And in the meantime, you can tell him to go to hell. I will not negotiate with thugs. He can keep the gold. Let the deaths of the civilians of this city be on his own conscience.'

'That is your final word?'

'Yes. So, are you going to kill me now?' His eyes went to the sabre on his desk.

'I didn't come here to kill you.'

'I thought that was what bandits did, when they didn't get their way? Not much of a man, are you?'

'I am a man, Johansson. But I'm not a killer. You know that.'

He gave a bitter laugh.

'You think you're not, but you are. Everyone is. We're all at war, Karl. It's just that some of us are too cowardly to face it.'

'I don't know what you're talking about.'

'You think you can live a life of softness and let other people do the fighting? Too good to get blood on your hands, are you, Clockmaker? It doesn't work like that. There's already blood on your hands. The blood of men, women and children. War will seek you out, will make you choose. It will find you.'

Were those *tears* I saw in his eyes? What on earth was the matter with the man? He had always been calm, collected, logical. Not like this. I was enough of a Kantarborgan to feel embarrassed at the display of emotion. I turned to leave.

'You'll be back, Karl!' he shouted after me.

I walked out to Charlie and the others, and we hurried away down the corridor, making sure no-one observed us.

Back in the nursery, to our surprise, we found the King, dressed in his Yule Father costume.

'Your Majesty, you should not be here!' I protested. 'You might be discovered.'

'Nonsense, Nielsen. What could be more natural than the Yule Father emerging from a chimney in a child's nursery?

What did Johansson say?'

'He refused the offer.'

'I thought as much. Well, no matter. We move on to plan B. Time to take the train.'

The King and the raiding party crawled one by one into the fireplace. I was the last man. I looked around one last time, to make sure no-one had seen us leave.

Something moved in a corner of the room. I watched, transfixed, as the figure of a boy, perhaps eight years or so of age, slowly emerged from the shadows. He was dressed in fine velvet clothes with a lace collar, and had long, white-blonde hair and bright blue eyes. He looked at me with no sign of fear.

'The Yule Father was here,' he said. 'Who are you?'

'I'm ... one of his helpers.'

'He brought me a present,' said the boy. 'For Yule.'

'What was it?'

'It's a secret. You'd better go now. The grown-ups are coming. Goodbye.'

'Goodbye,' I said and crawled into the fireplace.

CHAPTER THIRTY-SEVEN

Frederik found Sarah Kaldur sitting on a chaise longue in one of the palace corridors. She was staring at the floor, her arms resting on her knees. He sat down beside her.

'So, did you see him?' he asked.

'Nah, I only got as far as his secretary. Some lieutenant or other. *I'm sure it's important, Mrs Kaldo...*'

The young man gave a snort of laughter. 'Mrs Kaldo!'

'*... but we can't go bothering the Commander with every trifling matter.* So I asked him, who are all these people, then? And he says they've all made an appointment. Rum-looking lot, they were, I can tell you. Soldiers in strange uniforms. And then he says I have to make a written application. *If it's a problem with the lighting, Mrs Kaldo, you should contact the maintenance department.* So I says, I AM the bloody maintenance department, you blithering idiot! And that's when he threw me out.'

Frederik laughed.

'Never mind, boss. You tried your best. On their own heads be it.'

Kaldur turned and looked into her assistant's eyes.

'I'm not letting this go, Fredo. This could be serious. I'm going to get to the bottom of it.'

She looked back at the floor.

'I told him to give Johansson my name, but it didn't make any difference.'

'Does he know you?'

'He damn well should. I was there in the King's Garden, night of the Blood Moon.'

'Well, so was I, boss. So were a lot of people.'

'Yes, but I opened up the armoury for them, didn't I?' Kaldur lifted her palace key ring and shook it. 'Nearly wish I hadn't, now. I thought we'd had a revolution, Fredo, but nothing's changed. You know what I think? I think we might have been better off ... in the old days.'

Frederik glanced around him worriedly.

'Er ... like you said, walls have ears, boss.'

'Yeah. Well,' she stood up. 'This is an electrical matter, and I'm the palace electrician. So it's my job to find out what the problem is, and fix it. And I intend to do just that.'

CHAPTER THIRTY-EIGHT

I and the other members of the raiding party had exited the shaft and were standing in a group around the King. I had decided not to say anything about the child.

'Well, that was Johansson's last chance,' said the King. 'Without gold, he will not survive the time to come. Now, we must leave quickly before he finds the shaft. The train is ready?'

Charlie nodded. But then there was a sudden commotion on the gallery above our heads. The King looked up.

'But I can't kill a woman!' pleaded a man's voice.

'Well then give me the sword and *I'll* bloody well kill her!' a woman retorted.

'Just a minute!' shouted the King, climbing the spiral staircase. 'What's going on?'

'A spy, sire,' said the woman. 'She came down the shaft. Your orders were to kill any intruders.'

They were holding a middle-aged woman by the arms, with a sword at her throat. The King peered more closely at the prisoner. She was dressed in overalls, and in her hand, she held what looked like a tool bag.

'I know you, don't I?' said the King. 'Weren't you on the palace staff?'

The woman said nothing.

'Let go of her,' he said. 'What was your name again?'

'Kaldur. Sarah Kaldur,' she said resentfully, putting down her tool bag and rubbing her arms.

'Are you a spy, Kaldur?'

'Do I look like a bloody spy? I'm the palace electrician! I climbed down to see who was stealing our power.'

'Indeed! Electrician, eh? Know anything about windmills?'

'Is the Pope Anglian, ya tosser?'

'What?'

'I'm an electrician! Of course I know about windmills. I helped set up the Great Windmill, didn't I?'

'Excellent. Then you must come with us. Bring your tools.'

'Do I have a choice?'

'Not really. We can't let you go, you see. You know about the fireplace. So it's either that or death, I'm afraid.'

'Oh well then, since you put it like that, I suppose I'd better come along,' she said, picking up her tool bag. 'Where are we going?'

'Just a little train ride.'

They led her down the spiral staircase and past the raiding party. Charlie winked at her as she passed.

'Sorry about that, Mrs Kaldo.'

'Oh, bloody hell. I should have guessed, shouldn't I?' she said.

CHAPTER THIRTY-NINE

'Joe? Joe? Are you awake?'

A muffled moan came from the floor beside the bed.

'Listen to this: *"Although prolonged and serious in its effects, the Long Winter was not the primary source of the great mortality that afflicted humanity after the Great Cataclysm. For War and Conquest were only the first of the horsemen – they were followed by Famine, for darkness was on the face of the earth, and without the blackstone people had neither the machines and fertilisers to produce their food, nor the means to transport it; and by Pestilence, for they had no medicines to combat disease – neither the old ones, for which there were no longer any vaccines, nor the new ones that emerged, and which they could not study. And so terror and superstition stalked the land, and men accused each other and fell upon each other, and died of strife and hunger and contagion in great numbers, so that whole nations succumbed."* Jaze, it must have been an awful time altogether.'

Joe appeared beside the bed, a blanket around her shoulders.

'Shut up about all that and move over, boy. I'm fecking freezing down there on the floor.'

Christopher made room, and Joe crawled in under the blankets.

'And no funny business,' she added.

'Not even a little cuddle?'

'Go to sleep, you miscreant. Give me an arm.'

Christopher put an arm around her. She seemed so slight of body, he thought.

'Joe, do you think we're going to live through this?' he asked.

'We will, if I have anything to do with it.'

'What do you mean?'

'I'm not planning to have a baby in a war zone, boy. We're getting out of here. One way or the other.'

'Yes, but how?'

'Never you mind. Shut up now and go to flipping sleep.'

She blew out the candle.

CHAPTER FORTY

A hundred or so men and women – the entire army of the King, such as it was – were standing on the platform of the underground railway station, waiting to board a train. The small platform could not hold them all, and many people were still queueing in the stairwell, awaiting their turn.

'Where's Nielsen? Get him over here,' called the King.

I pushed my way through. He took hold of my arm.

'Did you manage to get your device down here?'

'It's in the rearmost truck, sire.'

'Good. Right then, Karl – now it's your turn to drive.'

'Do we have room for everyone, Majesty?'

'I certainly hope so. There's no time to lose. When I give the signal, go.'

I looked back along the train to estimate the weight. We would not exactly be travelling in style. There were five closed trucks, two of them sealed and presumably filled with gold coins, and several more open ones at the back. I caught sight of Charlie shepherding Sarah Kaldur onto one of them.

I climbed into the cab, and the King, carrying his sceptre, climbed in behind me. Standing at the controls, I readied the machine. We had five pods. It ought to be more than enough for an hour's journey, but the load was heavy. I turned over the clutch lever and felt the jolt through the cab floor as it engaged with the main drive. The King leaned out, looking back along the train, where people were jostling and scrambling to get on board.

'Now, Nielsen!' he said after a minute. 'Go!'

I released the brakes and eased out the throttle. The locomotive emitted a loud metallic squeal and began to move into the darkness. As we picked up speed, the generator began to run and I turned on the forward lamp.

'Only a short distance at first,' said the King. 'We'll need to make a stop in a minute, so keep it slow.'

He was watching the tunnel ceiling. After about five minutes he suddenly said, 'Right, that's it! Stop here.'

I stopped the train. He pointed back at a round hole in the tunnel roof, through which a small amount of grey light penetrated from above.

'That's the chimney that I came down on the first night. It was an air shaft originally. We're directly under New Square here. Now, take the train past that, and then install your monster underneath the hole.'

I did as the King requested. As soon as I had set up the device alongside the track and bolted it firmly fast, a draught caught the sail and swung back the arm. A loud, deep moan filled the tunnel, reverberating along the walls. The men laughed, but Charlie hushed them.

'Excellent!' said the King. 'That will give them something to think about.'

I went back to the cab and started up the locomotive again. I brought the speed up to the equivalent of a fast run – no more than that. The tunnel ahead looked clear and the track in good condition, but you never knew what you might encounter down here – as I knew better than anyone. We were, after all, deep inside the Irrational Layer. The next monster we encountered might not be a fake one.

In the trucks behind, quite insouciantly, the soldiers began to sing. I recognised the tune: *The Recruiting Sergeant*. Like all such marching songs, it was bawdy and boisterous, borderline insubordinate:

And the first thing that the sergeant saw, it was an old hat-stand
He gave it a lieutenant's cap and he put it in command-ay-oh
For you can be a useful, very, very useful
Very, very useful thing
In the service of your country and the army of the King!

Some new verses seemed to have been added since the last

time I had heard it.

And the next thing that the sergeant saw, it was an old baboon
He made him an ambassador and he sent him to the moon-ay-oh
For you can be a useful, very, very useful
Very, very useful thing...

I glanced at the King, but he was paying no attention. Having spent so much time among soldiers, he no doubt knew what it was expedient to hear – or not to hear.

'They're in good spirits,' I remarked.

'And so they should be,' said the King. 'I have promised them three months' wages in advance.'

'In gold?'

'Just so. They haven't realised yet that it is worthless.'

'How so, Majesty? Is it fake gold?'

'Oh no, it's real gold all right. But gold is only worth what you can buy with it, isn't it, Nielsen?'

I didn't know what to make of that, so I said nothing. After a few moments, the King said:

'If I had my way, you know, we would have taken the contents of the library vaults instead. All that knowledge. That's the real gold. But the trouble with politics is that it has to be financed. It's all subject to what the ancients called the Golden Rule.'

'What's that?'

'He who has the gold makes the rules,' smiled the King.

The track stretched on ahead, mile after weary mile of tunnel, almost entirely straight. I began to grow drowsy. The King noticed my fatigue.

'Not much further!'

How do you know? I wondered.

Finally, after about an hour, some signs suddenly appeared at the trackside. They flashed past before I could read them, but they seemed to be written in Old Kantish.

'You can start braking now,' said the King. 'Take it slowly up to the entrance.'

I brought the locomotive down to walking speed as we rounded a curve. Up ahead, I could see a narrow platform. I drew up slowly alongside it and halted the train. The King switched on a wind-up lamp and pointed it out of the cab. At the other side of the platform was what looked like a giant, square metal door, painted with a black and yellow symbol of obscure import, made up of three triangles in a circle. The King handed the lamp to me and jumped down onto the platform.

'Everyone stay in the train!' he shouted. 'We must first check for access.'

Carrying his sceptre, he marched across the platform. To the right of the door was a small panel with a socket at its centre. Once again he took the sceptre, inserted it into the hole, and turned the shaft grip. The enormous door slid gently aside, revealing a dark corridor.

'Home sweet home!' said the King. 'Regan Palace!'

Reptilicus

A solemn warning to the citizens of Kantarborg!

On the eve of holy St Nicholas, in defiance of the decrees
of the CHURCH OF GOD and the precepts of common
morality, a minister of the so-called government, the
DEVIL WORSHIPPER JOHANSSON,
attempted to steal the gold of the citizens of Kantarborg
and offer it as a Yule sacrifice to the subterranean demons.
But none who deal with the creatures of the netherworld
and defy THE LORD THEIR GOD shall escape
the consequences. Through his foolhardy actions, the
NORTHLANDER TRAITOR
has set loose the dragon REPTILICUS, which did prey
upon the citizens of this city in ancient times! By this
means, THE LORD shows that HE is not mocked. Dire
punishment and a terrible DEATH await all those who
venture into the IRRATIONAL LAYER and release
the demons there!

Kantarborgans! Embrace the path of
RIGHTEOUSNESS
and throw off your oppressors! Obey THE LORD and
let NO MAN NOR WOMAN enter the subterranean
world, on pain of death and eternal
DAMNATION!

CHAPTER FORTY-ONE

'Me? What does he want to see me for? You're the designer.'

Christopher was straining at the pump by the sink, trying in vain to get it to cough out some water.

'I've no notion,' said Joe. 'He didn't say. Just said to send you round.'

'Maybe he's looking for a pumping expert. I've a load of experience. How the heck did they manage to pump up the water for our ballast tanks in Mont-Saint-Michel? That tower was even taller than this one.'

'They had a windmill,' said Joe.

'Fair play to them. Wish we had one. This thing'll be the death of me.'

At last the pump vomited out some water into a wooden pail. Joe took the pail, poured the water into the tin bath on the floor, and handed it back.

'One more and we'll be there.'

'Aren't you going to warm it up, at least?'

'What for, boy? No harm in a bit of cold water. Freshens you up.'

Christopher pumped out some more water into the pail.

'I'm not sure all this washing is good for you, Joe. You'll catch your death.'

'I'll be grand. Sure don't I have the stove to warm up with afterwards?'

Joe poured out the water into the tin bath, then pulled the habit off over her head and stepped in. Christopher came over and placed his hand on her belly.

'Get your paws off me, boyo,' said Joe. 'I'm a man, remember.'

'You could have fooled me.'

Joe removed Christopher's hand and looked at him.

'I'm a man and you're a monk until the Pope says otherwise. We have our immortal souls to think of.'

'Boy or girl, do you think?'

'I don't mind as long as it's a child,' said Joe. 'A normal child. Not like that kid in the palace. He was weird, I'm telling ya.'

'With his stories about the Yule Father in the fireplace, heh.'

Christopher began feeding more wood into the stove.

'Just as well he never met the real Pope Nicholas. I couldn't imagine that fella going down any chimneys.'

'Yeah, or handing out gifts,' said Joe. 'He wasn't much of a Yule Father, that's for sure.'

Joe took a jug, filled it with water from the bath, and poured it over her head. Christopher felt cold just looking at her. And warm at the same time.

'So what's the big deal with all these Yule Fathers here?' she asked.

'Part of their solstice traditions. It goes way back, apparently.'

'There's one on nearly every street corner. There was even a rumour going around that the King had smuggled himself into the kingdom dressed as one of them.'

'Where'd you hear that?' asked Christopher.

Joe stepped out of the bath, picked up a towel from beside the stove, and began to dry her short-cropped red hair.

'Tillonsen told me,' she said. 'Just some palace gossip. Can't be true, though, can it? The King's away in the far north.'

Christopher said nothing. Joe glanced over at him curiously.

'What?'

'Joe, what was it the young fella said to you again? In the palace?'

'Ah ... something about the seventh wall. And the Yule Father wanting to meet us behind the fireplace.'

'Do you know what, Joe? I think we might be after making a very big mistake. That could have been a message from the King.'

'But he's away up north.'

'Yeah, that's what Johansson says. But how do we know that's true? Those two are sworn enemies.'

'Feck's sake, if the King was here and wanted to meet us, he could just have said.'

'He couldn't give the game away, Joe. He must be in hiding somewhere here. So he gave the message to the boy.'

'Ah, for ... So now what do we do?'

'I think we'd better find that fireplace. In a hurry.'

CHAPTER FORTY-TWO

Four calling birds

'If you ask me, it sounds like the most appalling nonsense,' said Brorsen. 'Though I grant you, the most appalling nonsense can sway the masses, sometimes.'

'Sway them, yes,' said Johansson. 'But cause them to flee in naked panic from their homes? And seek shelter in a foreign land, among their enemies? It would take a great deal more than just rumours, Brorsen. *Something* must be happening over there.'

Johansson looked over towards the opposite shore. The ice had spread out now across the Sound almost as far as the eye could see, and the tracks of birds and animals could be seen in the snow on its surface.

'I hear the boats have stopped coming?' said Brorsen.

'They can't get through the ice. That doesn't mean that whatever caused them to flee has vanished.'

'So what exactly do they claim to have seen? The flightings?'

'None of it really makes any sense. Some say wolves, some say monsters or the Beast of Revelations.'

'And you think the Witch might be behind it?'

'I don't know. But she made certain threats. And do you not find the cold … unusual for this time of year?'

'It's a cold December. Such things happen in our part of the world from time to time. There is nothing sinister about that, Lord Commander! The rest is all just superstitious nonsense.'

'I hope you're right, Astronomer. I saw many strange things in the north.'

The two men walked on. A group of gulls wheeled overhead, crying out to each other. Johansson looked up at them. Were they hungry, too?

'The word has got out, you know,' he said. 'About the robbery.'

'Yes. It was rather clever of the old fox, I must admit,' said Brorsen. 'A classic double bind. You could either accede to the Pretender's demands and lose everything, or else refuse and give him the wherewithal to fund a counter-revolution.'

'Will that be his next move, do you think?'

'Not immediately. Now that he has the gold, he will go to ground for a while. He will wait for you to weaken. Then, when things are desperate, he will pounce and make his grand entrance into the city, showering largesse and presenting himself as the saviour of the people. That is my guess. So you must hunt him down at once.'

'I can't. You haven't heard the worst of it. The royalists killed my men on the train. The bodies were mutilated. Scratches on the hands and faces, like the marks of claws. A pamphlet is circulating saying that they were attacked by a monster from the underground.'

'Oh, very clever! And people believe it?'

'Some do. The Church has been warning about the subterranean perils for years, after all. And some people claim they have heard a monster roaring in the depths. So now, if I try to order my men into the tunnels, I could end up with a full-scale mutiny on my hands.'

'You must retain order, Commander. Order above all. You must not lose your nerve.'

'Do you think I am? Losing my nerve?'

'No, but I think you are embattled. You are under a great deal of pressure.'

'We must do something soon. People are panicking. There was a riot yesterday. I had to send in the militia to quell it. Three people died. And of course I am being blamed.'

'Of course you are. And that suits the Pretender very well, doesn't it? But there is a way to counter that, you know.'

'What is that?'

'The classic way. Blame some minority. You have those flightings in your custody. You must concoct some story or other that they are to blame for the lack of food. Put it about as a known fact. And then eliminate them all. Show yourself to be a true patriot.'

'I'm not sure I have the stomach for that, Brorsen.'

'Oh you have the stomach for it, all right.'

The older man was staring sharply at Johansson with eyes that were suddenly as bright and hard as winter stars.

'What do you mean?' asked Johansson, surprised.

'Don't play the conscience-wracked innocent with me, Lord Commander. I know how you got rid of the Thorne woman. You had to, didn't you? Otherwise she would have derailed the whole project. When it comes to ruthlessness, you have plenty of steel in your soul. It is a quality I rather admire in you.'

Johansson looked straight in front of him. *Say nothing*, he thought.

CHAPTER FORTY-THREE

The Cold War

I lay in my bed, listening to the King snoring in the bunk above me. I had been a little surprised when he suggested that Charlie and I share his room, but he probably had his reasons. To keep watch on us, no doubt. Or else because he was getting nervous of sleeping alone. Perhaps both. I was curled up tightly on the lower bunk beneath the grey army blanket, with all my clothes on, trying to retain some warmth in my body.

It had been a long, tiring day. The vast underground complex was dark, damp and icy cold. Not at all the warm refuge I had imagined. We occupied only a fraction of it, and I had no idea how large it might really be. In the absence of powered light, we were winding up lamps all the time. The King had given me and the electrician Sarah Kaldur the job of restoring some more permanent illumination. Lady Amalia, he told us, had provided a windmill for us up on the surface.

Kaldur and I, accompanied by some of the King's men, had taken some tools and climbed a steel ladder to a round emergency hatch, the rusted lock of which had to be blown off with a gunpowder charge. We emerged into the snow on top of a mound surrounded by woodland. I was glad enough to get out in the open and see daylight again, if only for a few hours on a grey winter's day. We found the dismantled windmill where the King told us it would be, on a forest track not far away, where it presumably had been delivered by Lady Amalia's people. We dragged it back to the bunker, where the King was waiting for us. He directed us to a large, flat, circular area to set it up. The surface here was made of the same concrete material as the rest of the complex, but when we had cleared away the dead leaves and scrub bushes, the faint outline of a giant letter 'H' could be seen, painted in white with a yellow circle around it.

'What do you think 'H' stood for, Majesty?'

'Well, since it can only really be seen from the sky, my guess is it must have had a ritual purpose. For the glory of God,' he said.

'The Holy Ghost, perhaps?' I asked with a grin.

'Well, you can laugh, but it isn't completely impossible. He took the form of a dove in the Bible, remember.'

'But were they even Christians back in those days?'

'The nobles probably were, the slaves and peasants probably not. Judging by the number of laygod figures we've found, paganism must have had quite a stubborn hold on the common people.'

For the rest of the day, while daylight lasted, we worked on setting up the windmill and securing it with steel cables.

That windmill! A ramshackle, outmoded contraption, probably rescued from the discarded junk in some noble's barn. It clearly hadn't run for years, and just getting its cogs to turn took a great deal of effort and all the lubricating oil we had.

Kaldur was a good and skilled worker, if somewhat brusque in manner. Understandably, she did not seem well pleased at having been kidnapped by the King's rebels. I wondered if she had a family who would worry about her – though I did not presume to ask, as she simply ignored any non-technical question I put to her. But we worked well enough together, and she appeared to respect my expertise, as I did hers. As we struggled to assemble the windmill tower, our fingers stiff with cold, I suddenly realised who she reminded me of: Handrasen, my old boss in the clockwork workshop at the palace. Another court survivor.

At one point, when we were both up on the windmill tower, tightening bolts on the frame with a heavy spanner, she glanced down at the soldiers beneath.

'Is it my imagination, Clockmaker, or are they watching you as much as me?'

'Probably,' I said.

'You're not a dedicated royalist, then?'

'Just caught up in it.'

She nodded, and said no more.

In the middle of the day we and the guards lit a bonfire and partook of a little tea and bread. We were an ill-assorted bunch, but we had a common enemy in the form of the cold and that damnable machine. It's funny what can bring people together. There was a comradeship there, despite everything, as we enjoyed our hot tea, toasted our bread, and cursed the snow and ice. Even Kaldur seemed to relax a bit.

'We'll need to come back up here tomorrow morning for a maintenance check,' she said. 'Just you and me, Clockmaker, all right? You can look at the cogs and gears and I'll check the electrics.'

'All right. If you think it's necessary.'

'I do, Clockmaker, I do. We'll need to see which way the wind is blowing.'

God knows there was little enough wind to catch in that place, in a clearing surrounded by forest, but in the course of the afternoon the windmill blades eventually began, rather grudgingly, to revolve. Some of the men cheered, but were hushed by an officer. I don't know why – there seemed little danger of us being discovered here. There was no sign of life anywhere. Even when I climbed up to the top of the windmill tower, I could see nothing but forest all the way to the horizon – not a single building, nor even the smoke from a chimney.

As the light faded we descended into the bunker again for our evening meal. The quality of our food seemed to have improved, although there were rumours among the men that the cook was adding centuries-old canned food, found in the larders here, to the pots. Whatever the reason, it tasted much better than the fare we had been offered in the library, and went some way towards compensating for the cold and damp.

After the meal, the King showed me the heating system, to see what could be done with it. The main boiler appeared to be designed to burn blackstone oil, of which we of course had none, but the King – who seemed to have detailed knowledge of this place, wherever he had obtained it – showed me what he said was a solid fuel backup boiler, for which we could gather wood from the forest above. The original electrical pump had long since solidified with rust, and in any case looked rather complicated, but I thought it might be possible for the water, once heated, to circulate by convection alone. The pipes themselves, remarkably, seemed to be in good condition.

'They were built to last,' said the King. 'They were taking no chances, you see. Heating would obviously have been very important to them during a cold war.'

'Who would have been down here? Apart from the royal family?'

'The King's ministers, some military officers. And the leading noble families of the day, of course.'

'How do you know that?'

'Well for one thing, the facilities are clearly marked 'Ladies' and 'Gentlemen' in Old Kantish. So this place clearly wasn't just for anyone. And it makes sense, you know – they had to protect the best bloodlines. Everyone outside would probably have died of cold, so they would have had to repopulate the country afterwards.'

I felt there were a couple of flaws in this Noah's Ark argument, but I suspected it would be pointless to take them up with the King.

'And how long do you think we will have to stay down here, sire?'

'Until we've won, Nielsen. Kantarborg cannot hold out long without gold. Certainly not now, with the blockade going on. And we will not be alone here for long – I hope that many of the other noble families will be joining us eventually, once we have made the place habitable. Besides, with what is happening right now, this may well be the safest place to be.'

'How do you mean?'

'Well, we don't know how long this winter is going to go on for, Karl. Or what it may involve.'

It was an odd remark, but he added nothing further to it.

'Johansson said something about a wolf winter?' I prompted. The King sighed.

'So you've heard about that. Karl, this is all in strictest confidence, all right? Not to be mentioned to anyone. And I mean *anyone* – not Charlie, not the Duchess, no-one. When I negotiated my release from the Witch, there was a condition attached. She said that if I made any attempt to take the throne away from the boy, she would unleash a terrible winter upon the world. She called it a wolf winter; one that would last three years and kill all of humankind in the northern lands except her and her people. Tribal nonsense, most likely, but of course with Ulrika you never know. She might conceivably have discovered some ancient secret about weather control. So my move was to castle the King.'

'To come here?'

'To a place especially designed to survive a cold war, Karl. So now, if she does carry out that threat, she will merely eliminate our enemies. And we will emerge victorious.'

But what kind of kingdom would the King regain, after such a winter, I wondered? Would it even be worth having? Once again, I felt there was a great deal I did not understand about the thinking of rulers.

Meanwhile, we had our own cold war to fight. Until we got the heating system working, we would have to endure the freezing temperatures. The men and women of the King's party seemed inured to it, but I was not as young as I had been, and had perhaps grown accustomed to more comfortable living. I found it unendurable, and that night I was quite unable to sleep.

I lay there thinking, of course, of Marieke. Bad enough that she was still in prison, but what if there was anything in these rumours? If there was going to be a wolf winter, I wanted her down here with me. I would make her rescue a condition before I did any more work for the King. In a winter like that, nowhere above ground would be safe.

I still had the document Johansson had given me, tucked inside my shirt. I had had no opportunity so far to study it, but now was perhaps my chance. The wind-up lamp lay on the floor alongside my bunk. As the King continued to snore above me, I picked it up and slipped it under the blankets.

With my head beneath the covers like a child reading in secret, I leafed through the dossier. As I had half expected, it was an absurd farrago of lies, like the confession the jailer Hartwig had once manufactured for me. It contained a somewhat inaccurate version of the King's plans to steal the gold. According to this story, the King had intended to raid the treasury on Yule Day together with a party of seaborne Northlander troops, with the aim of forcing the surrender of Kantarborg through starvation and ultimately restoring the King to the throne. Marieke and I were co-conspirators in the plot. The statement had been inexpertly noted down by some official. Marieke's signature at the end looked genuine, but of course they could easily have forged it.

I turned off the lamp and lay there in the dark, thinking. There was something very odd about all this. If this supposed confession had simply been concocted by Johansson in order to condemn Marieke and me, why not make it conform more closely to the facts? For one thing, the robbery had taken place on Yule Eve, not Yule Day, and no Northlander forces had been involved. But Johansson had clearly expected the raid to come on Yule Day, which was no doubt why he had tried to move the gold the day before...

And then, of course, it all finally fell into place. I felt, first of all, a hot flush of shame at my own stupidity, then a white rage. And I knew what I would have to do, to save her. I had to get out, right now.

I sat up as quietly as I could, reached under the bed, pulled out my boots and put them on. In this underground cell, the darkness was total. I could literally see nothing at all – not even my hand in front of my face. I stood up, slowly. The King was still snoring. Charlie, in the top bunk on the other side of the room, was quieter, but his breathing sounded deep and rhythmic. Very gingerly, I put out my hand in the direction of the head of the King's bunk. My fingertips touched the soft fabric of his pillow. Beneath it, I could sense the hard edge of the royal sceptre.

Holding my breath, I very gently inserted my hand beneath the pillow and took hold of the end of the sceptre. The King muttered something in his sleep and turned over. My heart was hammering so hard that I felt sure it must be audible. Gently, I eased the device out from under the pillow. As the last bit suddenly slipped out, I almost dropped it on the floor.

I waited for a second, but there was no reaction from the King. Then I felt around in the dark and found my jacket, hanging from a coat hook on the wall. I slipped the unlit lamp into my pocket, put on the jacket and quietly opened the door to the corridor, holding the sceptre in my hand. I stopped to listen. The King did not stir. I stepped outside and gently closed the door behind me.

In the corridor, I turned on the lamp. An ancient yellow stripe ran down one wall. I knew that if I followed it, it would lead me back down to the railway.

I suddenly remembered that I had left the so-called confession behind, under the blankets of my bunk. Too risky to go back for it. Well, what of it? Let him read it – then he would know why I had gone.

It took me a good ten minutes to find my way back down through the silent passages and stairways to the underground entrance. No guards had been posted – with an impregnable iron door, they had probably thought there was no need.

I shone the lamp up at the giant door. No obvious opening mechanism was visible. On our way in, the King had inserted the sceptre into what must have been a control box mounted on the wall – so, logically, there ought to be something similar on the inside, at around the same spot. I put the lamp down on the floor and began to feel around the edges.

'What are you doing, Nielsen?' asked the King.

I swung round. By the light of the lamp I could see he was standing there in his nightgown, his sword in his hand. There seemed little point in pretence. I just stared back into his brown eyes. There was a look in them I had not seen there before. A wildness.

'Don't leave me, Karl,' he said. 'You must not leave me. I will not permit it.'

'I must, Majesty.'

'Why?'

'You know why.'

He stepped forward, and I backed up against the iron door.

'You are my only friend, Karl! But if you try to betray me, I must kill you. You know that. Don't make me do this.'

He drew back his arm and pointed the sword at my chest. I closed my eyes. But I would not, could not, say the words he wanted to hear. My loyalty was to her, not to him.

'*Each man kills the thing he loves.* I'm truly sorry, Karl.'

There was a sudden flash of light and an explosion that felt like a blow to the head. The King dropped his sword and crumpled to the floor. A figure stepped forward out of the darkness, holding a flintlock pistol.

'Up the republic,' said Sarah Kaldur.

CHAPTER FORTY-FOUR

The secret to being anywhere you're not supposed to be, as Christopher had long ago learned, is to walk purposefully, keep your nose in the air, and look as if you know exactly what you are doing. No-one will challenge you. In any case, he had the summons from Johansson in his hand, so he could always claim that he had got lost in the palace corridors. Nor was that entirely untrue – the place was a rabbit warren.

Which fireplace? There were dozens of them, some lit and some not, and all apparently equally useless at warming the draughty old building. He had looked into some of the ones not in use, in empty rooms and along the halls, but could see nothing unusual. A group of young courtiers passing by glanced in amusement at the monk staring up the chimney.

'Looking for the Yule Father, uncle?'

'That's right!' Christopher called cheerily back. *No word of a lie.*

He began to feel a little foolish. Maybe it was all his imagination. It wouldn't be the first time he had put two and two together and made four million.

Where had Joe seen the boy? It must have been somewhere around here, near Tillonsen's office, otherwise she wouldn't have just run into him like that. Unless he was looking for her, of course. Or could Joe have wandered into the royal apartments? Would she have been able to do that unchallenged?

Ahead of him in the corridor, Christopher saw a pair of open double doors with golden handles. Beyond them, the floor covering changed from parquet to red carpet. *Bingo.*

He glanced around, but could see no guards. Stepping onto the carpet, he had to suppress an almost irresistible urge to sneeze. Dust. Was this place never cleaned?

He could hear a whirring sound coming from a room up ahead. Like some kind of clockwork device. The door to the room was open.

Christopher approached the doorway and looked inside. A white-haired boy was sitting on the floor of the room, playing with a golden clockwork train. A toy fit for a prince. Running around on an oval track.

'You're too late. He's gone away,' said the boy, without looking up.

'Where did he go?'

'Back into the fireplace, of course.'

Christopher glanced around, but could see no fireplace.

'Right ... Did he leave any message for us?'

'He says he has a present for the Pope. He wants to know if you can take it to him.'

'We're working on it. When will he be back? Can we meet him?'

'He's coming back. He promised he would. But I don't know when.'

'Well, if you see him, tell him we have an important message for him. But we have to give it to him in person, all right? We're in the Round Tower, if he wants to find us.'

'Alright. I will tell him that.'

'How will we know that it's the real Yule Father?'

'He has a magic wand,' said the boy. 'A rod made of gold. It opens secret doors. He is the only one who may hold it. You'd better go now. Before they find you here.'

'Who?'

'The grown-ups. They're bad. They kill people.'

They kill people. Christopher sat opposite Johansson, who had taken to wearing his full naval uniform lately.

'You are the explosives expert of the two of you, I understand?' asked Johansson.

'I've been known to blow up a few things in the past, Commander, yes.'

'Before you became a monk?'

'Er ... also afterwards, to be honest. A couple of times. Not always on purpose, though.'

'All right. Look, I will tell you frankly, I am starting to have my doubts about whether the cannon device designed by your companion will ever work. There seem to be insurmountable technical problems. One after the other.'

'No doubt Joe will overcome them all in the end.'

'Yes, perhaps, but we don't have time for that. The blockade must be ended now. The threat from those ships must be eliminated. The city needs food. And to be honest, your colleague does not seem to be fully committed to the task.'

'So what do you suggest?'

'What if, instead of a cannon, we were to adapt the boat so that it could haul a couple of barges, under the water?'

'Why would you want to do that?'

'We have no shortage of gunpowder. It is a proven technology and requires no new inventions.'

'Ah right, I get your drift,' said Christopher. He thought for a minute.

'You'd need a timer. And some way of detaching the barges, one at a time. And they'd need buoyancy tanks to keep them at the right depth.'

'But could it be done?'

'I'd say it could. The crew would be pulling a heck of a load, though, if they're using pedals.'

'We don't need pedals. Our device has clockwork engines, powered by pods.'

'OK. So you want to haul the barges out and attach them one by one to the ships? And then ... boom.'

'That's the idea. Design that, and we have a deal.'

'And then we'll get our airship back?'

'If you can get those barges designed and built very quickly.'

'I reckon we can. And can we trust that you'll keep your side of it?'

'You have my word. As a Kantarborgan.'

Christopher smiled.

'As a Kantarborgan? All right, then. Nugget for nugget!'

CHAPTER FORTY-FIVE

'So what was your plan, eh, Clockmaker? What were you going to do if you got through that door?'

Sarah Kaldur and I were slogging through the snowy woods in the early morning darkness, keeping more or less to the trail. The path was difficult to see in the gloom – I kept stumbling over roots and rocks. Kaldur had slung the tool bag on her back. She refused to turn on the lamp, saying we should let our eyes get used to the dark instead.

'I just knew I had to go,' I said.

She paused and looked back to listen, then marched on again.

'I thought you and the Mad Monarch were friends?'

'He betrayed my wife.'

'Your wife?' She sounded surprised.

'Johansson has her in custody. The King used her to pass on false information, so that he could steal the gold. He knew she would be tortured. He made use of that.'

'So what were you going to do?'

'Take the gold back to Kantarborg.'

'Just out of the goodness of your heart?'

'Well, it's theirs, they need it. And ... Johansson promised to release my wife if I revealed the King's whereabouts.'

'And you believed him, did you?'

'He has my wife in a torture chamber, what choice do I have? But I think he's a man of his word, despite everything.'

'Johansson, a man of his word!' she gave a contemptuous snort. 'Johansson is the man behind this whole so-called crisis, my friend. He's in the pay of the Northlanders.'

'Just because he comes from a Northlander family, you think he's in league with them?'

'It's not something we think, Clockmaker. It's something we know.'

'But he organised the rebellion against the King!'

'Yes, while the King was safely elsewhere. And then, when the people rose up and were about to storm the Rose Castle, who was it that spirited the Queen away to Northland in the Royal Airship?'

That was true. I hadn't thought of it that way before.

'So don't expect too much of our Commander Johansson, Clockmaker. He's a republic of one. Not exactly known for his loyalty to old friends.'

'Is anyone?' I asked sourly.

'Not at this level. Not when you're playing for high stakes. Then the only thing that counts is ...'

She patted the weapon in her tool belt.

'Where did you get that thing, anyway?' I asked. She took it out of its holster and showed it to me.

'Screw the barrel off and it looks like any other electrician's tool. And they even asked me to bring my tool bag with me, the fools, so it was easy. But you rightly screwed up the plan, you know, going off at half cock like that.'

'There was a plan?'

'I tried to tell you yesterday, but you weren't listening. We could have slipped away the same way we came out just now, by the windmill. It would have been hours before they'd noticed we were gone. As it is, a dead body is a bit of a giveaway. They'll be after us on horseback soon.'

'They don't have horses, surely?'

'The Duchess does. And she's not the type to forgive and forget. She was planning on becoming queen, you know. You've rightly screwed that up now. You're going to have to keep looking over your shoulder for the rest of your life.'

Me? I thought.

'She did realise he had two wives already? He hardly needed a third,' I said.

'Yes, but he'd petitioned the Pope to have the first marriage annulled. The one with the witch woman – Queen Ulrika. And the other one was never consummated, or so it's rumoured. So that would have left him a free man, if it all went through. And of course, that's what the gold was for.'

'What do you mean?'

'A Yule gift to the Church, of course. Keep them sweet. Not *quite* buying their decision on the annulment question, he couldn't be that blatant about it. But the Church needs money, so a charitable donation would be very welcome.'

If this story was true, then everything else had merely been a smokescreen. Including my involvement in it all. But how much of this could I believe?

I stumbled again, and she stopped to wait for me.

'Do you want me to shoot you,' she asked casually, 'if they catch up with us? You wouldn't want to fall into their hands after ... what's happened.'

'What about you?'

'Well, afterwards I'd shoot myself, obviously.'

Or else you'd tell them you had killed the king-slayer.

'No thanks, I'll take my chances. I've been lucky so far.'

'The gambler's fallacy, Clockmaker. Anyway, the offer's there, if you want to take it.'

She might have been offering me the loan of a cart.

'Call me Karl, for God's sake,' I said. 'It's my name.'

'I'd rather not get too familiar with you, Clockmaker, if you don't mind. Just in case I do have to kill you.'

A little while later we reached a place where the forest track curved down to ford a small stream, rushing too fast to be frozen.

'OK,' said Kaldur. 'This is a good point to leave the trail. We go down to the edge of the water, then turn around and double back. Walk in your own footsteps. Like this.'

She demonstrated, stepping into the footprints we had left behind us in the snow. We walked back the way we had come like that for perhaps five minutes, until we came to a tree that lay fallen alongside the path.

'Get up onto the log,' said Sarah. 'Then jump as far as you can into the woods.'

I did so, and landed in some bushes. She followed me.

'Now, up the hill. And let's pray they don't have dogs.'

With difficulty we made our way up the wooded slope, deliberately scrambling through bushes and vegetation rather than taking a more direct route.

'You've done this before,' I gasped.

'You might say that.'

At the top of the ridge, she suddenly turned and gestured to me to be quiet. I heard the hooves almost at once in the distance. We crouched down and watched the riders pass by below – five, six, seven, eight. Armed with swords and muskets. The hunt was on.

'No dogs yet,' Sarah murmured. 'But they won't be long finding some. And we'd better be far away by the time they do.'

We moved off down the other side of the slope, into a more open area with fewer trees. I kept looking back the way we had come, worrying that we must be very visible now. Some light snow was falling, but not enough to cover our tracks. She noticed my glance.

'Don't worry, they won't come up that way. Not with horses. And they'll be expecting us to head south, towards the city. But we're going north.'

'Why?'

'I'm taking you to Alsina, Clockmaker. You're going to meet some of our people.'

'Your people?'

She looked at me with a half-smile.

'The less you know, the better. Surely you've learned that by now?'

'But you're one of these ... radicals, I take it? Like Erika Thorne.'

'She was our leader. Until Johansson betrayed her.'

'Johansson? But he was her ally. They tried to kill the Queen.'

'Sure about that? The original plan was for her to kill the King. But Johansson got him out, then warned the Household

Guard. And they killed her.'

'Why would he want to save the King and Queen?'

'Isn't it obvious? He needed them alive. For his deals. So he needed *her* dead.'

We trudged on in silence for a while. It was food for thought, certainly.

'I knew her, you know,' I said at last. 'Erika Thorne.'

'I know you did, Clockmaker,' she sighed.

'I suppose now you're going to tell me that that was all part of the plan, too? Me and her?'

She looked at me pityingly.

'Of course it was. No offence, but what interest do you think a woman like that would have in someone like you? You were a friend of the King, that's all. Her way in. It was Johansson's idea.'

'You're wrong. She learned nothing from me. And Johansson tried to keep us apart.'

'Oh really? And who do you think let her into the Round Tower? On the day the bomb went off in the King's Garden?'

'That had nothing to do with it!'

She shrugged.

'Believe it or don't, Clockmaker, it's all the same to me. But it's a bad old world out there.'

We walked on. It could not be true. Erika was not like that. She had never lied to me, never deceived me. All right, she had deceived me. Once. But only to save my life. And she had never asked me anything about the King or the court. Even on that day when she knew she was probably going to die. It could not be true. It could not. And I was damned if I was going to let Sarah Kaldur play these games with me.

'So who is your leader now?' I asked.

She hesitated.

'Ever hear of Olav Bertramsen?'

'No.'

'He's a historian. He wrote a book called *The Necessary Republic*.'

'Oh, that! Yes, I've read it.' She glanced at me in surprise. *So you don't know everything after all, Sarah Kaldur,* I thought with satisfaction.

'Is that who we're going to meet?'

She shook her head.

'Johansson has him locked up at the moment. But not for long, Clockmaker. Not for long.'

As the day grew brighter we found a muddy livestock track, now frozen hard. Sarah said we should follow it, as it would help to throw the dogs off the trail. But the uneven, churned-up ground was exhausting to walk on. The snow was still coming down, and it made the ruts slippery. When we reached the brow of a hill, Sarah stopped and pointed ahead.

'The railway line's due east of here. If we're careful and keep our eyes open for royalists, we can walk it all the way to Alsina.'

'I'm going to need to rest soon,' I said. 'I'm not in as good condition as you.'

'All right, ten minutes, then,' she said. 'It's all we can afford. We'll have to keep going all day.'

Across a field lay the ruins of an ancient church. We crossed a low stone wall and tramped through the snow towards it. The roof was long gone, but the stone porch offered a little shelter. We hunkered down opposite each other in the doorway.

'So what do you think will happen now?' I asked.

'Best not to think about things like that.'

'But the King is gone. You've won.'

She did not reply. I looked up. She had leaned her head back against the wall, and her eyes were closed. In her overalls and boots, she did not look much like a revolutionary. She looked like an electrician. But she, not Erika, was the one who had finally succeeded in eliminating the King. So maybe it took an artisan to get the job done in the end, I thought bitterly.

I put my head down on my arms and closed my eyes, too. And then, silently, I wept. Like a small child. For my lost friend.

I was awoken by a kick to my boot. Sarah Kaldur was standing over me, holding the gun and a chain.

'Give me your hand,' she said.

'What for?'

'I'm going to visit the bushes, Clockmaker, and then I'm going up ahead to reconnoitre. I want to make sure you stay put till I get back.'

'For God's sake, Sarah, you know this is not necessary.'

'Your hand, Clockmaker.'

I raised my arm and she padlocked one end of the makeshift shackles about my wrist, then wrapped the other end around the remains of an iron fitting that had once supported the long-vanished church door, and padlocked that, too. Then she left, still holding the gun.

It was snowing heavily now. Immobile as I was, I was shivering with cold. Time passed. I was about to call out for her, then thought better of it. These woods were reputed to be full of bandits, and I was helpless. The thought occurred to me that if she did not return, I could die here. But she must surely have been planning to come back – for one thing, she had left her tool bag behind, just out of my reach.

I was slowing down her escape – so why not just kill me, or abandon me? Indeed, why had she taken me with her at all? I thought we were making an escape together, but it was becoming obvious that she considered me a prisoner, not an ally. Maybe I was worth something, somehow. Was there a price on my head? She was a palace employee, she would have known about it if there was. And Johansson would certainly like to get hold of me and interrogate me about the King's hiding-place. But that would do him no good now – the King was dead, after all. *But Johansson doesn't know that yet.* Kaldur's group could offer me to him, in exchange for ... what? Money? Food? *Bertramsen!*

They wanted to swap me for their leader. And they would have to move swiftly, before word of the regicide reached Kantarborg.

Clearly, if I did want to end up in a torture chamber again, I would have to try to escape at once. *You told me a bit too much, Sarah Kaldur.*

I stretched my body out as far as I could on the stone flags and tried to reach the tool bag with my foot. It was no use. Then I took off my belt and attempted to use it as a lasso, but the bag was still a foot or so too far away. I tied the other end of the belt to my ankle and tried to swing it over the bag with my leg. At the fourth attempt, the buckle snagged on the handle of the bag and I was able to drag it a few inches closer. After a few more tries I could just about get my foot around it – by which time I had acquired a bracelet of red welts on my shackled wrist – and I pulled it over.

Inside the bag was a set of tools, and, to my surprise, a fair quantity of gold coins. At some stage, Kaldur had helped herself to the booty. Some of the tools were unfamiliar to me, but there were several small screwdrivers and pliers. To my frustration, though, the keys to the padlocks were absent – she had no doubt taken them with her. But locksmithing is part of a horologist's training. It took me a lot longer than usual, working mainly with my left hand, and without my usual tools, but eventually I was able to dismantle the mechanism sufficiently to release myself.

So now I could make my escape – but where was I going to go? I had no food and little idea of where I was. The sensible thing to do would probably be to head east, as she suggested, find the coast, and then follow the railway line north to Alsina and the fortress of Sythorn, where Marieke was being held. And then what? Was I planning to storm a fortress strong enough to hold off a whole army? But what else could I do?

It was at that moment that I heard an echoing shot, not far off. Quickly, I picked up the tool bag and hid inside the roofless church.

Not long after came the sound of horses' hooves. I heard them stop. They must have been looking across at the building, evaluating it as a possible hiding place for fugitives. Luckily the snow had been falling steadily, so perhaps our footprints would be erased by now – and we had come across by the churchyard, not by the main pathway to the entrance, which was still pristine and undisturbed.

I took a chance and glanced out through the porch. A man, his sabre drawn, had dismounted and was wading through the knee-deep snow towards the church. I ducked back, my heart thumping hard in my chest.

I heard him approach the porch. There were a few moments of silence, then a hissing sound as he urinated against the wall. One of the men on horseback called out something, and he laughed.

The minutes passed. Finally, I heard the horses move off. When I dared to look out again, they were gone. Heading south, back the way Sarah and I had come. They must have taken a short cut and lain in wait for us. And if they had caught Sarah, now they would be looking for me.

I took the tool bag and hurried off in the direction they had come from.

It was not long before I saw a smear of colour up ahead in the whiteness alongside the path, though I hoped it was something else – a bundle of clothes, or a discarded sack. Not what I knew it must surely be.

Sarah's body was lying at a point where the track we had been following crossed a wider road. I found the flintlock pistol lying in the snow. They had ambushed her here, and she had kept her vow not to be taken alive. I picked up the weapon and put it in the tool bag. As I did so I heard a click behind me. I dropped the bag and raised my hands above my head. My freedom had lasted all of half an hour.

'Give her a decent burial, at least!' I barked. Irrationally, I felt more angry than afraid. I turned around slowly to find myself facing, not the band of royalists I had been expecting, but a group of half-naked men and women wearing an odd assortment of clothing, and carrying muskets and bows and arrows, all pointed at me. Several of them had painted faces. An older, bald man, dressed in a black leather jerkin and a red tartan skirt, and with a ring through his nose, came over and peered at me close up. He grasped my chin and turned my head this way and that to examine my features. Then he turned back to the others.

'Karl Nielsen,' he said.

CHAPTER FORTY-SIX

Three French hens

She was a little girl, perhaps seven or eight, standing in her father's workshop. The smell of sawdust and varnish. He was showing her his latest piece. A noble had requested a cabinet in which all of the many drawers could be locked and unlocked by the turn of a single key. Hendrik had solved this through a system of brass rods that were kept out of sight behind the facing. Counterweights and pulleys reduced the effort involved in turning the key. It was immensely complicated, but for the user it looked simple. The art that conceals art, her father said proudly. There is always a way. It may not be easy, or elegant, but there is always a way.

Marieke awoke, lying in her prison bunk in the early morning. Outside, she heard the courtyard clock strike five. What did the dream mean? *Think,* she said to herself. *You must think.* What did she know for certain? She knew that someone in the prison was of the King's party. Someone who was willing to plant that document in her cell, even though it might mean death if it was discovered. Marieke had followed the instructions carefully, and had torn the sheets of paper into tiny pieces and flushed them away with the contents of her chamber-pot when slopping out in the morning. But whoever gave her the papers had to trust that she would do this.

That is one thing I know. What else?

When they were fetching the water for her interrogation, they had taken her through the staff canteen in shackles. Four or five guards were sitting at the tables, eating. They turned away from her, but she saw. It was gruel. The same gruel they were giving the prisoners.

Yesterday, when they were standing out in the courtyard, one of the guards had fainted. His companion had quickly helped him up and taken him inside. The prisoners had mostly ignored the incident, but Marieke had noticed.

Then there were the prisoners who were being 'moved to better quarters'. They were mainly Northlanders, but De Vries, the Meijers, the whole Janssen family, too. The militia came to get them, the train left, and that was that. So how long before they were all 'moved'? She guessed a week or so. If she was going to act, it would have to be now.

When the guard came and unlocked her cell, she told him she wanted to see the governor. She had urgent information. No, no-one else would do. Only the governor.

The guard was reluctant, but grudgingly shackled her, brought her to the governor's office and knocked on the door.

The governor actually smiled as he opened it. He was an older man, perhaps sixty or so. He looked, Marieke thought, more like a teacher than a prison governor. His desk was sparse, with nothing on it but a writing pad and a few pens. He nodded to the guard to wait outside.

'Mrs Nielsen! Our star prisoner,' he said in attempted Northlandish as he went back to his desk. 'I must pass on the compliments of the government on your confession and all the useful information you have divulged.'

She ignored the sarcasm.

'You have a problem,' said Marieke.

'*I* have a problem, Mrs Nielsen? I don't think so. As I see it, you are standing before me in chains. I rather think that you are the one with the problem, don't you?'

'Your men are starving. You have been abandoned by Kantarborg.'

'Well, I'm sorry to disappoint you, but that information is quite incorrect. We have no shortage of rations.'

'You are starving,' repeated Marieke. 'And we know where there is food. Lots of food.'

'By 'we', you mean who, exactly?'

'The Lowlander prisoners.'

'Not the others?'

238

'The Northlanders know nothing. It is hidden somewhere they are afraid to go.'

The governor looked thoughtful.

'What kind of food?' he asked, after a few moments.

'Potatoes. Carrots. Turnips. Root vegetables. All the food the Northlanders will not eat. We have it in abundance, because we have been unable to sell it in Kantarborg since the blockade.'

'And how do I know any of this is true?'

'You don't. But it is true nonetheless.'

'So what do you propose?'

'Find a boat and take the prisoners back across the Sound. All of them. As the price of their release, I will arrange for the Lowlanders to give you food.'

The governor laughed softly.

'You are seriously suggesting that I release my prisoners?'

Marieke shrugged. 'Call it an escape, if you want.'

'And what about the blockade?'

'The city is blockaded. Alsina is not. There are no North-lander warships between here and the far shore. And in any case, we are civilians of their own nation. They will not fire upon us.'

'And the ice? The harbours have not been cleared.'

'You have explosives, use them. On the Northland side, you can use a cannon to clear a channel, if need be.'

'Thought of everything, haven't you? But I'm afraid you cannot win your freedom that way, madam. You are a criminal and a spy, facing a possible sentence of death.'

'We all are. I know what is going on. Why the prisoners are being moved.'

The governor looked sharply up at her.

'I do my best for the prisoners in my custody. I have nothing to do with them after they leave here. That is a matter for the military.'

'They are innocent people, and you know what is happening to them. That is complicity. If you care anything for your immortal soul, release them. I know you must keep me here. I am a pawn in the game, but they are not charged with anything.'

'And what do you think my superiors will have to say about that?'

'Your superiors! What the hell does it matter what they think?' said Marieke hotly. 'Do your superiors in Kantarborg care what happens to you? Do you have a wife? Children? Are they hungry?'

The governor was silent a moment. Then he got up, walked over to a corner of the office, and fetched a chair.

'Sit down,' he said.

CHAPTER FORTY-SEVEN

The Irdai village smelled just as I remembered from the Westlands – wood smoke, animal skins and humanity – though the huts, arranged roughly in a circle, looked rather more ramshackle here than they had back then, as though they had frequently been moved. The roofs were made of rough planking rather than thatch, and here and there a tarpaulin had been slung across to cover a leak. A couple of bonfires were burning, with children standing around them, staring at me as I was dragged before the throne in the central clearing and pushed onto my knees in the snow. Chief Ragnar stared balefully down at me, his naked torso crossed by leather ammunition belts, a fur cloak about his shoulders. He had aged; his once lively and engaging look was stern now, almost bitter. The throne was made of wood, but was otherwise, so far as I could tell, a close copy of his former metal throne in the Westlands. A young man stood at his shoulder and acted as interpreter.

'You are Karl Nielsen, companion of the King of Kantarborg,' said the chief, the Old Kantish words more or less intelligible to me, but repeated by the youth in the modern idiom.

'I was,' I said. 'The King is dead.'

There was a murmur among the onlookers.

'Did you kill him?' inquired the chief.

'No. But I was there when it happened.'

'Your king brought us into the land of bondage.'

'I know.'

'But you served him?'

'I did.'

'Why?'

'He was my king. And my friend.'

This admission might cost me my life, but in truth I was past caring. If I was going to die now, let me die with some kind of integrity.

'Did he betray you, too?' asked the chief.

'Yes.'

'Then he was not a good king or a good friend. Such men die young. How did you serve him?'

'I was the King's ... I made ... devices in metal. Small machines.'

I remembered something.

'I made the King's gift to you. The airship.'

The chief gestured to one of the warriors, who disappeared inside a hut and to my surprise returned with the model of the royal airship *Freya* that I had constructed all those years ago. It looked a little battered, but still quite splendid in copper, brass and wood. Several of the brass cannons had come loose, and one of the small tin motors had become detached and was hanging off.

'You made this?' asked the chief.

I looked at my guards and indicated that I wished to stand up. The chief nodded, and I approached the throne. I took the model, turned it over, and showed him the letters carved into the base.

'KN – Karl Nielsen.'

'Can you repair it?'

'Yes. I think so.'

The chief looked at the model wordlessly for a few moments. Then he said: 'Give him food.'

Teema, the young man who had acted as interpreter, brought me a bowl of boiled potatoes and some other vegetables, then sat down with me at the bench table. He was an attractive, dark-haired youth, with the faint shadow of a moustache on his upper lip that made him look adolescent, although his build suggested he was around eighteen. I am ashamed to say I ate quite greedily – it had been some time since I had tasted real food of any kind, and the simple meal did me a great deal of good. When I asked him where the food had come from, he told me that the tribe had cleared some areas of the wildwoods to use as gardens.

'Far away from here,' he insisted, waving his arm in a vague direction. I doubted that – it would scarcely be practical – but they probably had good reasons to keep the whereabouts of their larder secret.

I complimented him on his good Kantish, and he told me that he had learned it at mission school in the labour camp for the King's railway.

'My school name is Timothy,' he laughed.

I found myself wondering how their old sky-god religion had fared after they had been betrayed by their own messiah, but thought it wisest not to ask.

After I had eaten, they brought me the model airship and Sarah Kaldur's tool bag – which included among its contents a soldering iron and solder. I put the end of the iron into their cooking fire until it was glowing red hot. The children of the tribe were inordinately interested in what the strange man was doing and crowded in around me until they were shooed away by Teema, who seemed to have appointed himself my personal guardian. I managed to fix the cannons easily enough, but re-attaching the motor to the model was tricky. I had to try it several times, re-heating the iron each time, before the seam took. It was not the neatest repair job in the world, but it would hold. For good measure I also polished the model up a bit. When it was finished, it didn't look too bad at all. Teema accepted it reverently and bore it away to the chief's hut.

They had given me a mug of water to drink, which gave me an idea. Using a magnetic screwdriver from the tool bag, I took a small sliver of copper that was left over from the work, and rubbed it until it was magnetised. Then I laid it carefully on the surface of the water in the mug, so that it floated. Teema returned and asked me what I was doing. I was worried that he might think it was witchcraft, so I explained as well as I could that I was making a device that would tell me which way was north.

'You mean like this?' he asked – and from a leather pouch on his belt, he produced a perfectly serviceable brass compass. Then he took out a map and asked me where I wanted to go.

I was woken in the early morning by Teema, after a less than entirely comfortable night lying on a fur-covered bench in an Irdai hut – although it was still somewhat better than the accommodation I had recently enjoyed in the King's service.

Outside the hut, in the early morning greyness, an elderly woman was stoking the embers of the previous night's bonfire, while children brought water from the stream. A dog came up to me to sniff the newcomer, barked once, then lost interest. Teema laughed. More snow had fallen during the night, but none of the tribespeople seemed much bothered by the cold. Teema and I ate bowls of steaming porridge – Do you grow grain, as well? I asked, and received an evasive reply – under the awning of the cooking hut. I asked Teema if I should say good-bye to the chief, but he shook his head.

'No need. He told me to show you the way.'

I suspected that Chief Ragnar would be glad to see the back of me before I brought bad luck on the tribe. They had had quite enough of Kantarborgans, one way and another.

Having eaten, we packed a little food – more potatoes! – and set off through the forest. Teema moved with the grace and agility of a young man who had never known any other environment, while I, the city-dweller, stumbled rather clumsily behind. He was dressed in the usual tribal motley, black leather mixed with ragged Kantarborgan cast-offs, and a bandolier from which hung tools, weapons and what I surmised were amulets of some kind.

I tried to make small talk with him, but he was reticent most of the time, tapping his ear by way of explanation. He was listening constantly, stopping sometimes and turning his head this way and that to better fix the source of some sound that was quite inaudible to me. I became hungry again quite quickly and began to gnaw on one of the boiled potatoes as we walked. I offered one to him, but he refused.

'Potatoes are good,' he said. 'But not in the forest.' Whatever that meant.

After about three hours we came to a nondescript clearing.

'Our gods go no further,' he said, and pointed. 'The railway is that way.'

He was clearly reluctant to go anywhere near it. Given his people's history, I suppose that was hardly surprising.

On the horizon, no more than a few miles distant, I could make out the sea. And beyond that, a sliver of land that was surely Northland, and home. If I had a home.

Teema had soundlessly vanished again when I turned around to say goodbye.

I tramped across the snowy clearing and clambered over the remains of some ancient stone wall. A cold, restive wind was blowing in from the grey sea. I thought I could make out the dark line of the railway, not far away.

There was a spinney of beeches to my left. Suddenly, from the corner of my eye, I thought I saw something in there, among the trees. There: a silhouette was moving. I froze on the spot. I had Sarah Kaldur's pistol in the bag across my shoulder, but I could not get myself to reach for it.

The figure appeared again. It seemed to be turning slowly around, almost as though dancing. And now I could see others, alongside it. Many others. Some moving, some not. They looked almost like puppets.

CHAPTER FORTY-EIGHT

Kramer looked up in irritation as Johansson entered his office.

'Whatever it is, Commander, it will have to wait. I was just leaving.'

'Ah yes, I heard you had a speaking engagement this evening, Prime Minister. I'm sorry to have to delay you.'

'Speaking engagement?'

'At the end of tonight's festivities.'

'I have not the slightest idea what you are talking about.'

'Oh well, perhaps I misunderstood something. You see, I heard that you had given all your men this evening off to celebrate Yule – sorry, Nicholastide – in the church hall of St Ignatius, where your gangs store the confiscated liquor. And that you had relaxed the prohibition on drinking alcohol, just for tonight. I must say I was surprised, but I suppose there is no reason why the men should not enjoy the fruits of their labours once in a while. It is quite a different matter when the righteous partake, isn't it? Wine is a sacred drink, after all. Not *akvavit* or anything like that, of course. Only wine and beer, made from good Christian plants, grown above ground. And tonight they may drink as much of it as they please.'

'Who told them that?'

'Why, you did, Prime Minister. In the invitation that you signed and sent out, for distribution to all your men.'

Johansson placed the paper on Kramer's desk.

'You forged my signature!'

'Oh, I don't think so, Prime Minister. I watched you sign this document in this very office not two days ago. On the same day that those two monks came to me with a most interesting story. It seems your trip to the Moon never actually took place, did it? Your whole movement is based on a lie.'

'So you've been talking to those fools. Even if what they say were true, Johansson, what difference would it make? I was elected because I am a man of God. I speak the voice of the people. The people do not want aristocrats like you as their leaders any more. That is what galls you.'

'Well, be that as it may, Kramer, I have received disturbing reports of a possible riot at this celebration tonight. So as Minister of Defence and Security, I'm afraid that for the sake of public law and order I am left with no option but to place you in protective custody. Just for twenty-four hours, you understand.'

Johansson opened the office door, and four members of the Watch entered. Belatedly, Kramer realised what was happening. He stood up.

'Guards! Guards!'

'I'm afraid your men have all gone to the festivities, Prime Minister. And are no doubt by now lying in sodden communion with their deity, waiting for their leader to appear. Except that now, I'm afraid he won't.'

'You won't get away with this, Johansson. My men will defend me.'

'Well, that's the thing about drunken men, isn't it? They are more inclined to fight, but on the whole rather less able.'

'Then you should have given them the *akvavit* as well!' said Kramer bitterly, as the Watchmen led him away.

'Ah well, the thing is, spirits have a rather special property, don't they?'

'And what is that?'

'They burn, Kramer. They burn. Like the very fires of hell.'

CHAPTER FORTY-NINE

Two turtledoves

Walking railway tracks is a wearying business, even more so than walking an empty road. The ties were not well spaced for pacing, and the line stretched off into the far distance without pause or break in the monotony. But my fury gave me strength. I was ready to kill someone.

It is strange how, even in such a fervid state of mind, reason insists on worming its bothersome way into your consciousness. *What good would it do? It won't bring them back, will it?*

'I don't care,' I said aloud as I tramped along the ties. 'Johansson was right. War seeks you out. I am a soldier now.'

I had to look at every one of them, to make sure Marieke was not among them. Twenty-six bodies, hanging from the trees like obscene Yule decorations. Men, women and four children. All of them dressed in prison clothes. One face I recognised: Magnus Petersson, the ship's chandler – a neighbour of ours from Sandviken. Their captors must have used the train – my invention! – to bring them here, to this desolate spot. Johansson had found a solution to his problem. But a black vengeance would befall him soon, if I had anything to do with it.

The line seemed to have been cleared of snow fairly recently – it had been shovelled up in piles alongside the track – so I could make reasonably good progress. After a few hours I could make out the towers of Alsina on the horizon, and by dusk I was at the harbour of the town. Up ahead towered the dark bulk of the fortress. I had some notion that I might be able to use the gold coins to buy some food in the town, if there was any to be had. But in the streets the snow came almost to my knees, and there was no sign of human life anywhere – not even the sound of a child crying or a dog barking. Nothing but the sighing of the wind, blowing the snowflakes into my face like sea spray. Perhaps I was dead. Perhaps this was what death was like.

In the town square, a tall Yule tree had been erected. At its base, some candles were scattered around. A sign lay on the ground: *Yule Collection for the Needy. Candles one penny each.* The collection box had vanished. I picked up a candle, lit it with the flint mechanism of Sarah Kaldur's pistol, and left it flickering gently in the snow, at the foot of the tree.

I went back to the railway line and followed it as it began to curve around towards the fortress. The tool bag was slung on my shoulder, and I had the firearm in my hand. I didn't know what I was going to do, but I knew I was going to do something.

The rails brought me to a gateway in the outer defences, which was open and unguarded. I followed the tracks through the archway under the ramparts, then under several more, until, up ahead in the shadows, I saw a train with closed wagons. I approached it cautiously, but there was no-one around. I took a look inside the cab. The locomotive was primed with several pods. Enough to get me back to Kantarborg, perhaps. But not without Marieke. I walked up the rising ground to the main gate, and hammered on it with the butt of the pistol.

A window opened in the wall above.

'Who's there?'

I am vengeance. I am the angel of death. I have come to kill you all.

'Karl Nielsen!' I shouted back.

'Just a minute, I'll come down.'

After a moment the gate door creaked open and a small bespectacled man peered out.

'If you've come to help with the transport, they're all down by the harbour,' he said.

'I've come for my wife.'

'And your wife is ...?'

'Marieke Hendriksdatter.'

'Who?'

'Mrs Nielsen.'

'Oh, right. I think she might be up in the governor's office.

I'll take you there.'

This was not all the reception I had been expecting. The man led the way across the courtyard, through a door and down a corridor. I discreetly slid the pistol back into the tool bag, but kept it where I could quickly get hold of it if need be. We ascended a staircase, and the man knocked on a door and opened it.

'Karl Nielsen, Governor. He's come about his wife.'

The governor stood up from behind his desk and walked over to me. He extended his hand. I took it, feeling utterly confused.

'Karl Nielsen! Well, it's been a while since we've seen you in here. Your wife is down in the harbour with the boats. The operation is going well.'

'What operation?'

At that moment, the door opened and Marieke walked in, accompanied by two men in uniform. She stared at me in shock.

'Karl!'

She rushed over and embraced me.

'I thought you were dead!'

'So did I,' I said.

CHAPTER FIFTY

Something had gone wrong. Something had gone very wrong. Brorsen had heard the rumours. Now he needed to find out the truth.

'I understand you had something of a showdown with the Moonies,' he said, as he and Johansson took their usual morning walk along the ramparts.

'Yes. But it did not go quite as planned,' said Johansson.

'How so, Commander? I hear you had them at your mercy.'

'In the church hall, yes. Drunk as lords, by all accounts. Ottesen reported to me that we had them surrounded. We were going to torch the building, cut down anyone who tried to escape.'

'But ...?'

'But I could not give the order, Brorsen. They are citizens of Kantarborg, and their crimes are minor. Not deserving of the death sentence. We arrested them instead. For public order offences.'

'But they are a threat to the state, Commander! And to you!'

'Are they, Brorsen? Religious zealots and bullies, certainly. They need to be reined in. But I will not have the mass murder of Kantarborgans on my conscience. I have enough blood on my hands already.'

So it was true. The older man stared at Johansson, naked horror growing in his eyes.

'Where is Kramer now?' he asked quietly.

'He is due to be released shortly. He is only in protective custody. We have nothing on him. It is not a crime for a politician to lie about his past, sadly. And the poor sap may even have believed his own fantasies.'

'Then why did you not charge him with corruption, or tax evasion?'

'Because he hasn't evaded any.'

'My dear Johansson, that is not the point! Do you really not understand what will happen now? To you?'

'What will happen, my lord Astronomer?'

'He will crush you like an insect!'

Johansson made no reply, but just stared out across the frozen greyness of the Sound. Brorsen grabbed his arm like a man drowning.

'How can you be so calm about this? You had your chance to eliminate your enemy, and you fluffed it. If you release him, you are finished, man! And I along with you. You understand what this means? I have backed the wrong horse!'

'Well, as you so often have remarked to me, Astronomer, there may be higher concerns than the fate of any one of us.'

Brorsen looked stupefied.

'This is insane. There must be some rational explanation. It's that witch woman, isn't it? You're scared of her and her ridiculous prophecies.'

'It has nothing to do with her.'

'Commander, listen to me. What this kingdom needs right now above all is a firm hand. There is quite enough hysteria in the land already. We need someone to assure the people that order will be maintained. And if you are not the man for the job, someone else will take over, that much is quite certain.'

'You, perhaps? How about the regency, Brorsen?'

'I am not about to lay my head on the block, Commander. Someone else can do that. I intend to save myself.'

CHAPTER FIFTY-ONE

Christopher was sitting by the window in the tower, sketching a design. Joe came over and placed a cup of tea beside him on the desk.

'Keep the hunger away. What's that supposed to be?'

'The barges for Johansson.'

'They look more like balloons.'

'All right, all right, I'll never be a draughtsman. Long as the boatwright can see what's what. That's the payload area in the middle, and them's the buoyancy tanks at the sides.'

'You pump the air out from inside the boat?'

'That's the idea. Through the hosepipes. Here and … here.'

'And what kind of weight are we talking about?'

'A gunpowder keg weighs about ten pounds. You'd need about twenty of them to blow a fair-sized hole in a ship. Then there's the barge and the tanks. So maybe four hundred pounds in all.'

'And you'd want one for every ship?'

'That's the idea.'

'Sure you'll never be able to pull that kind of weight with a clockwork motor. You don't have the traction, and they'll be submerged, have you calculated the water resistance? You'd be able to manage one, maybe two at a time. Or else you'd need to make them smaller.'

Christopher looked up with a smile.

'Are you telling me how to make the weapon more efficient, Brother Joe?'

Joe looked at him, and at the drawings.

'Are you saying what I think you're saying?' she asked at last.

'Let's just put it this way. If it works, it's good – and if it doesn't, it's even better.'

'Ya cute hoor ya!'[5]

'I learned from the master, Joe. I learned from the master.'

---

5 'Cunning bastard'.

CHAPTER FIFTY-TWO

Marieke, the governor and I were sitting in what had once been the great banqueting hall of the fortress, back in the days when Sythorn had been a royal palace. It was a vast space, with an ornately tiled floor, brass chandeliers, exquisitely scrolled furniture and tall windows with long velour curtains. Enormous oil paintings of ancient monarchs adorned the walls. Nothing I had seen, even in the Rose Castle, could match it for grandeur. But like all such distinguished places in the kingdom, it had seen better days. Dust lay everywhere, and several of the windows were cracked. My guess was that it had been quite a number of centuries since anything approaching an actual banquet had been held here.

We occupied one small corner of the hall, where a large map of the region had been spread out on an old oak table. Marieke was outlining her plan. The shipments from across the Sound would continue, and the train would bring the food to Kantarborg.

I had told them about my escape from the underground fortress, but I said nothing of the King's fate. The thought of my name being forever associated with what would surely be a historic event appalled me. And since no-one had seen who had really fired the pistol, I would probably fall under suspicion. I was not anxious for that business to begin any earlier than it had to.

'What about the Northlander warships?' the governor asked Marieke in his half-Northlandish. 'You are undermining their blockade. Aiding the enemy – us.'

'They are not watching this part of the coast,' said Marieke. 'The passage here is narrow and we can bring a lot of food over before they notice.'

'Yes, but technically, this is treason towards your country, isn't it? You could hang for it, you know.'

She shrugged.

'People are starving on both sides of the Sound. The southern provinces of Northland are convulsed in chaos. My guess is that they will have other things on their mind besides warfare.'

'I can drive the train,' I said.

'No,' said the governor. 'I cannot allow that, Clockmaker Nielsen, and you cannot risk it. You cannot just turn up in Kantarborg as though nothing has happened.'

'But surely, if I arrive with food ...'

'Releasing the flightings in exchange for food is one thing. They are not charged with any crime, and it will alleviate a major problem for Kantarborg. Two major problems. I will probably be commended for it rather than disciplined. But I cannot release the two of you. You are both felons in the eyes of the state...'

'You cannot be serious..!' I began, my voice rising.

'No, listen to me. *Listen to me!* If you return to Kantarborg now, you will be arrested and put in a cell. You may well end up being executed. Your good intentions will count for nothing. What you must do now is *escape*. Go back to Sandviken. Then, when the dust has settled, I promise you that I will make your case to the authorities. I cannot guarantee it, but a pardon may well be forthcoming. I will certainly recommend it.'

I looked at Marieke.

'He's right, Karl,' she said.

'But will we be safe in Sandviken?' I asked her.

'They tell me that things have settled down a little there. The Northlanders are scared and exhausted. My people are arranging for emergency feeding stations to be set up in the southern towns. It may help to heal the wounds a little.'

'Will they eat the vegetables?' asked the governor.

'If the alternative is starvation, yes, I think they will.'

'And there will still be enough left over for Kantarborg?'

'We have enough,' she replied. 'All the food we had grown for the market in Kantarborg is being kept in storage, but it must be used soon, or it will rot.'

'Where do you keep it?' asked the governor.

'Where they are afraid to follow.'

'Where is that?' I asked. I had never heard of this place. To my surprise, Marieke's only reply was to smile and sing a line in Anglian from an old Yule song:

'*Sire, he lives a good league hence, underneath the mountain...*'

'There is also another thing that is worrying me,' said the governor. 'If the people of Kantarborg hear a train has arrived with food, there will likely be a riot. The Watch won't be able to contain it. Or worse, it will all disappear before it reaches the people who need it most.'

'What if we say nothing to anyone?' said Marieke. 'We just distribute the food, starting with the poorest districts. Give each family a bag of vegetables.'

'That would require considerable organisation,' said the governor. 'You would need the militia. Which means getting Commander Johansson to agree. But if we can get the train to Kantarborg, I will negotiate with Johansson and try to persuade him to get the militia to help out. If we offer to feed the soldiers and their families first, that will probably grease the wheels a good deal.'

'Does it have to be the militia? Couldn't the Watch distribute the food?' asked Marieke.

'They will need to keep order and ensure that everyone gets their fair share,' he said. 'I can only see soldiers being able to do that, under the circumstances. And even they will have trouble, as soon as people see food arriving. We will have to be very careful to ensure that things do not get out of hand.'

'Perhaps we could take the food out at night,' said Marieke.

I could not take my eyes off those long velour curtains. They were a deep red colour.

'Governor, do you have any people here who can sew?' I asked.

'Sew? There's a whole sewing workshop. The ordinary prisoners produce uniforms for the military. Why?'

'I have a bit of an idea.'

CHAPTER FIFTY-THREE

Brother Christopher walked down Woolmerchant Street, carrying his drawings. He was feeling rather grumpy after an uncomfortable night. There had been a lot of shouting going on in the city, the sound of glass breaking and rioting. Joe, thankfully, had slept through it all.

There had been nothing for breakfast except re-brewed tea – they had not received the military rations for several days, and had been making do on leftovers. Christopher wondered whether the rations had stopped altogether. If even the soldiers weren't being fed, things must really be bad.

What the hell were you thinking of, bringing a pregnant woman into this? If any harm comes to her or the child, it will be your fault. Just couldn't bear leaving her behind, could you? Should have thought it through. Church missions are never straightforward, whatever they tell you.

It was oddly quiet now on the street. There were no traders about. The smell of smoke drifted on the wind. A few bands of scavengers were out, ragged children mostly, but their pickings seemed to be meagre. They looked as thin as wraiths, some of them barefoot in the snow. They watched him silently as he passed.

The guards outside the palace seemed lethargic and indifferent, and the palace halls themselves were almost empty. Walking down an echoing corridor, he thought he saw someone stuffing brass candlesticks into a sack at the other end. It was all very odd.

There was no-one in the outer office, so he knocked at the Minister's door, opened it and looked in.

'Commander..?'

Johansson was standing by the window, looking out.

'Good morning, Brother Christopher,' he said grimly, and sat down. He looked pale, as though he had not slept. Christopher sat down opposite him and placed the drawings on the table.

'Well, the good news, Commander, is that the barges are ready. In tests, we've been able to get them to function quite well. The bad news is that it seems the submersible boat can draw no more than two of the requisite size at a time. So you'd have to make a few trips. I'm not sure how practical that might be in a battle situation. There are a lot of ships out there. But there's not really much we can do about that.'

'No...' Johansson seemed preoccupied.

After a pause, Christopher continued.

'So I was wondering ... about our airship?'

Johansson looked at him in silence. Christopher began to feel uncomfortable.

'When are we going to get it back? I mean, now that we've kept our side of the bargain?'

'It may be difficult,' said Johansson at last.

Christopher waited, but no more information was forthcoming.

'You mean there'll be a delay? For how long?'

'I don't know. We have other problems right now.'

Christopher was about to ask more, but Johansson looked away and was clearly in no mood to discuss it.

'I see. Well, then perhaps ...'

Christopher got up to leave.

'I don't know much about monks,' said Johansson abruptly. 'We don't have any in the kingdom.'

Christopher sat down again.

'What is it you wish to know, Minister?'

'Are you also ordained? Like a priest?'

'Some monks are. I am.'

'I'm afraid my time here may be coming to an end. I will quite likely be arrested and put on trial.'

Johansson looked over at Christopher.

'So would you hear my confession ... Father?' he asked.

CHAPTER FIFTY-FOUR

Conciliatory, conciliatory. That is the tone to adopt, thought Brorsen to himself as he strode down the palace corridor in the direction of Johansson's office, holding the document he had hurriedly drafted. *Ignore whatever foolishness the man may come out with. It is a question of survival now.*

It had been a trying morning, to put it mildly. Arriving at the palace at his usual hour to attend the Crown Prince, he had knocked at the nursery door and, hearing no answer, had opened it and entered.

The boy was sitting on the floor, playing with a clockwork toy. Brorsen could not remember having seen it before. Perhaps a Yule gift.

'When Your Highness is ready,' said Brorsen, in what he thought was an appropriately peremptory tone.

'Is it mathematics again?' asked the Prince, without looking up.

'I'm afraid so, Your Highness.'

'I think I've learned enough mathematics for now, don't you, Brorsen?'

The astronomer stiffened.

'I would be pleased if Your Highness would refer to me as Mr Brorsen, or as my lord. It is a question of respect.'

'I shall call you whatever I please,' said the boy, without looking up from his play. 'If I want to call you Mr Pig-face, I will.'

'Then I would resign my position at once.'

'No you wouldn't. You're just like all the others. They don't resign until it is too late.'

Brorsen did not know what to say to that. He watched the mechanical toy, running around and around on its metal track. Surely it would stop soon? The boy had built some kind of tunnel across the track, made out of books. He noticed Brorsen's gaze.

'This is where the King my father went under the mountain,'

he said, pointing. 'And this is where he came out, and met my mother.'

'Indeed, Highness. But nonetheless, it is time for mathematics now.'

'Oh, mathematics, mathematics! Here's a mathematical problem for you, Brorsen. How many bushels of flour does it take to feed a city?'

Brorsen had never heard him talk so much before. The precociousness was disconcerting.

'Indeed I do not know, Highness.'

'Fourteen hundred. Every day. And do you know how many bushels are left in the Royal Storehouses?'

Brorsen spread his hands by way of reply.

'Fifty-three,' said the prince. 'Perhaps those are the sort of mathematics we should be talking about.'

Brorsen said nothing. The train continued to run round and around, gradually slowing down.

'You think I'm odd, don't you, Brorsen?'

'No, Highness. You have perhaps had an unusual upbringing, but ...'

'You do. You look at me and see a strange child. You should not. You should see the future monarch of this nation.'

'A monarch would refer to me as *my lord*!' Brorsen snapped.

The boy looked at him for a long moment. Then he smiled.

'You are right. You are quite right. I shall do so from now on, my lord Astronomer. And as I am the future monarch, perhaps you should consider your own position. In that scheme of things. As it were.'

'I'm not sure I follow, Your Highness.'

'Where is Mr Kramer, my prime minister?'

'He is in temporary custody until tomorrow, Highness. For his own protection, as I understand it.'

'So who is the acting prime minister now?'

'Why ... Commander Johansson.'

'Then we have what I believe is called a window of opportunity, do we not?'

'Your Highness?'

'I understand you have been offered the position of regent. I think you should accept that offer. Now, while Johansson can sign the order.'

Where did the boy learn language like this? Brorsen felt dizzy, as though the situation were unreal.

'Why do you wish me to do that, Highness?'

'You need not take it as any sign of affection on my part. It is a question of survival. The kingdom is falling apart. The royal line must survive. I need a grown-up to get me out of this situation before it is too late. You will do. I place myself under your protection, my lord Brorsen. And I, in return, will save your life.'

Brorsen allowed himself a slight smile.

'And how do you intend to do that, Highness?'

The boy looked at him seriously.

'My lord Brorsen, kindly do not underestimate me. You will see that I am not without agency. I wish you to accept the position of royal regent and return here immediately. Then we will talk about the details. Do you understand?'

The boy was insufferable, but Brorsen gave a slight bow.

Conciliatory, conciliatory. Brorsen arrived at the door to Johansson's outer office. His hand was shaking slightly as he opened the door.

'Does the Commander have a moment?' he asked.

'He is in conference at the moment,' said Johansson's secretary. 'Perhaps my lord would care to take a seat?'

At least someone around here shows a bit of common respect, thought Brorsen, as he sat down to wait.

CHAPTER FIFTY-FIVE

Johansson's profile was silhouetted against the palace window. The day was already growing dark, but Christopher had lit a candle on Johansson's desk instead of turning on the electric lights. It gave, he felt, an appropriately confessional atmosphere. Theatrical means were not to be despised, if they could provoke contrition.

It had been a very long time since Christopher had heard anyone's confession. He tended more often to be on the other end of the stick. *I'm not the right man for this job*, he thought. *I never was.* It was the abbot who had insisted on his ordination, against his protests. *When a man is sick and goes to a doctor, Brother, the doctor must heal him. He has the training and the authority. Whether the doctor was once sick himself is entirely irrelevant. It may even be an advantage.*

Johansson was sick in his soul, that much was clear. He was a man in torment.

'I saw the flightings,' he was saying. 'They were smitten with some contagion that was not of this world. Their eyes were dead. They would have infected us all.'

'So you decided to do away with them?'

'It is my job to protect the kingdom. They must have been deliberately sent to infect us. There is no other rational explanation. They were a weapon of war.'

'You didn't think they might just be hungry?'

Johansson turned to Christopher with sudden vehemence.

'I know hunger, priest! This was not hunger. This was something else, something demonic. It is not murder if you kill people who are no longer human, who are possessed by the devil!'

Christopher sighed. A small, sad suspicion had begun to germinate in his mind.

'If you believe otherwise, say so!' said Johansson.

'You said it was a bad harvest in Northland?'

'The year was very damp, and the grain harvest was poor, yes. I hear there was very little bread to be had.'

'And they couldn't make do with other crops? Potatoes, for example?'

'The Northlanders disdain food grown beneath the ground. As does Kramer's faction. They believe it imperils their immortal souls, so they feed it only to their animals. But what the devil does that have to do with anything?'

Christopher was silent for a few moments. *What would a real priest say?* he thought. *Or the abbot! What would the abbot say?*

'All right. Listen to me, Johansson. What I say to you now, I say not as your confessor, but as a monk of the scientific order of St Michael. The task of our order is to preserve and copy ancient documents, and keep the knowledge of the past alive. So we read a lot about the ancient times. About wars and strife, and times of conflict. And also about disease.'

He paused.

'Have you ever heard of something called St Anthony's Fire?'

Johansson shook his head.

'It's a disorder of the body and mind. A bad one. It's caused by a fungus that grows on the rye plant. Like all fungi, it spreads best under damp conditions. In some ancient languages, it was known as *the tooth of the wolf.* Eating it can cause convulsions and hallucinations.'

Johansson stared at him, and gave an appalled laugh.

'You can't be serious. Something like that could not possibly have affected an entire population!'

'By itself, probably not. But when combined with fear and hunger, who knows? It used to be quite common. Some ancient writers believed it to be the explanation for historical witch burnings and other outbreaks of mass hysteria.'

'So you think it was all just a matter of what they *ate?*'

'Tell me, are all the flightings infected with this malaise?'

'No ... not all of them. Some do not seem to be affected.'

'The ones you call Lowlanders?'

Johansson looked away.

'Yes ... the ones the Northlanders call *potato pigs*,' he said quietly.

Christopher said nothing.

'So you're telling me that this was murder?' asked Johansson.

'I don't need to tell you, do I?'

Johansson put a hand to his forehead and closed his eyes.

'It was my duty to my country. I had no choice.'

'*We have no choice* is the excuse of despots. There are always choices. And each of us is responsible for them. Do you repent of what you did?'

'What use is that? No forgiveness is possible for me,' said Johansson.

'Listen to me, man,' said Christopher, leaning forward. 'I've been something of a sinner myself in my time, let me tell you. If God can forgive me, he can forgive you, too. God offers forgiveness to every one of us. No matter what we've done. But you must refrain from evil and do only good from now on.'

'What kind of good?'

'You know what the Bible says. Feed the hungry, clothe the naked, care for the sick. No matter who they are. Just as God loves each of us here on earth, without distinction.'

'I may have very little time left,' said Johansson. 'The trap is closing around me. But I will try.'

'Good. For your penance, say a decade of the rosary. *May God give you pardon and peace, and I absolve you from your sins in the name of the Father, and of the Son, and of the Holy Ghost. Go in peace, and sin no more.*'

Johansson looked up in surprise.

'That's it?

'If you truly repent, yes. In the eyes of God, you are forgiven.

Whether your fellow human beings will forgive you is another question. That can be rather more difficult to achieve. But as you said, you can try.'

CHAPTER FIFTY-SIX

Brorsen walked away from Johansson's office in a fury. It was the end. Johansson had lost his reason. This latest piece of lunacy had left the astronomer reeling, almost speechless. Brorsen had gone to him, man to man, in all humility, to tell him that he had changed his mind and would accept the regency. He had expected to at least be interrogated on the reason for his change of heart, but there was no reaction from the man at all. You would think Brorsen had merely been remarking on the weather, not on a matter of constitutional importance to the realm. Johansson had barely glanced at the document as he signed it. And then he had started rambling on about some insane plan – if you could call it a plan – that had been cooked up by the governor of Sythorn in connivance with his own prisoners. Brorsen had been unable to hide his indignation.

'Forgive me, Lord Commander, but as your advisor it is my duty to say that I think that is the most preposterous idea I have ever heard.'

'On the contrary, Brorsen, it seems to me most ingenious,' said Johansson. 'We need to get the food out into the poorer streets without causing a civil disturbance. And who could be more above suspicion than the Yule Father, bearing a sack on his back?'

'But there will be dozens of them!'

'Well, there are dozens of them in the city already, if you haven't noticed.'

'And you seriously think you can get the militia to take part in this ... masquerade?'

'They and their families will be the first to receive the rations. I can assure you, there will be no shortage of volunteers.'

'And then what? One trainload of potatoes and carrots is hardly going to relieve the situation of this city.'

'Indeed. Which is why we must proceed to negotiate with the Northlanders to get the blockade lifted.'

'You mean surrender!'

'Whatever it takes, Brorsen. I can no longer stand by and watch the people starve. If we don't do something soon, we will have no city, no kingdom, nothing left to defend.'

'But what of your plan to destroy the Northlander fleet?'

'That was a pipe dream. Completely impractical. It may well be that underwater warfare has a future, but it could take us ten years to develop it. We don't have the time.'

Brorsen had protested, but Johansson was implacable. *When the Minister of Defence refuses to defend the kingdom,* thought Brorsen as he marched down the corridor, *what other name can you give it but treason?* His only hope now was the boy. The kingdom was not defeated as long as the prince was alive.

The door to the nursery was open, but he knocked anyway.

'Come in, my lord Astronomer,' called Prince Valdemar's voice from inside. It sounded like he was playing with that damned toy again.

Brorsen walked in – and stopped. There was a bearded stranger in the room, standing beside the boy. Beside him, on the floor, lay a large sack.

'Who are you?'

The man in the red and white outfit spread his hands.

'Isn't it obvious, Astronomer? I'm the Yule Father.'

'Not the real one,' said Prince Valdemar.

'How did you get in here?'

'He came out of the fireplace,' said Valdemar. 'Like the others.'

Brorsen looked at where the prince was pointing – at the open cabinet doors, and the old marble fireplace behind them. Brorsen strode over to the man, took hold of his beard, and pulled. It came away in his hand.

'You!'

'I've got a million faces, Uncle!' said Charlie.

'I'm calling the guards.'

'No you won't, Uncle. Because blood's thicker than water, ain't it? And because I bet you're curious to hear what I've got to say.'

'You have nothing to say that would be of the slightest interest to me.'

'Oh, I think I do. First of all, I've got a bit of good news for you. The Young King is dead. We were down in the tunnels. The clockmaker tried to escape, and there was a scuffle. Next thing, bang, and the King's lying dead on the floor. I saw it.'

'The clockmaker killed him?'

'Nah, it was the woman, Sarah Kaldur. She shot him. Then they escaped together.'

'Kaldur? The palace electrician? What was she doing down there?'

'The King kidnapped her. Couple of days ago. He need someone to wire up his lair.'

'And how do I know this is not just another of your stories?'

'Well, with your permission, Uncle ... I have a little Yule gift here for you. Just a small token of my familial affection.'

Charlie reached into the sack on the floor and brought out the golden sceptre. He held it in both hands and offered it reverently to Brorsen.

'Now ain't that a nice bit of kit? Never left it out of his sight, he didn't. So now you'll have to admit, either I'm a very clever thief, or else he's a very dead king. Not that the one necessarily excludes the other, mind you.'

Brorsen took the sceptre and examined it. It was clearly of ancient manufacture, covered in arcane designs of obscure significance. He had heard of it – it had once been part of the crown jewels, but had been lost for years, presumed stolen.

'The key to the kingdom, that is,' Charlie continued. 'And what's more, I've got the gold as well. I've brought the train back to Kantarborg, on the underground line. Now, before you say anything, I know what you're thinking. You're thinking, what bleeding use is that to me now? The city's in chaos, the ground is burning beneath me. *Things fall apart, the centre cannot hold.* Am I right? But outside the city, I reckon gold is still worth its weight in gold, if you know what I mean.'

'What on earth are you raving about? And stop talking in that ridiculous proletarian manner!'

'All right,' said Charlie, and continued in his cultivated voice. 'The coins that Johansson had minted – are they the real thing? Pure gold?'

'Of course they are. Not like the junk that was circulating in the days of the Young King. We needed a proper currency to trade with. Kantarborg gold has a good reputation now.'

'Right. And you're in a bit of a tight spot, as I understand it? I hear rumours that Johansson is planning to surrender.'

'What is your point, wretch?'

'Well it seems to me, Uncle, that I could help you out of a sticky situation here. Because if Johansson goes and surrenders to the Northlanders, you know what will happen to the boy they call Ulrika's bastard son. More to the point, you know what will happen to you. But you see, I've got a bit of a plan for us. But we'll have to move sharpish, because I've got the duchess and her whole household guard on my trail. She's not too happy about me borrowing the train, see. Not to mention all that gold. So you help me, and I'll help you. All right? *Noget for noget.*'

Brorsen regarded Charlie sourly.

'What is your proposal, then?' he asked.

'Well, as the dearly departed monarch said to me, in time of crisis, it's vital to protect the royal line. And right now, that means this young fellow.' He turned to the prince, who stared back with expressionless eyes.

'I know that, you fool!' said Brorsen. 'But how?'

'You're royal regent now, he's your charge. So you have the authority, and I have the wherewithal. And you have an island in the Sound. And a magic boat that can get us there, past the Northlander warships.'

Brorsen hesitated.

'We don't have the men.'

'I can get the gold down to the harbour tonight on the train.

I know the way. We just need some people to help us get it loaded, and someone to sail the boat. One of the men who know the controls. Issue the command to the militia, immediately. In the name of Prince Valdemar. And then tomorrow morning, we all go into the fireplace.'

'This will not end well, Charlie.'

'Nothing ends well, Uncle. We all die in the end. But we have to do what we can, don't we? For the sake of the Kingdom. And our family.'

CHAPTER FIFTY-SEVEN

'Prime Minister! I've been expecting you.'

'I'm sure you were, Johansson. You know what you have done.'

'Do enlighten me!'

'You were plotting to surrender the Kingdom to your compatriots across the Sound. The legal term for that is treason. You know the penalty.'

'I do.'

'And that doesn't concern you?'

'Not anymore, Kramer. Not anymore.'

CHAPTER FIFTY-EIGHT

And a partridge in a pear tree

Christopher burst through the door of the apartment in the Round Tower.

'Joe! Joe, where are you? We have to get out of the tower. Johansson's been arrested. Our guards are gone. It's all gone to pot down in the city.'

At the kitchen table, Joe was calmly packing a sack with cooking utensils. Alongside her were ranged a number of brown paper bags, with potatoes, carrots, turnips...

'Where the heck did you get all that?' asked Christopher.

'What?'

'The food!'

'Somebody left it outside the door last night. I don't know who. They left some for Marchas, too, but he's gone, so I took that as well. So I thought to meself, now's the time.'

'The time for what?'

'To make our getaway, of course.'

'But ... we don't have our airship. And, er, it might be a while now before we get it back.'

'Sure we were never going to get the airship back. That's why I was working so hard on the design.'

'What design?'

'The submarine, you eejit! I told you I wouldn't make a weapon of war, and I didn't. I was designing something else entirely.'

'What?'

She turned to him and handed him a large sack.

'The most useless weapon in the history of warfare. But not a bad escape vehicle. Now – fill that up, will ya?'

Joe and Christopher scurried nervously along the quay, carrying the sacks on their backs. The bored guards at the gate had recognised the two chief designers and let them pass.

On the quay stood a clockwork locomotive and a couple of empty trucks. They hurried past them to where the submarine and its barges lay semi-submerged at the dock, the dark harbour water slopping across its hull. A gull, perched on the conning tower, regarded them with suspicion.

'You go on board and fire her up, I'll cast off,' said Christopher.

Joe made the slightly perilous crossing to the boat, which swayed as she stepped onto the hull, then Christopher threw the sacks of provisions across. Joe took them and went below.

'Flip's sake, what are they after doing here?' said Christopher.

'What is it?' Joe called up.

'Someone's after padlocking the quick release handle. What did they do that for? I can't get the barges off.'

'Never mind, we'll sort it out later. Let's just get out of here now.'

Christopher cast off the ropes as Joe started up the clockwork motor, which began to whine and cast up white froth in the water behind them. Christopher, standing in the conning tower, took the wheel and turned the vessel away from the quayside. The boat and its barges eased slowly out into the harbour.

'Hey. HEY!' came a shout from behind him.

Christopher looked back to see a man dressed as the Yule Father running down the quay and waving. He was holding something in his hand. Christopher pulled the throttle lever and disengaged the motor.

Joe looked up through the hatch.

'C'mon Chris, let's go!'

'Just a sec, Joe. Holy God, I think that's him.'

'Who?'

'That fellow there dressed as the Yule Father. I think it might be the King!'

Joe climbed halfway up the ladder and looked out of the cockpit.

'Sure there's loads of them in the city.'

'Yes, but he has the golden rod! It must be him, Joe!'

'Chris, we don't have time to hang around.'

'I know, I know, but he's the one we were supposed to give the message. That was the whole point of our mission. Pass me up the loud hailer.'

Joe ducked back down and brought up the conical brass device. Christopher put it to his mouth.

'Hey Yule Father! We have a very important message for you!'

The man stopped running and stared. It was hard to read his expression behind the long white beard, but he seemed rather agitated.

'Listen to me! The annulments have come through! Both of them! The Pope says you're a free man! You can marry whoever you want. Congratulations!'

The man looked bewildered. Then, to Christopher's astonishment, what looked like a whole army of Yule Fathers, carrying swords and muskets, suddenly appeared at the harbour gate and began running along the quay. The man with the golden rod shouted something to them and pointed at Christopher and the departing vessel. Some of the men went down on one knee and aimed their weapons. Puffs of smoke appeared.

A musket ball whistled past the conning tower.

'Uh-oh, outstayed our welcome,' said Christopher. 'Take her down, Joe, they're shooting!'

Christopher swung himself down into the boat's interior and screwed the hatch firmly closed above him. Joe put the craft into a shallow dive while Christopher began to pump the air out of the buoyancy tanks.

'Don't think they've quite got into the seasonal spirit. You wouldn't think they'd get that annoyed about a bleeding boat!'

'Did he hear you?' asked Joe.

'I think so. Jaze, what's in them barges? They're going down awful fast.'

'They're heavy all right,' said Joe, watching the gauges. 'We can only barely pull them. But we just need to get under the surface, then we'll be safe. They can't shoot through the water. So it doesn't matter if we're a bit slow getting away.'

'But the harbour mouth is frozen over, Joe. How will we get past the ice?'

'We'll go under it. The pods have about an hour of power in them. That ought to be enough. And if we stay submerged, we can sneak past the Northlander warships as well.'

'Isn't technology a marvellous thing?' said Christopher.

'It's the engineers that are marvellous, boy.'

'But what about when the clockwork power's all used up?'

'Then we have a sail. And a retractable mast.' Joe glanced back at Christopher with a grin. 'Tillonsen couldn't understand why I wanted that put in.'

'Aren't you the smart one! *And* we delivered the message. I'd say that's mission accomplished, Brother Joe! Let's go home.'

And so it came to pass that Josephine Caffrey and Christopher Columba, brothers of the order of St Michael and emissaries of the See of Birmingham, departed Kantarborg on the last day of Yule, the feast day of the Visit of the Magi, bearing with them the entire gold reserves of the Kingdom.

CHAPTER FIFTY-NINE

Underneath the mountain

'What *woman*?' I asked in frustration. 'There is no woman!'

Marieke turned and looked into my eyes. 'Yes, there is.'

Our apartment, miraculously, had not been torched – perhaps because there were also Northlanders living in the building. But every scrap of furniture was gone, except for a single chair. We were standing in what had been our living room. Once again, we had nothing and were starting from scratch – an appropriate time, I thought, to try to re-establish things between us. But my attempt at an honest discussion had not gone well.

'Marieke, I swear to you, there is no-one.'

She kept her gaze on me. 'You swear that there has never been anyone else since you met me?'

I sighed and looked away.

'All right, there was someone. Once. But that was a long time ago, and she's dead.'

'She's *dead*?'

'Yes, years ago!'

I thought that would comfort her, but it seemed to distress her even more. She sank down upon the chair.

'Did you love her?' she asked, looking up at me with a fierce expression.

'I ... I don't know. I suppose I did. But not like ...'

'Don't, Karl. Don't. I always knew. Always.'

'But she's gone!'

She stood up.

'Karl ... you understand nothing. I can fight for you against any woman alive. But I cannot compete with a ghost. You will always love her.'

'Marieke, that's crazy. You and I are here now. You and I. That's all that matters, surely?'

She shook her head, took her cloak, and walked out without another word. I watched her go in complete confusion. She was right about one thing – I understood nothing.

I thought at first that she had just gone to be on her own for a while, but when she had not returned after an hour, I went out looking for her. The town was beginning to fill up with people again. There was a queue at the feeding station, although Berendina Jansen would not be opening it for another hour.

Marieke's footprints in the snow had been obscured by others and were impossible to follow. I ended up just walking and walking through the town, with no direction, unable to stop because of the fever in my heart. People saw my expression and stepped out of my way.

I always knew, she had said. Perhaps, but she had misunderstood. Yes, I am sometimes a silent and secretive man. My life at court has taught me to hold my tongue. A word out of place can easily put someone in danger. Words can kill. It becomes a habit – never say more than you have to.

And yes, damn it, I had loved Erika. But in a different time, and in a different place. Erika and I would have been a disaster as man and wife, and we both knew it. And yet, for all these years, had Marieke really thought I was pining for another, and that I had only married her out of ... what? Convenience? A man of the court, down on his luck in a provincial town? Surely she knew me better than that? *How would she know you better than that? She has never known you at all, you fool.* But it was not like that. It was not! I loved Marieke, and her only. And now I was going to find her and tell her. *Then for once in your life, for God's sake say what you truly feel.*

I found myself on the outskirts of the town, standing at the bottom of the hill leading up to her father's house. But she would not have gone there – she had told me there was nothing left but a blackened ruin. Where, then?

Think, Karl! *We go where they are afraid to follow.* Where was that? Where were the Northlanders afraid to go?

Sire, he lives a good league hence, underneath the mountain...

There were no mountains anywhere near Sandviken. But there was high ground outside the town that went by the name of *Trollberget*, the troll mountain. People said there were ancient mine ruins up there, and that they were haunted by the ghosts of dead ancients.

I was desperate and sick with worry. I had to try something, anything. I took the path near what was left of Hendrik's house, down into the valley where they fetched their water from the now-frozen stream. I crossed by the stepping-stones, and then walked up the other side to the foot of *Trollberget*. There were footprints here in the snow – the marks of clogs. I placed my foot on one. It looked to be her size, but of course it could have been anyone.

I followed the trail up along the hillside. Here the pathway disappeared beneath the snow, and if it had not been for the footprints, I would not have known where to tread. The wind was bitter, and being a Kantarborgan, I was unused to navigating such inclines and kept slipping. But I had to hurry – it had begun snowing heavily, and the footprints would soon be covered up. I crossed the remains of a fence by a stile, and came down into a flatter area, and what looked like an ancient roadway of some kind. It curved away to the left, among the trees, and disappeared. I followed it, and after about twenty minutes it ended in a giant iron door in the hillside. The door was well rusted, clearly of ancient construction, but looked much too heavy to be moved by any human power. A faded symbol painted on it in yellow and black could just about be made out: three triangles bounded by a circle. It looked familiar. I tried to recall where I had seen that before.

A loud, metallic, groaning sound. *Reptilicus!* I whirled around, to see a man standing in an iron doorway set in the rock, about ten yards away.

'Karl! Over here.' It was Marieke's father.

He held the door for me as I went in and down a set of steps.

Inside, the only light came from a few candles, but when my eyes got used to the gloom, I could make out an enormous cavern, as big as the inside of a church, that seemed to have been carved out of the rock face itself. The floor was covered with row upon row of hessian sacks. Hendrik led the way.

'Dark, dry and cold. Very good for storing vegetables. Not so good for people,' he said.

Nonetheless, there seemed to be quite a few people down here. I could hear murmuring in the Lowlander tongue from many sides in the darkness. Men, women and children. I followed Hendrik to a side passage that provided a small living space, where a candle had been set up on a table, with a few chairs around it. Marieke and her sister were sitting there. They stood up when they saw me.

Hendrik said something quietly to Gertrude, and they withdrew.

'So, you are not the only one with secrets, Karl,' said Marieke, when they were gone.

'Why couldn't you tell me?' I asked.

'We don't even name this place to each other. It's our last place of refuge. When this happens.'

'When this happens? How can you go on living among them, like this?'

'What would you have us do?'

'I don't know. Flee? It will surely happen again one day.'

'And where would we go? Our ancestral country is gone. And you saw what happened in Kantarborg.'

The thought occurred to me, not for the first time, that other people sometimes live lives that are rather more serious and perilous than my own. It made me feel unworthy.

'Marieke, please listen to me. I love you. I love only you. I can't live without you.'

She came over to me and embraced me, her head against my shoulder.

'We'll see what happens,' she said.

It was enough. We stood like that for a long time, in the silence of those who have said everything and have nothing left to say.

On the table, the candle flickered gently.

CHAPTER SIXTY

[From the correspondence archives of Cooley Abbey, undated]

Dear Father Abbot –
I hope that this finds you in good health. Now, the good news
is that despite a couple of bumps along the way the mission went
very well. Our airship was destroyed, but we met the King of Kan-
tarborg and gave him the message, and he gave us a great gift of
gold altogether for the good purposes of the Church.

I know the Jarl is putting about the rumour that we stole the
gold with the underwater boat, but that is completely untrue.
First of all, we didn't even know it was there till we made landfall
in the Alban isles, and secondly we realised then that the King
must have put it there, in accordance with the agreement. Quite
how he knew when we were planning to leave on the submersible
is a bit of a mystery to me, but the Lord moves in mysterious
ways, as you know. (I suppose to be honest the question of whether
we stole the boat itself is a bit more ambiguous. It kind of depends
on how you look at it.)

Anyway, I hope when it is all counted out there will be enough
to get the Church back on its feet, and maybe enough left over to
pay for the mission to America as well. And by the way, Brother
Joe is still going on about the clockwork railway system they have
in Kantarborg, powered by the wind. If the Church could fund a
small research project into this area I think it would make our Joe
very happy indeed.

Speaking of Brother Joe, I must now write of a rather more
delicate matter. I'm afraid we had a bit of an accident on the way
home. Shortly after we arrived here at the monastery on Holy Isle,
Joe gave birth to a baby girl. I hope this isn't as much of a shock to
you as it was to the abbot here. He says it's the first time in a
thousand years they have recorded a birth to a monk. Joe and the
young one are both doing fine.

The occasion of sin was all my fault, as I'm sure you can

imagine – Joe is very devout as you know. So I hope you will see your way to giving us both absolution and penance when we return, despite everything. And if you could release us from our vows now and turn Joe back into a woman, too, that would be grand, before we get into any more trouble. The other monks here are calling us the Holy Family and it's getting a bit embarrassing.

When Joe is rested up a bit we'll be making our way back to the Rock, and then, with your blessing, I hope we'll be able to marry. I don't think the Order will have too much of an objection to us leaving, seeing as we're probably the worst monks in the history of the Church. I am, anyway. But we might make a better go of it as a family, who knows?

Yours in Christ,

Brother Christopher Columba

CHAPTER SIXTY-ONE

It was a Saturday night and the speakeasy was crowded, mainly with young people. The pianist had barely room to play, squashed up against one wall, and people kept jogging his elbows and putting glasses and bottles on the small upright piano.

He was playing a quiet, reflective melody. A young couple, wearing the latest *jazz clothes*, pushed their way through the crowd. The man, in a bow tie and a straw hat, placed a glass of *akvavit* on the piano top.

'Play something good.'

'You don't like this one?' asked the pianist, without pausing in his playing.

'It's all right. It's a bit churchy.'

'*Round Midnight*. It was written by a monk.' He played the concluding chords.

'Can you play *Alley Cat*?' asked the girl. 'We want to dance.'

'I don't play that one.'

'Why not?'

'I play jazz. That's not jazz.'

'Miss Andersen plays it. And she plays jazz.'

'It's an old Kantish melody,' added the young man. 'Traditional.'

'Yes, I know, but it's not jazz.'

'Stuck-up prick,' said the girl. 'You'll play all that foreign aristo stuff, but you won't play a good old Kantish tune. Who do you think you are, royalty?' She walked away, her tasselled dress swinging.

'Go on, grandad, give it a try,' said the young man. 'Then I might buy you another one of those.'

He walked off in the direction of the bar.

The pianist sighed. He looked at the small glass of *akvavit*. Shame to waste it. He'd have to get it off the piano anyway, or it would spill onto the keyboard before long. He picked up the drink, knocked it back, and began to play the lively opening bars of *Alley Cat*. A small cheer of recognition arose from the crowd. Several couples took to the tiny dance floor.

The pianist stared off into space, as though dreaming of somewhere else, as his fingers found the familiar notes. His dark brown eyes twinkled with reflected candlelight. It was going to be a long night.

THE END

Acknowledgements

I am once again deeply grateful to my friends and colleagues for their help during the production of this book, particularly beta readers Titia Schuurman, Michelle Asselin, Pia Björke Bengtsson, Margaret Schroeder, Dagmara Meijers-Troller and Veronica Lambert Hall for your extremely helpful and useful comments on the first draft. Thanks also to Andrey Dorozhko (andreydrz.com/art/) for another stunning cover picture, to Liz Cencetti for help with French, and to Haydn Rawlinson for expert advice about pinball machines.

My thanks are also due to my son Christopher for the back cover artwork and help with the cover, as well as for his fantastic VR work to promote all the books of the series, to my daughters Catriona and Ciara for marketing advice and, not least, for keeping my feet on the ground, and to Charlotte, my muse and fellow dreamer, without whom there would be no Kingdom.

The title of the book refers of course to *A Christmas Carol* by Charles Dickens. Even if my tale here has little in common with his marvellous story, at least on the surface, he has certainly been an inspiration.

The paintings of the wonderful Otto Frello have also frequently been a source of inspiration. Chapter 17 is based on his painting *Læsende pige* ('Girl reading') (1979), which also contains, at least in my imagination, the only known pictorial representation of the Grumfel. (I have been asked whether the Grumfel is real. I can only say that he strongly denies it.)

The Round Tower of Copenhagen is a real place, and well worth seeing if you are visiting the city.

Regan Øst is also a real place, but is not, as far as I am aware, equipped with a secret underground railway. (But then again, how would I know?)

About the author

Originally from Ireland, Billy O'Shea was educated at Trinity College Dublin and the University of Copenhagen. He has so far failed at being a grape-picker, a dishwasher, a dock worker, a TV sound technician, a diamond sorter, a pirate radio DJ, a musician, a translator and a writer. He lives in Copenhagen, Denmark, with his wife and three children.

A Clockwork Carol is the third book in the Kingdom of Clockwork series. The paperback versions of the books are available at the Round Tower of Copenhagen and from www.blackswan.dk. Kindle versions are available from Amazon, and audio versions from Audible and StoryTel.

Facebook community: facebook.com/KingdomOfClockwork

If you have enjoyed A Clockwork Carol, please consider leaving a review on Amazon or Goodreads. Thank you!